THE RACE

THE RACE

A NOVEL OF POLAR EXPLORATION

BY KÅRE HOLT

TRANSLATED FROM THE NORWEGIAN BY **JOAN TATE**

A Merloyd Lawrence Book
DELACORTE PRESS/SEYMOUR LAWRENCE

Originally published in Norwegian by Gyldendal Norsk Forlag
under the title KAPPLØPET
Copyright © 1974 by Gyldendal Norsk Forlag A/S

English translation copyright © 1976
by Michael Joseph Ltd. and Dell Publishing Co., Inc.

Manufactured in the United States of America

First American printing

Library of Congress Cataloging in Publication Data

Holt, Kåre.
The race.

Translation of Kappløpet.
1. Amundsen, Roald Engelbregt Gravning, 1872–
1928—Fiction. 2. Scott, Robert Falcon, 1868–1912
—Fiction. I. Title.
PZ4.H75845Rac3 [PT8950.H72] 839.8′2′372 76–21752
ISBN 0-440-07198-4

AMUNDSEN

A young man wearing too-tight patent leather shoes and a bowler hat ran through the streets of Kristiania trying to sell a human skull. He had been ordered by his mother, a strong-willed woman, to study medicine whether he liked it or not. When she died, he had broken off his studies. Now all he had left was the skull, and he was selling that to pay for books about the polar regions.

He was a well-built determined youth; he had few friends, being silent and rather anti-social; he had never had a lover. Nor had he shone particularly at school. His spelling showed an originality that suggested stubbornness rather than stupidity. His capacity for hatred was to prove great: his capacity for loyalty to his friends no less great—as long as those friends recognized his superiority and allowed him to use them. There was a streak of opportunism in him which he never managed to get rid of, and he knew how to play on this in a masterly way when it came to gaining the advantage. He chose as colleagues men not unlike himself—but men of smaller stature, lesser leaders who deferred to him, the supreme ruler. On his own, as he planned the great expeditions of his life, he was a genius. He was the first man to reach the South Pole.

We see Roald Amundsen hazily as a recruit: before reveille he would leap out of bed and go on a training run. When his company was on Sunday morning parade and the captain called for volunteers to sacrifice themselves for church parade, he was always the first to volunteer. Otherwise, he never set foot inside a church. Later in life, he reaped great honour for this behaviour. It was insignificant enough and false enough to appear genuine, which is not to say that he acted dishonestly. On the contrary, he was being true to a profound need in himself always to be first. In every situation where he risked being number two, he made use of this tremendous willpower—and dishonesty.

His family came from Havaler and had been connected with the sea as far back as they could remember. His father and uncles owned their own ships and sailed all over the world. There was a strange mixture of wild boldness and dignified gentility in the family. His father had four unmarried sisters, and he built a house for them, near his own, where they occupied their days with pot-plants and lavender.

According to some, Roald's father was a slave-trader; according to others, he was the white commander who had survived when a mob of coloured bandits rose in rebellion, while he was sailing a cargo of Chinese coolies from China to Havana. He had three hundred of them on board, shut up in the hold. They had to have enough fresh air to survive—they had a specific cash value—so they were let out on deck for an hour at a time, in small groups of ten or twelve. But then one of them got hold of an axe belonging to the carpenter, and they decided to take over the ship. The skipper was standing by the rail, staring out over the horizon when the Chinese attacked him from behind. He whirled swiftly round and the edge of the blade slashed his cheek, instead of striking his head. All hell broke loose. The Chinese were driven back into the

6

hold, where they started a fire to force their way out. The crew battened down the hatches. The smoke began to suffocate the Chinese, and they were being consumed by their own fire. The skipper was bleeding profusely. His young wife was also on board: she had not yet given birth to Roald, the polar explorer. She stitched up the wound with a darning needle and thick wool. The skipper gave his orders to the Chinese. 'Sentence the man who led the revolt yourselves—or die!'

Then the man was hanged by his own people.

An effective policy: complete fearlessness and clever tactics. One of the anonymous leaders of history had been sacrificed. He was wise enough to understand the situation: My own men may hang me, but they can continue the struggle if they survive. Had the rebellion succeeded, Roald would not have been born and Scott would have been the first to reach the South Pole.

Roald had an elder brother, Leon. They were very close for many years, but their friendship ended in hostility. Once, when they were young boys, they went on a long midwinter trip across the Hardanger plateau. In some ways, it was just as risky an enterprise as many of the expeditions Roald later carried out. They took sleeping-bags, but no tent. They ran into a blizzard and started going round in circles. We sense their determination: they *had* to succeed. We sense their brotherhood too, their capacity to push themselves to extremes. In the account of this trip that Roald wrote shortly afterwards, the tone is simple, harmonious, expressing a friendship for Leon and a strong self-reliance kept in check. On this trip, it was his brother who saved Roald's life. One mild evening, on their way back to civilization, they dug themselves in on a ridge. The plateau stretched all round them, the darkness of night made a close roof. Each dug out a hole in the snow. Roald crawled in head first, dragged his sleeping-bag after him and crept into it. He lay down snugly and fell asleep.

Later in the night he woke to find it had grown cold. One of his arms, which had been outside the sleeping-bag, was frozen fast in the ice and he couldn't free it. He noticed that the space was hermetically sealed, the air decreasing. His head was throbbing. He tried to kick himself free but the bag and his feet were frozen fast to the surface below. When he shouted to his brother, the shout seemed to come from a deep cellar of ice. It was dark, but a weak light seeped in through the layer of snow. It seemed to mock him—or perhaps it was a faint farewell from the life he had so far had time only to taste.

He felt he was beginning to suffocate, and the feeling grew stronger the more he struggled to get free. Perhaps Leon was frozen in too. He imagined the wide plateau and his own cramped ice chamber ... he lost his self-control and hysteria overcame him. He kicked his feet wildly in the bag. It didn't shift. Suddenly he heard a slight sound. He didn't know if it was in his imagination, a false hope, or if it came from his brother, trying to dig him out. The moment that hope returned, he regained his cold, calm ability to plan, staking all on this one card. Breathe calmly, he told himself, don't waste oxygen. If it was Leon, this was his only chance of survival.

It was. It took him three hours to dig Roald out. Then they went back to civilization. To Leon and to no one else, Roald disclosed his bold dreams of following in the wake of Sir John Franklin to the North-West Passage. Later, Leon was his only confidant when he changed course from north to south to try and reach the South Pole before Scott. But in the end there was a court case between the two brothers. Looking back, in *My Life as a Polar Explorer*, Amundsen refers to him in the wastelands as his 'companion', never by name, nor as his brother. He refers to his only confidant during the planning of the South Pole expedition as his secretary. But when he comes to the court case, he uses his brother's full name, and fills page after page with harsh words. We sense at this stage, towards the end of his life, that the man was shattered—by superhuman physical wear and tear, by the storms over the Antarctic, by boundless ambition. His concern for money had become overriding—the money he had pressed for to accomplish his unique achievement. He felt naked before posterity, his glory worn thin. He sensed the stern judgment of history. But he was wrong there. There is a chilling distance about genius, and he was certainly short on humanity. He had paid the price of success, and he had won—or lost. He had kept quiet about his plans—to be the first in a place where no one else had been before, and where no one had any business being. But he was great in his loneliness, Roald the loser is brother to us all.

Young Roald Amundsen was playing cards with Death. He was twenty-five, and coxswain on board the *Belgica*. The expedition was led by Baron Adrien de Gerlache to explore the seas round the South Pole. Following the current fashion, the coxswain had a narrow moustache and a small, well-groomed, pointed beard. Abundant hair covered his forehead. The air hung heavily in his small, uncared-for cabin, as the ship was ice bound. Outside, ice floes thundered as they rose up on end, ground against each other, mashed to slush, pressed together round the ship's sides and swept over the deck. Darkness covered both ship and men—an unbroken darkness. Roald was sitting on the edge of his bunk, playing cards with Death. Danco, the young scientist, had scurvy and would soon die. His face was yellow, his eyes had a reddish glow in the half-light of the cabin. He cried: 'Play cards with me. I'm going to die soon.'

They all had scurvy, Roald too, and the American doctor, Frederick Albert Cook. Even so, those two still had their strength, having found a remedy against death: they drank blood. Now and again a seal would poke its snout up in a channel before the floes were pressed together, and penguins appeared occasionally. The two men would sneak up on the birds and animals in the dark, stab them and put their lips to the open wounds, drinking while the bodies still twitched in death-throes. They dragged the meat back to the sides of the ship and tried to force the others to eat it raw. But the leader of the expedition refused—on behalf of his men as well as himself. Madness began to shine from the inflamed eyes of Adrien de Gerlache. He suspected that the two hunters wanted to kill the others on board. Orders went out each morning: no one was to drink blood!

Young Roald sat there with blood on his pointed beard, disobeying the order, and playing cards with his dying friend. Roald lost time and time again, but Danco was still clearsighted enough to see that his opponent was letting him win. He cried out in torment: 'You think I'm already dead!' Then Roald played seriously and won. So Danco cried: 'You've no pity for me, I'm going to die!' Roald tried to coax a piece of meat into his dying friend's mouth, but he knew it was no longer any use.

De Gerlache's ship was fast in the ice because of his own ignorance, his lack of knowledge of the conditions in the Antarctic. A storm had come up from the north as they were tacking along between the ice floes. Experienced men would have immediately headed out to sea, but Gerlache found a channel direct to the south. He didn't think that the storm could reach them in there; nor could it. They froze fast and lay in the ice for thirteen months.

Roald said later, without boasting, that he had foreseen the danger. He realized that Gerlache should have done exactly the opposite of what he did. But, Roald said, no one consulted me, so I kept quiet. Opportunist? Perhaps. If so, one with his nerves under control. After several weeks in the ice, Gerlache retired to his bunk and made his will.

Then Roald Amundsen was the real leader on board. But on one point, Gerlache remained inflexible: 'No one must drink blood.' Roald was equally inflexible: 'Everyone must drink blood.' But the men on board the *Belgica* feared raw meat more than death. Word went round that the Norwegians wanted to kill the others by pouring blood into them.

As a result of this year in the ice, Roald formed a deep respect for the American, Dr Cook. Later Cook came back from another Arctic expedition saying that he had conquered the North Pole, and was exposed as a fraud. Cook was also involved in financial swindles, and ended up in prison in Kansas City. After many years, when Amundsen had become a world-renowned figure, he went to Kansas City to give a lecture. There he visited his friend in prison, and was violently attacked in the American newspapers for supporting the swindler. Amundsen must have realized this would happen even before he had knocked on the prison door in Kansas City. But as always, he was inflexible.

What the two of them talked about, no one knows: perhaps about the sailor on board the *Belgica* who became a megalomaniac as Danco lay dying? About the stealthy footsteps on deck, the sound of ice floes being crushed like the shrieks of desperate human beings? About Danco jumping to his feet and hitting his head on the cabin roof, fainting, coming to again and crying: 'More will die! Play cards with me.'

Perhaps they talked about Danco's last journey? The first grey light shone over the ice mass, over the ship which was leaning over so that they had to haul themselves up by ropes. Everyone came up on deck, even Baron de Gerlache, most of them like living corpses, yellow, cavernous, toothless. Only two men were still full of life, and had maintained their strength: the blood drinkers.

Danco was sewn into a sailcloth and the body ballasted

at its feet. When a few words had been read in the cold and the wind, Roald and Dr Cook shoved the dead man out. The body stood upright in the sea, then sank slowly, while two floes squealed against each other as if the corpse were having one last laugh.

They had to get out of the ice or die there. A channel occasionally appeared, but closed up again before they could get the ship free. Cook suggested cutting their way out, and Roald supported him—two strong wills against many weak ones. The crew had no strength to work: it was hundreds of metres to the open channel, they had no tools, they were doomed to stay there ... and doomed to die.

But there were two strong wills against many weak ones. Amundsen never forgot his gratitude to Dr Cook. *Belgica* got out of the ice.

But how can we tell at what cost? Even for the strongest, there are the boundaries of a shattered mind. Next time they met, one was a swindler. The other eventually brought a court action against his own brother.

There is a photograph of Roald Amundsen sitting in a kite: it must have been commissioned. He's hanging on to a chair well above the ground, wearing a bowler hat, collar, gloves and patent leather shoes. There is an air of gentility about our hero, and he appears to have used lipstick. He knew he was going to be photographed and held fast to his dignity—the respectable citizen who doesn't offend anybody by taking his gloves off. He was original in his choice of props—the kite was to lift him over the ice mass and give him a better view—but fastidious to the point of vulgarity in his behaviour. He never contradicted anyone who in his own eyes stood above him in the community, and he was in the habit of disagreeing with every subordinate.

Nansen and Amundsen first met in 1900—the one

already a world-famous figure, the other a coxswain. No one had yet taken any notice of Amundsen, few knew of his insane longing for glory. From his account of his meeting, written a quarter of a century later, we have some idea of his cringing entrance, his humble stance throughout the meeting, his profound gratitude on his departure. And—though he doesn't mention this—a touch of envy was apparent too. The two men were strongly dissimilar. Nansen was more than just a man of powerful intellect: he was a man of the world with a feeling for politics; a scientist, prepared for confrontation—and he had in addition a strong sense of the ridiculous. Amundsen was introverted, sensitive, petty. He was quick to take offence if he felt he wasn't being treated with respect, and his horizons were bounded by that compulsion to be first on the map where no one had ever been. And that was exactly what he achieved. He was both genius and snarling tiger: a weakling who bowed unnecessarily as he left. The two of them could hardly have been more different. No friendship ever grew between them.

Later Amundsen deceived Fridtjof Nansen, by a deliberate suppression of the truth, and therefore a lie. It was at this first meeting that Amundsen put forward his plans for finding the North-West Passage; Nansen promised to give him all the support he could.

He was standing in a barge half full of water, testing to see if the grease kept his boots watertight. Grease was just one of the many problems for the man who wanted to conquer the North-West Passage. He had bought a cockleshell of a boat, the *Gjøa*; she was only a few metres long, hopeless at sea—a death trap, according to many people. Now he was painting the outside of the *Gjøa*; standing in the water in his newly greased boots. He had tried all the existing greases, but none of them worked, so he boiled up his own concoction, swore and spat into the mess, diluted it with urine, then tried the result again—the boots had to stand six hours under water. Finally they were watertight.

The expedition was to carry provisions enough for five years: 1800 days, so he had to think carefully before acting. The preparations took two years. Amundsen was the man behind the scenes, the solitary master, who cross-questioned the experts, didn't comment on their answers, and went his own way. Sir John Franklin had fought his way into the North-West Passage with 134 men and two large ships. None came back. During the next ten years, fifty expeditions were sent out to rescue him. Many never got through. Amundsen, waiting in Tromsoe while the *Gjøa* was being overhauled, took the opposite course: a small ship which didn't run aground so easily; a few men who could do everything that had to be done—and more. How did he go about choosing his men? Not only for their ability to obey, although that was the first commandment. If you look at the many men who followed him, a pattern emerges: they were all good with their hands, and perhaps this was as important as the requirement that they be physically strong and experienced skiers. Practical men first and foremost—and men with a willingness to obey their leader. Only one of his colleagues didn't conform on that point, and he was dropped from the team that was to conquer the South Pole. This demand for submission should not necessarily be dismissed as arrogance: Amundsen knew that an expedition of this kind, composed of a small group of men who admired their strong leader, would have the greatest chance of succeeding. And the only happiness lay in success. Unfortunately, this desire to dominate other people got out of control. Gradually he must have measured the men's smallness against his own greatness with pleasure. The cancer of arrogance was within him, and towards the end of his life the infection was to become more apparent.

But on his way through the North-West Passage he was

still the wise leader, able to show humility when required, young, strong and inflexible. Every expedition to an unknown region needs money, and his was no exception. He had yet to make a name for himself, but had to go cap in hand as if he were a world-famous explorer. The man in the watertight boots wiped the grease off his fingers, cleaned himself up with an old newspaper, trimmed his beard with sail-maker's scissors, found he had to change his trousers. He went behind a couple of crates and did so. Put on a stiff collar. Got a spot of grease on the collar, solved this, practical man that he was, by turning the collar round. He changed his face, too, becoming a humble, cringing person, bowing and scraping his way in through heavy doors, bowing and scraping his way out. He flattered the rich by implying that wealth was evidence of moral strength. Then he spat in the driveway on his way home; but he lost part of his soul. A cold contempt for humanity began to grow inside him.

Just before they were due to set sail in the *Gjøa*—they were in Kristiania now—one of the purveyors wanted the ship confiscated for debt and the captain arrested. Amundsen never disclosed the man's name, probably for tactical reasons, thinking he might well need help later from other firms with which the man had connections. He acted quickly, collecting the men in the middle of the night. The *Gjøa* sailed.

The Ferder lighthouse outside Oslo marked freedom for him, and Amundsen was a happy man. It was rare for him to find genuine words for genuine feelings, but he did so then. Leaving all his money worries behind, protected from heavy seas in the fjord, with a handful of obedient men on board gladly following him towards adventure—that was happiness.

Getting through the long winter months was no problem to him: his relationship with the icy wastes was like that of a worshipper before a crucifix. He knew no fear of death—or perhaps he did, but treated the question with academic interest. He thought of death as a challenge, increasing the risk of failure—another problem to be overcome. He didn't talk effusively about death. Before the last enemy—or friend—he disciplined his language into obedience. In his dealings with the Eskimoes, he was wise, quite often displaying a warm humanity. This could simply have been good strategy. He established his superiority early on, in a dramatic encounter. A crowd of Eskimoes was approaching with bows and arrows. Amundsen and his companions had guns. When they were close enough to shoot, Amundsen called: 'Throw down your guns.' The men did so. Then the Eskimoes threw down their bows and arrows.

He helped the Eskimoes and they admired him. He could drive dogs and sleep in the snow. He bargained and paid well, with sewing needles (again the result of creative planning: sewing needles found a place even on board the overloaded *Gjøa*), but he could be a stern master when he thought the situation warranted it. When one of the Eskimoes stole a couple of tins of food, he called them all together, thundered in a language they couldn't understand, demanding that the guilty one be handed over— then dismissed him. No mercy because—well, for several reasons, but compressed into one—such a theft could jeopardize the success of the venture. And he did get through the passage where so many had failed.

In the ice on the west coast, he came upon a wrecked whaling ship. The skipper, a certain Mogg, was on his way to the nearest telegraph station to wire for help. Amundsen wanted to go there too, burning with desire to give the world news of his victory. Anyone would have felt the same, but he felt it more.

Amundsen was penniless, but Mogg had money, so the victorious conqueror had to accompany the shipwrecked man through the wastelands like an obedient child. Ahead,

Amundsen raced over the snow, the dog-team behind, Mogg sitting dozing on the sledge. The man who had conquered the North-West Passage felt as if he were being whipped into submission. Between two overnight stopping places he threatened to turn back. Mogg couldn't manage on his own; it was miles to the next station, so he agreed to pay up and the telegrams were sent. Amundsen went out under the white stars and thanked Almighty God. Perhaps he thought the Almighty ought to have thanked him too. Next the South Pole.

Before we start on the journey to the South Pole, we should mention some events from his later life. By bearing these in mind, we can better understand the man who won the race to the Pole by deceiving the world. The genius who played for such high stakes emerges as a man perhaps not so great in stature as his contemporaries thought him, but greater than we now tend to give him credit for.

After the journey from the South Pole, he entered a difficult period which was to last for the rest of his life. His next expedition wasn't as successful as the first two. His plan now was to sail through the North-West Passage and then drift across the Arctic Ocean as Nansen had done. But the First World War broke out, and Amundsen became a mercenary, earning money on German submarines. At the same time, he showed his justifiable contempt for German submarine warfare by sending back a medal he had received from the Kaiser. He seemed not to see the contradiction: analysis of double standards of morality wasn't his line. In his description of the episode, he seems to have been quite proud as he stood before the Ambassador. He read out a written speech, bowed, handed over the medal and left. With a half-embarrassed, slightly sly smile, he mentioned the money he had earned as a result of that same submarine warfare.

His new ship, the *Maud*, was not a success. The drifting

over the Arctic Ocean and everything that followed was an exhausting period for Amundsen. He didn't achieve great results; he seemed to become sour. It was as if he had hardened (if that were possible) and he developed a total contempt for death. On the other hand, his distrust of human beings appeared to grow, and his aggressive attitude to those who didn't meekly mould themselves to his leadership became more noticeable.

Small personal mishaps added to his troubles. A broken arm, not irreparable in normal circumstances—but he was on the ice without a doctor, and his shoulder swiftly stiffened. It required an iron will to exercise the arm—a little higher each day, each night. The ice creaked and packed together, tired men snored; he was suffocated by gusts of air from sour stomachs, surrounded by grim faces. Endless monotony, the days like frozen grey potatoes, all stories already told, the smell of other men's jokes—and his arm aching as he tried to raise it a bit higher every day.

He was knocked down by a bear and had the flesh torn off his backside. Later, he tried tersely to make a joke about the event. 'If only I had received the wound in my chest, I could have shown it as a medal for bravery.'

After this, he suffered a bout of carbon monoxide poisoning. This was the most serious accident of his life. His heart began to give way under the strain. When he got back to town and was examined by doctors, he was told that his condition was serious, and he must put an end to expeditions. So he went on with expeditions. A few years later, he carried out the most gruelling march of his life during a stay in Alaska—sixteen hundred kilometres with skis and dogs over sixteen days. He was justifiably proud of that.

But he was bitter too. That became apparent. The latent hysteria of his youth, which had been revealed only occasionally, now emerged in full force and was there like a threat, though perhaps it was also a source of strength.

He stamped on the ice; he waded in the slush. Nothing worked. He couldn't pull off another stroke of luck. He was no longer a young man.

We know little of the women in his life. But he dropped a few discreet hints about them, and in such a way as to suggest he was hiding something else. Could he, a ruler of men, have been homosexual? If so, he held his desires sternly and puritanically in check—and perhaps a feeling of vulnerability in this respect strengthened his uncontrollable desire to impress others. Maybe there was something in his lonely mind which found peace in the isolation of the ice. External challenges can be controlled. Inner ones are sometimes ungovernable. There was one moving episode in his life which demonstrated another side to his character. He rescued two small Eskimo girls, looked after them and took them home with him. He had always been a practical man; the two girls went to a Norwegian school. No doubt he was aware of the gossip, but he ignored it with a scornful smile. Then he sent them back. This might seem brutal, but the girls were getting in the way. He was off on new trips. How could an explorer look after children? From then on no more was heard of them.

Towards the end of his life, he took his own brother to court. The indispensable brother, Roald's only confidant, the one who had crossed the plateau with him and saved his life—later Leon was the first person to whom Roald disclosed his change of plan before dashing south and deceiving the world. The finances had always been his brother's business. The legal wrangles that are part of every large expedition had lain on the brother's shoulders. Small enterprises seemed to have been hatched out jointly by both, Roald taking the outward responsibility, Leon the shadow, the man who stands silently and knowingly in the background. Suddenly the brotherhood between them was swept aside by an icy gust from the Pole. It was painful. They acted in full public view. Even so, it seems that Leon was keeping some of his aversion back, while Roald was merciless in his exposure. A dam had broken inside him; his mind had disintegrated. There was some hurry to reach the North Pole. Men from many nations were on the point of going.

Amundsen's most hysterical plan, little known, was his wild attempt to fly from Alaska to Spitsbergen in a single-engined machine, with one companion on board. The plane foundered at the start. Was he seeking death now, feeling himself a broken man? Did he remember Scott, finding that his great rival had won in the end— losing, and dying? He sat in a New York hotel room, not knowing whether or not to pick up the phone. It rang. He was bankrupt. The glory of his earlier trips had all gone. So many people were against him. His lecture tour through the States had become a fiasco. It was such a long, long time ago since he had steered course up the fjord at home, and small boats had come out with flags and pennants, while Akershus had saluted him so that the timbers thundered. Should he answer the telephone? It rang and rang. Was it some anonymous crank, to curse him, or a busybody or someone with wild plans to bring themselves glory and himself expense? Answer it. 'My name is Ellsworth: I'm a rich man.'

The expedition these two carried out was one of the boldest in the history of polar exploration. It was a bull's eye—Amundsen's last fling. With him he had men who followed him blindly, who valued his greatness and ignored the rest. Ellsworth was a noble man, but insignificant. Two planes started northwards. They found a channel, one of the very few; then the engines began to fail. It was a thousand kilometres to civilization. They had 225 grams of food per man per day, for twenty-four days. Then they got one of the planes up and got home safe and sound. It couldn't have been better. This would vanquish Scott himself: first the defeat, death so to speak, at the last

minute transformed into victory and life. The world had
feared their death, adjusted to it, prepared themselves to
acclaim the dead heroes—then the heroes were resurrected.
It was miraculous. What did they want with the Pole now?
Everyone was awed by the incredible. There again he
stood, in the centre of the six men, having got past the evil
of the court case. The small boats streamed with flags and
pennants, Akershus fortress saluted; Amundsen in a bowler
hat, ladies' white parasols, a dog tearing itself free and
biting a constable in the foot, three hundred little boys
fighting at Karl Johan because they all want to be Amundsen, and the six men in an open carriage, riding to the
palace, cabinet ministers in black frock coats. Happiness.

But his last trip, with the airship *Norge*, was a disaster.
His rival in this venture, Nobile, was an Italian, and to
increase the glory of Italy he intended to garner the largest
possible quota of the glory that Amundsen had taken for
his own. As a flying achievement, the trip was a daring
one. Around it raged battles about uniforms, about medals,
struggles for rights feebly camouflaged by cries about the
demands of science and the triumphs of exploration. Then
the airship *Italia* set off, flew for 132 hours and crashed.

This time Amundsen had his back to the wall. The
whole world knew of his relationship with Nobile. If he
refused to take part in the rescue operation, people would
say that he was too mean to risk his life for an enemy. If
he said yes, he would receive an extra bouquet of roses.
If he succeeded in rescuing Nobile, the triumph would be
magnificent. If he didn't succeed, and they were killed, the
memory of the unhappy circumstances between them
would reflect nobly on the rescuer for all time.

Remember that he was a schemer of genius. We don't
know what he was planning. But it's reasonable to suppose that he didn't reckon on living to be an old man. He
was now fifty-six years old. He had subjected his body to
unparalleled extremes. And he only had one heart.

Whether it were big or not, it was to highlight a mystery which was never solved. Glory has a tendency to tarnish. It must be constantly polished to keep it bright. One last magnificent gesture, and then exit? Death carries a lot of points. He died and took the trick. Was he thinking of Scott when he died?

SCOTT

Victoria was on the throne. In her Empire, a man either had to repress his sexuality, or conquer the world. John Edward Scott was among the former, but he dreamt of being one of the latter. He owned an old brewery in Plymouth, suffered ill health, and was a dissatisfied man all his life. Nevertheless, in time he acquired a wife, much to the astonishment of many people, whose astonishment increased to the point of embarrassment when children came into the world. His elder son, Robert Falcon Scott, became one of the greatest explorers in the history of the Empire. When he set out on his first journey to the South Pole, he had not yet seen snow.

The father had four brothers. They sailed the high seas, or were in the Indian Army. They stood to attention for the Queen, they had the legal right to conquer a woman with a warcry and then throw her aside. John Edward, on the other hand, had resident in-laws to look after. Slowly they grew older and more and more fragile. They spoke with respect of the Queen, and flushed slightly when it was mentioned in passing that she too had children. The brewery was a rather precarious business. John Edward Scott won neither honour nor fortune.

But he must have had a strong character. He didn't drink

his own beer. It would hardly have been surprising if we had seen him drowning slowly in tankards of beer, then progressing to bottles of whisky. He didn't drown. We see him struggling against misfortune; disagreeable, embittered, often sick; he consulted scores of doctors, but no one could find out what was wrong with him. Perhaps one of the doctors suggested: 'If you joined the Indian Army...?' John Edward lived such a boring life that people observed him with increasing interest. The Conservative Party discovered him. He was invited to stand as a parliamentary candidate, a secure rigid clique in which people drank beer and bored each other, had in-laws, and talked about the Queen. He was certain to be elected. However, he had to refuse the offer. A candidate not only had to pay for his own campaign, but also had to contribute to the party. He couldn't do that. Possibly, if he had become a politician, he might not have had any other contribution to make.

He was a loser—in life and in his marriage. For some time he had no sons. Historians haven't yet managed to explain how Victorian men and women, with their subdued silence on sexual matters, nevertheless managed to seek each other out and procreate. The existence of the new-born child was denied for the first few weeks. Rumours that the child also had a sex were made known rather reluctantly to an inner circle. Nevertheless, the father must soon have been told that that child and the second were daughters. He admitted within a select circle that he felt this to be an injustice.

But then a son came into the world. Though there is no evidence, we can imagine how the father's secret joy now soared. In his imagination, his son became a victorious admiral returned from great battles—wounded but still alive, with flecks of blood on his fingernails, laboriously scrubbed away for a visit to the Queen at Windsor. Then to everyone's dismay, the boy turned out to be like his father—delicate in health, disagreeable and inclined to nausea.

This was the cruellest blow of all, but John Edward struggled against it. Guests came to the house and said with genteel malice, 'He'll probably make a good brewer, like you.' We know that the father's antagonism towards a life in brewing was soon passed on to Robert, but a strong antagonism can become a strong will—hatred can turn into hope; in this case, hope of conquering an empire.

There wasn't much left to conquer. The Queen's ensign flew over all the oceans. True, Sir John Franklin had failed to return from the North-West Passage, and the fifty expeditions sent out to find him had no luck either. The South Pole still lay untouched—it was the last continent with no footprints on it, and this was the last generation that could hope to set foot on virgin soil.

Robert was not especially clever at school. This surprised his father, but didn't disappoint him too much. There must have been many frank conversations between father and son. We do not know what disciplinary methods the elder used, for the son was silent on this subject during his relatively brief life—with exquisite loyalty, he expressed only respect and affection for his father. But the relationship can't have been based on affection alone. There must also have been some naval discipline in their dealings—the Navy that the father had once dreamt of joining, perhaps not to be disciplined, but to discipline others. In a flash, we can see the father's dark eyes change and whiten, hear the son's weak cry, note his embittered resistance, sense that his character is hardening. Women glide uneasily past in the corridor. They had no right to know what was happening. That was an integral part of the glory of the Empire.

The father grew increasingly hysterical. The son kept up a controlled façade, but occasionally something moved below the surface, a pain perhaps, a subdued rebellion, a

violent, growing strength. The father became weaker
and constantly more disagreeable, the son stronger and
constantly more friendly. But it was an impersonal friendliness: his smile was pleasant but he remained politely
withdrawn, always willing to say the right thing, wise
beyond his years, with a slow toughness inside him and a
capacity for steady work. In addition, he was a modest
youth. Everyone is in agreement over this. At no time did
he show any foolish desire for glory.

But, as has been mentioned, he was inclined to nausea.
So he shouldn't go to sea.

Robert was thirteen years old when his father got him
into the Navy. Dartmouth was a port with a wealth of tradition in the history of the Navy. It was from there that
Englishmen had sailed out to sea to crush the Spanish
Armada. In Dartmouth, an old ship called *Britannia* was
berthed. She stayed afloat out of habit, and was used as
a training ship for future officers in the Navy. One hundred
and fifty boys slept in hammocks which hung so close together that only the slimmest could slip into his own without making that of his neighbour whip round. One
hundred and fifty thirteen-year-old boys had to keep quiet
and sleep to order, wake to order, pray to order, and smile
discreetly (in a military manner, of course) if it pleased
the officers to make a joke. They seldom deigned to do so.

Some of these one hundred and fifty boys had difficulty
in getting the discipline firmly ingrained. One such was
Robert Falcon Scott. Later, he became a man with a great
sense of discipline, but at this stage, as long as he belonged
to the subordinate side in the game, he didn't like it too
well. No doubt he admitted this—but only to himself. He
had already learned to keep his mouth shut, to pretend,
to make the situation appear different from the reality.
In this way you could put on a pleasant smile, stand to
attention with an expression that implied this was the
greatest happiness in the world ... and yet know that you

hate what you are doing. He had instilled in himself one of the principles of great leadership: never tell the truth to the men. But when you tell them something, say it with such conviction that everyone thinks it's the truth and nothing but the truth, confided to them alone—a pleasant or an unpleasant truth, which they will probably repay by showing greater loyalty to their leader.

He learned during those hard, bitter, boring months to concentrate on details. He had a good memory—and a selective one. He knew precisely what he had to remember and what he could almost certainly afford to forget. He was wise enough not to acquire the reputation of an opportunist. And for that reason too, he was noticed by his officers.

He was not, and never became, an unpleasant person. He had one quality that went deep and never left him— real friendliness, with a genuine smile in addition to all the smiles that were tactically determined. He knew how to phrase his comments carefully when dealing with educated people. A cadet in the British Navy had to pay for his own uniform. Robert's father was without resources. But Robert always kept his complaints about shortage of money under control and this showed a certain compassion for his father. Then his criticism of the government was also mild— because the government didn't issue cadets with free uniforms. Most people who knew him thought that he would be a good officer.

But no one thought he'd be more than that. Neither the dissenter nor the dashing sailor, nor the man on the horizon who balanced on the steep slope and scratched his ear as he stared downwards. Those who underestimated him, underestimated his sense of duty and self-control. They also underestimated his ambition.

To make matters worse, he suffered from sea-sickness. It was a weakness which could easily have given rise to much hilarity on board—at his expense—in the company of one hundred and fifty young men. All of them were martyrs to a military system. Every day they were stuffed with principles—one of them being that a seaman doesn't vomit into the sea. Robert was sea-sick and he vomited. His first great victory, engraved in his memory and buried with him, was the conquering of this weakness without making life intolerable for himself as a cadet in the British Navy.

Then he was given a command. It was a slender, tiny beginning—a cause for amusement among the many who had long been in the ranks, and who now enhanced their own superiority by smiling at the modest start of others. Hitherto he had been a nonentity. Then suddenly he stepped out of the ranks and acquired a new dimension. In one way, there was something magical about what happened. He was just as friendly as before—towards those in his command, too; he continued to be inflexible in the performance of his own duties; and he kept his private life to himself, now as always—very few were ever to be allowed to intrude there.

After a number of years in the Navy, he was allowed on an ocean trip. An ocean-going squadron was to go to the West Indies on manoeuvres. On board the flagship was one of England's many eccentrics—a cartoon figure, like a pencil drawing in the margin of a thick book on the South Pole—the Secretary of the Royal Geographical Society, Clements Markham. He had mutton chop whiskers and a longing to conquer a continent. As a young man, Markham had been in the Navy, but he couldn't stand the discipline. In his day, young officer-cadets were whipped for insubordination. Markham left. Later, he praised the discipline on board British ships. He cultivated young men who seemed to have a taste for it. Now he made Robert Falcon Scott's acquaintance.

Clements Markham had taken part in one of the expeditions sent out to rescue Sir John Franklin. Later he undertook journeys in Peru, wrote books on his discoveries and nursed his great dream—that the English should conquer the last continent still unconquered, the land round the South Pole. He considered this a task for the Navy. Perhaps it had dawned on him that a task of such huge dimensions would demand discipline. Perhaps he attached great significance to the opinion that the vast ocean wastes down by the South Pole would be best tackled by the Navy. But he didn't seem to realize that the journey south would only truly begin when the ships could penetrate no further. Apparently it did not occur to him that snow and ice would be a problem. He had never worn skis in his life. Clements Markham was a man of unusual perseverance. He knew that even in a country such as England, with her tradition of great discoveries, trying to raise money for new conquests was like wading through a swamp. He pursued his single-minded struggle with authorities and private financiers, newspapers, schools and societies. He pulled every available string—and there were plenty of them. Then he went on manoeuvres to the West Indies, invited in his capacity as Secretary of the Royal Geographical Society. One day, a regatta for small boats was arranged. The competitors were not only to sail as fast as possible, but also to dismantle mast and sail before the run was completed. Robert Falcon Scott was the winner. Clements Markham commented: 'That fellow will conquer another continent for Britain.'

Later, the young officer was invited to Markham's cabin, and behaved in an exemplary manner. Only gradually did he allow his great qualities to unfold in the company of his new and older friend. He assumed the qualities of leadership modestly and discreetly. Their relationship was always to be a profoundly human one.

But Robert Falcon Scott had still never set eyes on snow. A long time would pass before he did.

* * *

We see him as a young naval officer, a boy on his way to manhood. Others went about finding women, but not he. He listened with a polite, somewhat awkward, rather irritating smile to what his colleagues had to say on the subject of their conquests. He never gave anything away. There are two explanations for this, the most likely being that he had nothing to say. Or perhaps he had put up an ingenious smoke-screen to hide his relationships, half shyly, half triumphantly, finding his greatest pleasure in keeping a conquest secret. We don't know.

Men younger than he now brought his food, and men he could make jump to attention kept order in his cabin. They saluted his comings and goings, as he did when officers of higher rank went past, in perfect style, and quite expressionlessly. Much to the surprise of those who had known him in his youth, he was positively bursting with good health. General opinion held that he hoped to go far. But when his superiors looked for a topic of conversation in a pause between two rounds of drinks, to their surprise they found themselves beginning to talk about him. 'He'll never get very far in the world, will he? Something's lacking.'

It was difficult to explain exactly what was lacking. He was colourless. He didn't swear in that good old British way. He was not just religious in the official way, the loyal servant of the Queen who believed in God in her honour, and because there was a law in England that Sunday should be kept holy. Robert Falcon Scott actually believed in God. It was miraculous.

We have a glimpse of an incident which occurred on his way to a new posting in Vancouver, on the west coast of North America. He was travelling on a passenger steamer which ran into a storm. The end seemed near. Waves began to flood the cabins. Women and children were scattered in confusion, men struggled against the sea, Scott among them. Later—but before he became a national hero—his behaviour was described by others who witnessed it. He was staggering along between the waves carrying a glass of water. It must have been quite a sight. Soaking wet, with a glass of water he mustn't spill—sea-sick, but gradually less sea-sick the more reasons there were for being so. A woman had asked for some water. She got it.

He returned through the storm, several people crowding round him; he had time and took the trouble to smile —fetched a pillow. It was wet, he said apologetically, 'But as you'll understand, we haven't any others. Shall I put it behind your head? Is there any danger? I don't think so. I don't think a modern ship like this can sink, but we must be prepared for a certain amount of unpleasantness for a few hours. Would you excuse me now? Someone's calling.'

Young men were prostrate too. He got them on their feet, speaking in a friendly way and shaking them, pulling an ear, lifting them on to his shoulders, surprising himself with his own strength. Without boasting, he established that he wasn't afraid. He cuffed a boy, saying, follow me or drown. The young man then drank a glass of water and regained his equilibrium, followed his great and still nameless leader—trying out a polite smile of his own on a woman calling for help.

After his stay on the west coast, Scott returned to England. Queen Victoria was still alive, though there were those who whispered she shouldn't be, and her ideas even less so. During this time, John Edward Scott died. He had sold the brewery and lived a few years with the illusion that he had money to live on. The illusion cracked. Then he died.

Robert and his younger brother were left in charge of the family. It was one of the Queen's principles that one should always be responsible for one's family. A year later, the brother died too.

So there he was, a young officer, still on modest pay, and

just as he was beginning to live for himself, he had to be responsible for others' livelihood. He had four sisters and a mother to look after. There was nothing to indicate, either then or later, that he ever felt bitter about this. Energetically he began to climb the Navy's long ladder for officers who want swift promotion. But things went so slowly in peacetime. He trained himself in the art of shooting torpedoes. It was a wise step for a young officer. Torpedoes were modern weapons.

Once or twice during the course of the twelve years that had passed since his first meeting with Clements Markham, the two men had met. They had talked about trips to the polar regions, about men and ships, but there was no closer contact between them. One day, Scott was in London, walking down Buckingham Palace Road. On the opposite pavement, he caught sight of Markham. Scott crossed the street to him.

We shall never know if he regretted it.

Markham, with dogged British determination, had been working on his great dream of Britain's conquering the last unconquered continent. The Norwegians had been there, a man called Carsten Borchgrevink the first to set foot on land. A Belgian expedition had also gone out. Neither Markham nor Scott had the slightest idea of the existence of a coxswain called Roald Amundsen.

Markham probably encountered enormous sympathy, but it was mixed with an even greater apathy, although England was the country which had discovered and conquered such large parts of the world. Fine words but no money. Nevertheless, he got the principle accepted that an expedition should be equipped and sent to the South Pole as soon as the money was available. All he had to do was find it. Markham remained convinced that the Navy should equip the expedition, provide officers and ships. But the Navy refused. Then two rich men donated large sums to the plan for the conquest of the South Pole—

to increase the glory of England ... and themselves. The
expedition could now become a reality.

Scott didn't know this as he crossed the street and
greeted Markham.

'Have you heard what's happened?'

'No.'

A couple of days later, Scott put in his application for
leadership of the expedition. What he didn't know was
that on Markham's list of possible candidates, his name
was as low as number six. A great many battles went on
behind the scenes: should a scientist have the leadership,
or an officer?

An officer it was.

At that point in time, Scott had still never seen snow.

Scott was a touching mixture of man and child when, as
the newly-appointed leader of the expedition, he went
to Kristiania to meet Fridtjof Nansen. Nansen was a famous
man, Scott a mere officer. The hero of the great wastelands received the newcomer with an open generosity
which made this polite young man seem ill at ease. He
had come to learn about the polar regions. He was very
keen to study sledges and their possibilities in a terrain
which presumably differed slightly from that in England.
He also asked Nansen's opinion on skiing. Were skis practical? Perhaps the older man turned his face away for a
moment. Scott still hadn't seen snow. He went inland to
do so.

This was the outward picture. The inner one showed
an inexperienced man who absorbed with impressive
strength all that the experienced explorer had to tell him.
Nansen wasn't slow on the uptake. He saw into Scott's soul,
and what he saw there was the raw material of a strong
and talented leader, made to solve great problems. Perhaps he saw too a certain naïveté which might prove costly,
and a lack of that brutality you need to save lives when

everything is at stake—or at least to save your own life, if not those of others.

Scott tackled the problem systematically, going through the plan as if it were a curriculum; he passed the exam with flying colours. He soon knew everything there was to know about polar journeys. But he hadn't got it in his bones—none of the mysteries of ski-bindings, none of the art of driving dogs. At home in England, the experts were quarrelling about the use of dogs. Clements Markham said no. The men would have to pull the sledges. Dogs would collapse. The English had had unfortunate experiences with dogs in polar regions. But the problem had not been properly analysed, and no one had given an adequate explanation of British failure on this point. Markham was an expert, difficult to persuade—not least because he was conscious that the expedition was primarily his work. 'No dogs!' Other men thumped the table and cried, 'Dogs!' Apparently Scott had no say in the matter. Finally, they reached an unsatisfactory compromise. Twenty-three dogs were brought from Siberia—too few to depend on them for pulling-power, and what good were they otherwise? The dogs were of different breeds. The sleds weren't built to suit dogs.

The ship which the Navy put at their disposal was called the *Discovery*. The ship and its equipment were simplicity itself. Negotiations deteriorated when it came to deciding on the ratio of scientists to officers on board. Which should be in the majority? The experts disagreed. The Navy refused to give up more men. As usual, it turned out that they were short of money. There was no more to be had without the most humiliating forms of begging. The Boer War broke out.

Scott was on the point of giving up before he had even started; he saw a tragic dimension in the financial charades, as did his rival and colleague—Roald Amundsen, now on his way to the North-West Passage. But even if Scott had the guts to accept defeat and withdraw, it had now become a matter of prestige to others that he went on. Half against his will, he was forced to continue, and at last the *Discovery* was ready and sailed out to sea.

Let's take a look at some of the men on board.

There was the great doctor, Edward Wilson, who was tubercular and had weak nerves; he had spent a long time in Norway recuperating from his illness, because he thought the cold air would improve his condition. On the same principle, a trip to the South Pole would do him the world of good. Wilson was a very fine artist, and made numerous sketches throughout the expedition.

He was wise, unassuming, with an elegant sense of humour, everyone's friend, though with a reticence which made his friendship invaluable to the only man he really gave it to: Scott.

The two of them were to die together.

Then there was Edgar Evans, an iron-hard, thickset Petty Officer, strong as a bear and amazingly practical. There was something uncouth about Evans. In many ways the complete man, he needed a strong leader to deal with his few weaknesses. In a critical situation, where the leadership didn't measure up, Evans's physical strength wouldn't be enough. Scott admired him, but overestimated his tenacity. One day Evans cracked up.

Ernest Shackleton was to play a considerable part in Robert Scott's life. He had applied early to be included in the *Discovery* expedition; he was an officer in the Merchant Navy, a Scot by birth, but with nothing to indicate any special qualifications for an expedition of this kind. So he was turned down. But he persevered, pursuing the matter with concentrated energy. Fortuitously, one of those appointed on board resigned, and had to be replaced at the last minute. A friend of Shackleton's was sent to Scott to try again on his behalf. Scott shrugged and asked one of his officers to try to find out something about the man.

It wasn't easy, and the officer found out nothing what-soever about him. But Shackleton came to be included. He turned out to be temperamental, fanatical, dedicated to achieving glory, perhaps dedicated to revenge, too. *Discovery* sailed.

There was some Norwegian dried fish on board for feed-ing the dogs. The fish itself was good, but had been badly stored. When the dogs later became weak and useless, most people thought this was the cause. This was some-thing Scott only knew about at second hand. He had heard about dried fish, but none of the men with him knew much about it. Perhaps maggots had got into the fish. Nansen was said to have shaken his head when he heard the story about the dried fish. That the dogs did not measure up on this occasion was to have sombre consequences for Scott on his next—and last—expedition.

At least the sea trip south went well. Scott and his men knew the art of sailing. Eventually they caught sight of the ice, which most of them on board had never seen before.

They made their way through the pack-ice, reached the Great Ice Barrier, struck land and put up a little hut at Hut Point. It was 1902.

Overwintering took place on board the *Discovery*. Here, as on the *Belgica*, men would go out into the darkness and scream—then make themselves be silent, force a smile. They would go back, find the side of the ship in the dark, crawl back on board. For a moment they would bask in the security of the ship, but this soon turned to hatred—of the men, the vessel, everything. Then they would go out into the dark again and scream.

Did everyone on board go mad? Was everyone equally disagreeable? There was one exception, one person who was consistently courteous, consistently friendly, nearly always content. On his bad days, he might be a little moody. That was all. He was their leader.

Scott formed a special friendship with two men on

board, Wilson and Shackleton. His friendship with Wilson was taken for granted. But with Shackleton there might possibly have been a streak of self-interest in it. Shackleton had a certain magnetism, and magnetism can easily be repelling. It's as if we see Scott, hand outstretched, in Shackleton's cabin, the ice creaking outside. A polite question, an embarrassed smile: 'Shouldn't we two be friends? It would create a good impression if we were friends, and besides, I personally would consider it an honour...'

Winter passed. When spring came, the expedition was to set sail for the south. But would they try to reach the Pole? This had never been stated in so many words, but must have been the secret aim of the trip. Scott himself was to be the leader. The other two were to be Wilson and Shackleton.

They had dogs with them, but no skis. The dogs were a disappointment from the very first day. The men were unskilled and couldn't drive a dog-sled. The terrain was terrible. They waded up to their waists in snow. A day's march covered a few kilometres.

Three friends went on this first melancholy trip south— but they didn't return friends. No one had ever been as far as this. Distant mountain peaks were glimpsed, then became shrouded in mist again. It turned out that the food rations were insufficient. At first, the dogs had to sit on the sleds and be drawn along by the men, then they had to be shot. The three men were forced to turn back 620 kilometres away from the pole.

Shackleton cracked up on the return journey. We'll never know the full truth of what happened, but we catch a brief glimpse of a sick man, now out of his senses. Had he been eating the poisoned fish? The other two wanted him to ride on the sledge, but he refused. Three men were in the icy wastes, with death a few paces behind them. Scott was the leader, but wasn't he too weak? Perhaps the intimate friendship between Scott and Wilson became the last mental straw which broke Shackleton's back. Scott had his Bible with him, though it was small comfort here.

Despite everything, they got back to Hut Point. There was now some fear for Shackleton's life. The *Discovery* was still frozen in, and an auxiliary ship had been sent for from England—the *Morning*, originally from Norway, where it had belonged to Svend Foyn.

Shackleton was sent back to England on the *Morning*. He was a sick man and had failed, but his failure suggested manic strength. The icy cold of the Antarctic had now penetrated his relationship with Scott.

Scott and his men returned to England the following year. They were greeted as heroes and deservedly so. Never, never, it was said, had men been so far, explored so widely, achieved such results. Who remembered Shackleton now? But his own memory was good and he was determined; there was a streak of hatred in him which made him a more efficient man than Scott. He lacked Scott's balanced mind, but imbalance has its own strength.

Scott became England's youngest battleship commander. At the same time, he fell in love. Even so, he still wanted to go back to the Pole.

So did Shackleton.

Both of them had now seen snow.

To his own surprise, Scott discovered he'd become famous. After all this time we can't be sure whether he enjoyed the feeling or not. Amundsen's unsavoury smile when he received ovations tells us clearly his reaction. Contemporary pictures of Scott show an expression of shrinking fear, shoulders hunched, an embarrassed twitch of his mouth which was probably meant to convey a happy smile. Around him are milling crowds, acclaiming their hero.

He soon learned to bear the weight of his medals. Here he was on familiar ground: as a naval officer, he knew the regulations on how many medals could be worn without injury to chest and back muscles. He had never been much of a public speaker, but he applied himself to the task: he learned rhetoric and developed a simple style which gained force in retrospect. He began to be more authoritative. Perhaps this was why there was now a touch of triviality about him which hadn't been apparent before. Shackleton had recovered, and wished to rehabilitate himself. Outwardly he wished to do so as Scott's friend. Inwardly his feelings were more hostile. Privately Shackleton gave it its real name—revenge on a man who had shown greater strength out in the ice and had sent the loser home. No doubt it saved his life, but even Scott was human, and probably took a certain pleasure in getting rid of a troublesome colleague.

Shackleton wanted to be off on an expedition of his own, and wished to make use of the hut on Hut Point. Scott reckoned it belonged to him. Scott himself wanted to be off, to further the cause of science, so it said in the newspapers—and perhaps that was the reason in his heart of hearts too—but somewhere, and he had a much deeper consciousness of it than would ever be publicly known, was the realization that the glory which would accrue to him by conquering the Pole was the real reason for his determination. So Shackleton should stay at home.

If we read between the lines of letters between Shackleton and Scott at this time, we can detect a certain irritability. Then Commander Scott's battleship collided during a manoeuvre; misfortune beset him; he fell in love.

He had had several lady friends, but they were casual acquaintances, no more. Then he met Kathleen Bruce, a sculptress. The photographs show a handsome woman, beautiful, gentle, with rather too firm a mouth. Fortunately, she was ambitious, too, and this ambition extended to Scott. His infatuation became an inner flame, a source of both pain and strength.

Was she right for him? How can we tell? He cruised

round her for a long time, like a commander of a battle-ship round an enemy craft, unable to make a battle-plan and thus go into attack. His Victorian upbringing had taught him that a man should take a wife. From that came children—if God so wished it, and if the King gave his permission. In his most frivolous moments, his thoughts might even have skirted the physical manifestation of the problem. He let weeks and years go by. Meanwhile Shackleton was moving in the direction of the South Pole.

But Scott was not a man to refuse to accept the moral consequences of his infatuation. This meant addressing himself to his chosen one in writing. He had a naval officer's sense of propriety, so his first problem concerned his family. His mother was still alive. He now earned enough to be able to keep both her and two sisters—and eventually, if that was to be his melancholy lot in life, a family of his own as well. It was after some pressure from his mother that he finally pulled himself together and proposed. He was accepted. He was a handsome young man. On the wedding photograph he looks more hunched than ever. Kathleen has assumed a proprietary air—and had good grounds for doing so: she had made quite a catch.

Kathleen quickly became pregnant.

Would Shackleton reach the South Pole?

The one problem was no less vital than the other.

Royalty had been on board to bid farewell before Shackleton sailed. England celebrated, all flags were hoisted, another hero was to conquer the world—and he almost managed it. He and three of his men travelled in the direction of the point in one of the most hazardous, daring, most exhausting trips the history of the poles has to tell. They had four ponies with them. In his choice of draught animals lay hidden something of Scott's later tragedy. On this point, he came to resemble Shackleton.

Shackleton and his companions got up on to the pole

plateau itself and were the first to see that it was flat land ahead to the south. There they had to turn back. Rations were short. But they were only 160 kilometres short of the South Pole.

They could have cheated if they had wanted to. No one was in a position to prove that they hadn't actually got there. But although Shackleton was difficult and uncompromising, he was honest. A few months later, Peary got to the North Pole. It's often said that there's no evidence that he did in fact reach it.

We can have some idea of Scott's secret hopes, although he was too wise to write much down about Shackleton and his journey. Nor does it necessarily detract from his greatness if even a part of him did prefer to see Shackleton fail. Shackleton returned to England and received a hero's welcome. The two men now met publicly. Their formal handshake gave way to genuine congratulations—heartfelt, demonstrative, two huge smiles breaking out. Behind them stretched an empire.

Inevitably, now it was Scott's turn. The opportunity had been created and he couldn't back down. Almost everyone was now out for the South Pole. It was claimed that Peary himself, the man from the North Pole, would soon be setting off. From Norway there wasn't a word. No one gave Norway a thought. England had sprung into action. Money was said to be available, much to everyone's astonishment; that proved something important was up. The South Pole was to be conquered.

It reflects to Scott's advantage—to his nobility, some would maintain—that on the day his son was born, he began preparations for another journey to the South.

Maybe his choice of timing also contained a touch of egotism.

Continuity was now secure. God and his son would exist, even if he had to die.

AMUNDSEN

Roald Amundsen visited Nansen again in 1907, this time with a request to borrow the *Fram*. Amundsen had returned from the North-West Passage, no longer an unknown coxswain, but nevertheless, not yet in the same league as Nansen in the minds and imaginations of the population. Now he wanted to drift across the Arctic Ocean as his predecessor had done, trying to reach the Pole itself. It wasn't an original plan. Nansen asked for time to think it over.

A few years earlier, two men had overwintered in a double sleeping-bag on Frans Josef Land. They had built rough stone walls around them to weather storms which sometimes lasted as long as a week. They ate walrus meat and possessed only one shirt each, which they turned inside out on Christmas Eve. One of them was Nansen, a warrior in mind and truth—in public opinion and in his own— perhaps the only person who had crossed polar country without impairing his soul; the other, Hjalmar Johansen, was a master at penetrating the icy wastelands, hard as iron, indestructible, but he was no great leader. However, he was intolerant of any leader except one—Nansen.

Each time one of them turned over in the sleeping-bag, the other had to turn too; when one breathed out, the other should be breathing in. This demanded strict self-discipline from both, and mutual respect. When one of them slept, the other had to sleep; when one felt the need to talk—driven to it by fatal boredom—the other had to force himself to listen whether he liked it or not. They were two men who fitted together like hand and glove, both wise: Nansen philosophical, Johansen slightly naïve, without the other's great stature, but honest to the marrow and with a doglike capacity for devotion—if the master were worthy of devotion.

There, in a hut on Frans Josef Land, Nansen thought out the details of his journey to the South Pole, the culmination of his life as an explorer. Very possibly he considered taking Johansen with him. This was the warrior's impressive remedy for depression in the polar darkness: planning another journey—in the same darkness, but as far away as possible from his present situation. Then the two of them came back.

Nansen thought about the *Fram*, and decided to refuse Amundsen. He was no longer young. If he were to embark on the journey south, then it would have to be soon.

Amundsen was already in the house, Nansen on his way downstairs to deliver his harsh refusal. But there was someone else in the house too—his wife, Eva. Perhaps she was already ill—she died not long afterwards. Eva put her head round the door and said: 'I know what you've decided.'

Maybe there was an element of reproach in her words: the two of them had drifted far apart from each other. 'You have decided, haven't you? Go your own way then.' The effect of her words was to needle him into changing his mind. It must have been a close thing: behind his decision lay the wish to spite Eva.

Amundsen got the *Fram*.

Let us take a look at him with his air of humility—back bowed, head slightly raised, a dog-like look in his eyes, the tip of his tongue protruding slightly. Nansen had risen from his chair and spoke frankly, barely suppressing his irritation: 'I'd thought of going south myself! But now you come along with your plans for the North Pole. Yes, yes, I know you have every right to go north. But it's not for my own sake that I am giving way and letting you go. There's still a great deal undiscovered in the north. But you should know that it's with some bitterness I'm letting you have the *Fram* ... I was to have her myself.'

Amundsen completed his bow, thanked him deferentially and left. He was not a man to allow himself to be delayed by other people's feelings. He began to plan the journey to the North Pole that same day.

The plans were made public, parliament granted the money, private contributions poured in. Essentially, Amundsen was to follow Fridtjof Nansen's route. Then came the telegram saying that Dr Cook had reached the North Pole.

Roald Amundsen's genius was inseparable from his fanatical ambition. The news of Cook's reported conquest of the North Pole must have been a crushing blow. We can picture him when the newspaper arrived: gasping for breath, he throws down the paper, tramples on it, picks it up, spits on it, wipes away the spit for a second look. Dr Cook has reached the Pole ...

Amundsen must have quickly realized that there was no way of knowing whether or not this was true, but what would people think if on his own journey to the Pole he maintained that his old friend Dr Cook had been lying? Tears ran down his cheeks. He hated the world, threw himself down on his bed, ranting and raving ... for a moment even contemplating suicide.

But he soon realized that he had to keep his feelings to himself.

Don't let anyone see that you hope it is a fraud. He brought himself under complete control, and went out to be greeted by journalists. He professed to believe utterly in the truth of what he had just heard. My good friend

Dr Cook has reached the North Pole. I sincerely congratulate him.

Then another telegram came. The American, Robert Edwin Peary, was also said to have reached the North Pole.

Peary accused Cook of lying. Cook smiled and defended his statements. Amundsen had officially aligned himself with one hero, and he couldn't now start siding with another. In any case, it was crystal clear that even if they succeeded in exposing one man, they could never expose both.

Now there was only one spot left on earth where no man had set foot.

Amundsen had an idea.

He stopped in mid-stride and looked round, swiftly running his fingers through his hair. The idea was so daring that it left him trembling.

He tried to ignore it, but couldn't ignore the joy bubbling within him as his strength and lust for life began to return. But keep quiet. Discretion at all costs.

Yes, discretion. Other explorers are making plans all over England, aren't they? They haven't got a monopoly, but if I disclose my plan, it will get into the Press and maybe I'll be stopped from going south because of our close ties with England. Shackleton got very far south, didn't he? Now Scott's setting out. Amundsen rested his head in his hands. His mind was buzzing with excitement, but even the excitement was controlled.

Then he met the Shadow, his brother Leon. The two of them discussed the matter. Roald disclosed his plan to the Shadow, the only man in whom he had absolute confidence, with whom he had crossed the Hardanger plateau. They knew each other's weaknesses, ambitions and raw strength. The Shadow was wiser than his brother, but didn't have his courage. He wasn't the chosen one, but he got his own back by being the truthful one—during those few chosen moments.

A strange moment, the two of them in a hotel room, two pairs of eyes glowing in the dusk. They didn't dare speak out loud in case someone overheard them. The first rough sketches, the feverish hunt for maps—who could get maps of the South Pole? We must have maps! Will they suspect anything if we go out and buy them? They know you down there: you were with the *Belgica*. The English have no monopoly.

Keep quiet.

If we succeed, all will be forgiven. If we fail, then everything fails and you'll have to face dishonour. I, the Shadow, can retreat into the background. You'll have to face the spotlight of disgrace. You're staking everything on one card. You must either be first, or be destroyed.

This plan reveals the breadth and character of Amundsen's genius. The boldest feat in his life was not that he reached the Pole, but that he had the imagination and courage secretly to reverse all his plans from north to south. It wasn't a question of morality. It was a question of willpower and the ability to accomplish his will. He won because he had the courage to take an imaginative decision.

The Shadow was behind him, unsmiling. Did Amundsen for a brief moment feel an oppressive weight from his elder brother? The clever brother who understood everything but wasn't chosen to do anything.

Later the two of them split up.

Roald deceived Nansen.

He deceived parliament.

He deceived the public and all his patrons.

He knew he would be vindicated if he reached the Pole first—and condemned if he were not first on the spot where no one had gone before, and where no human being should presume to go.

Amundsen decided to set up winter camp on the sea-ice at

the Bay of Whales, in Ross Sea. Assuming Scott went on land where the *Discovery* expedition had overwintered, Amundsen wished to be a whole degree, eleven Norwegian miles, nearer the Pole than Scott. When Shackleton sailed into the Ice Barrier in the Bay of Whales in 1908, he was greeted by a terrifying sight. Huge floes broke off and stood upright, then were ground to slush. A constantly shifting and heaving mass, the ice would erupt in new shapes which glinted weirdly in the sunlight before vanishing into a sea of mist. Then the ship, a mere dot in the turbulent channel, with frightened men on board, turned and made its way back to the mainland at Hut Point. Amundsen knew of this. It is an illustration of his independence and courage that this knowledge did not stop him. Before his departure he got hold of a map and studied it. It wasn't in his nature to make rash decisions, but after hours of lonely walks during which his mind ground the problem to pieces, the way the current grinds down an ice floe, a plan matured. He would strike camp and overwinter at the Bay of Whales on the ice in Ross Sea.

At first glance, it wasn't a good plan, but he had arguments to forestall all his critics. If Shackleton had passed the Bay of Whales a day later, or the night before...? Would the sea and ice have been equally disturbed? Was there no sign that indicated ... and he dug out all the old arguments, went over his own experiences in the *Belgica* with a fine toothcomb, using all his skill in an imaginary debate. Wasn't there any evidence that the Bay of Whales was shallow, that farther in, some of the projections were islands that would bind the ice and make it relatively firm?

Generally speaking, an expedition should feel secure overwintering on the ice. Generally speaking—but if he was right, he would win world acclaim. If the expedition failed, he probably wouldn't be given a chance to answer the criticism. It was true that he was risking his life. But

47

what was life for if not to be risked? If there was a problem, it was whether to allow all of them to go under, or none.

He took the decision to set up winter camp in the Bay of Whales, and stuck to it, refusing to budge an inch, carrying the plan through without batting an eyelid. But he didn't mention his reservations.

Didn't mention them to the men, either. It was best that his worries were shared with one person only.

Now Scott arrived in Kristiania. He was newly-married and had his wife, Kathleen, with him. She was smart and friendly, very willing to show off her husband, a woman with bold features both physically and spiritually, cultured and intelligent.

She certainly impressed Nansen, who was a man of considerable culture. He had been the Norwegian Ambassador in London, and was familiar with English ways and customs. He could kiss a hand and raise an eyebrow simultaneously, if necessary. He was friendly, as usual—and helpful, as always. Scott was wearing a boater. He was more assured than when the two had first met, but he had retained his modesty. Nansen was still the master and he the pupil: these two rôles suited them both down to the ground, Nansen especially. They took trips into town to look at sledges, and again discussed the problem of skis. The older man let his wealth of experience flow, the wife chattered, her husband bowed politely. Three happy people ... one of whom was going to the South Pole to die.

Scott was currently absorbed in motor-sledges. This was something new and the work on them took up a great deal of time. He should have known that new inventions were seldom successful at first. A trial run was for experience, not achievement. For the experience, I should take the sledges along. If I hope to conquer the Pole, I should leave them behind.

He took them with him, for the experience.

Nansen asked: 'Dogs or horses, Mr Scott?'

'Herr Nansen, all the experts are quarrelling over that in England.'

Scott was to go inland first to find snow so that he could try out the sledges.

'But first of all, Herr Nansen, my husband and I would like to meet this ... what's his name? The man from the North-West Passage.'

'I agree with you, Kathleen. We should meet him. He's going to the North Pole, isn't he?'

'You mean Herr Amundsen, madam. I'll have my secretary ring him.'

The phone rang and rang. Engaged.

Or not engaged, but a voice said that Amundsen was out, Amundsen was in town, Amundsen was at sea, he was not at home.

Out at Uranienborg, in the house in Oppegård which Amundsen had now purchased, he had given his orders. He stood in a corner, letting the phone ring. He knew what he wanted and was willing to pay the price; his face tense, muscles knotted, eyes darkening as he turned away.

'Pity we weren't able to meet him, Herr Nansen. He's going to the North Pole, isn't he?' They never did meet, those two.

In the garden of Amundsen's house, out at Oppegård, a hut was being constructed in sections, to be taken on the journey north. An observation hut, they said—rather strange, as the hut was large enough to hold many people; no one with experience in the northern ice could make out what it would be used for. But it grew swiftly and surely, for Amundsen was a master at finding practical men to work with him. He had employed a young man called Jørgen Stubberud. Jørgen could handle tools exceptionally deftly, and had a capacity for admiration which stood him in good stead later on in life. Amundsen was the perfect

employer, full of consideration for the simple Jørgen—
making small observations, praising his work, helping
when there was a rush, possessing an almost uncanny ability
to know the appropriate thing to do and say to such an
honest and friendly soul. Hjalmar Johansen came to visit,
on orders from Fridtjof Nansen. Amundsen had no choice
but to receive him. So the two met, both experienced men,
but Johansen the more so. There was no denying it: compared with the ski-trip to the North Pole, every other
journey into the polar regions paled into insignificance.
Amundsen was physically strong, Johansen stronger. Both
were good skiers, Johansen better, as it turned out. Practical men, both with an unusual capacity for survival when
everything was at stake. Each knew his limitations. One
of them was a formidable leader as long as he himself
could choose men to suit his nature, but edgy and stiff,
unable to lead people who didn't admire him enough.
Johansen had the capacity for admiration, but the object
had to deserve it. He had known only one man worthy of
his admiration and that man was not Amundsen. And even
Johansen had been affected by the icy wastes of the north.
They hadn't crushed him, but they had battered him and
left their scars on his mind. His return home from the
expedition with Nansen had turned into something of a
party. He wasn't quite the man he had been, though just
as clever, just as strong, still able to turn cartwheels when
people clapped. His nerves were still good when something
was happening. But nothing was happening in Oppegård.
So why should he go round admiring a man who wasn't
as great as the man he had admired? Hypocrisy wasn't in
his nature.

The two met and disliked each other on sight.

Nansen had authority and warmth.

Amundsen had authority, but he was entirely lacking
in warmth.

The man from the North-West Passage never became

friendly with the man from Frans Josef Land.

Amundsen was on familiar terms with the dogs which had now come to Kristiansand. There were ninety-seven of them. Amundsen had contacts everywhere and used them with a mixture of charm and cleverness, insolence and energy. They were Greenland dogs, carefully chosen through contacts in Copenhagen, well-fed without being fat.

He understood dogs. It must have been a natural gift, as he hadn't had any experience with them. The dogs understood him, with their profound, tactful understanding. He radiated firmness and friendliness. He wasn't afraid of an unknown jaw. He scratched them thoroughly, rolling them over and over, lifting them up by their pelts and letting them go; he was not generous with titbits, withholding them before graciously handing them over. He examined every dog minutely, studying their legs and their back muscles, quickly getting to know them and remembering the names of every single one of the ninety-seven. But at the same time, he was calculating quickly and coldly: they will eat each other; and we will eat them. Why shouldn't a man be able to eat a dog?

He had a whip with him and thrashed the ones who disobeyed.

One of Scott's problems was that he felt compassion at using the animals out on the ice. This didn't deter him, but the feeling of doing wrong weighed heavily on him.

By now Amundsen was working night and day on his equipment. He constructed a boot that looked like a barge. It had to be both stiff and pliable. A foot, he said, is dressed from morning to night. You can't come to its rescue if it freezes. You soon lose contact with it. The foot becomes an independent creation without feeling when it is frozen. To prevent that, it must have room. So the boot should be soft; but ski-bindings required a hard boot. That was the problem. The success or failure of the expedition could depend on the relation between boot and foot. He solved the problem in theory, then he found a shoemaker who could do the job.

Next he turned to the problem of making underpants thick enough at the back. If there's a storm behind you, victory or defeat can hang on whether your underpants are properly made. They have to be sewn of suitable material. He got two hundred old woollen blankets from the Navy. They were the right material, but could he find a tailor to take on such inglorious work? He went off to the tailor and took all his powers of persuasion with him. That was one of his talents, one not often brought into use, but there all the same. Inventive lies mixed freely with broad, homely humour and a radiant charm which would melt a tailor. 'You see that the material is imported. Feel this, the stuff's beautiful. Look at the colour. I think it would be easy to work with for a skilled man like you. Have you thought what the length of a pair of underpants could mean to a hero in a storm?'

'Are there women there?'

'No. But then, a man's a man for all that ... he's got his male equipment, and thank God he has, but we mustn't let it get frozen, must we?'

'The way to the Pole lies in these underpants.'

Amundsen stumbled out, sneering, filled with self-loathing, needing someone to talk to. There was only one man who would do, his brother, Leon.

His fingers trembling, the man stood in front of the Shadow, seeking comfort from him; they emptied a bottle of brandy between them.

But an aversion began to grow in Roald. One day it broke out.

The Shadow had no chinks. It knew too much.

The *Fram* was a sorry sight on its journey across the sea,

resembling a barrel in motion, unworthy among craft of a nobler kind. The *Fram* rode the waves like a piece of planking, apparently without hope of survival, but like a plank, she couldn't sink; half-seas over, with small sails hoisted and an engine rumbling with the muffled snore of a drunken old uncle after a good dinner; a gypsy-boat full of remarkable gear and no less remarkable men. They were in a hurry to get south. The ship was to round Cape Horn and then sail north through the Pacific, then into the Bering Straits—so they thought. Only one man on board knew the truth, and he kept quiet. Only he knew the real reason why there was such a hurry. They had to reach the Bay of Whales before Scott. Amundsen had the sudden thought that Scott might also be hoping to set up winter camp there to be nearer the Pole.

The leader had his friendly smile pinned on as though with safety pins. It could quickly vanish. At night in his cramped cabin he was like a caged animal, sometimes running up on deck, stumbling over dogs; the crew in total ignorance of his scheme. They had been hired for several years in the northern ice. Tough contracts had been signed by tough men, who held a pen as if it were a ski-pole. They had agreed in the contract that they would go with Amundsen, obey Amundsen, subject themselves to Amundsen. But they assumed that Amundsen would tell them the truth, which he had not done.

He kept himself busy by helping the crew with all their tasks. There was nothing that he, the leader, was too grand to do. A man was kept swabbing the deck clear of dog excreta. Amundsen joined him, swabbing the deck, too. This he could do, waltzing around in shiny sea boots on deck, swabbing until his boots were as foul as the deck. He gained popularity this way, but at the same time there was something repugnant about him—and he knew it; he repelled the crew at the same time as he attracted them.

There was one other person on board who would have

53

to know where they were going: Nilsen, the skipper. He was a seaman, and not much of a thinker. He stood steadily on deck and didn't stumble over his feet or his conclusions. Amundsen had made sure that Nilsen knew everything at an early stage. You can't fool your skipper. To deceive a skipper on board his own ship was an insult. So the two of them had a private conference, first a firm handclasp, then a few words. 'You see, Nilsen, I know I can trust you ... Do you see what I mean?'

Nilsen nodded, but he didn't really understand, nor did he realize he was already half won over. The leader leaned across the table, the hero, the man in the headlines; gimlet-eyed, he even managed to force out an expression of need: 'Nilsen! Can you keep your mouth shut?'

'Yes, yes.'

'Then I'll tell you everything.'

So saying, he took out of his wallet a carefully drafted document. Nilsen signed it. He would be as silent as the grave. Amundsen told him everything.

Out in the Atlantic, without having mentioned to Nilsen that any others were to be initiated into their secret plan, Amundsen further reduced the number who might refuse when he decided to announce the truth. There were two lieutenants on board, Gjertsen and Prestrud. The wily leader took one lieutenant aside first, on his own: 'Only the captain and I know—but we can trust you, can't we, Prestrud? Will you sign?'

Then the other one. How could he refuse when the first had promised to keep his mouth shut?

Now only the crew was left.

The *Fram* was a hell-hole of dogs. With ninety-seven of them on board, they were tethered everywhere, always in the way; the men tripped over dogs, scratched dogs, patted dogs; when they got into the trade winds and tried to sleep on deck in the warmth, they found they were lying on dogs. One of the characteristics of Eskimo dogs is that they howl in chorus. One would start off—a secret leader, divinely chosen--with a voice to make mountains tremble and storms fall silent with shame. This leader would start up, then the others followed, rising and falling in scales and notes with dazzling power across the ocean, the ship vibrating with sound and taking in waves over her deck. A man rushed out from the cabins, cursing. Another came out and kicked one of the dogs, but not the right one, not the leader, now wisely keeping its mouth shut. The other ninety-six doubled their contribution and the howling rose to the stars and sky. Two more men came on deck, clenching their fists. One of them was wearing clogs: he took one off and aimed, missed, the shoe landing in the sea. He noticed his companion smiling. He hit him—one blow too many. The two men began fighting. Then the skipper roared, and miraculously the howling ceased for a brief spell, while the canine choir drew breath to start again. Fighting between men became fighting with dogs. Soon everyone was fighting everybody else, each man against six dogs, eight dogs, ten dogs. But the dogs carried on howling and the *Fram* chugged on across the sea—a quiet breeze to starboard and an old-fashioned, brave little engine. At last the dogs fell silent.

The deck was covered with dog-shit. The dogs had been busy as they howled. The men on board vomited.

Let's take a look at one of them. He had never set foot on deck before, and was now struggling against sea-sickness. He came from the isolated Morge valley and knew little of what lay outside it. He was the best skier in the world. They had taken him to Paris and he had skied in France. He had had to be told what country he was in, but he had won the race. On a railway station in Hamburg, the Norwegian ski-troop had met Amundsen. Olav Bjaaland had said: 'Can I come with you on your next trip?' He hadn't known where Amundsen was going. 'I expect that can be arranged,' had been the reply. And here he was.

But Olav Bjaaland was a force to be reckoned with. He hadn't much education but his Norwegian prose savoured of earth and sweat as he wrote in his journal on his way to the Pole. He was a practical man, a man of few words. Strong as a young horse, he could put up with the extreme cold as no one else could without getting frostbite. He was tolerant of insult and free from great ambition. Clarity of thought was not always his strong point, but he genuinely felt that beneath Amundsen's less likeable qualities lay a wealth of admirable characteristics. So he was faithful, not uncritical, but always loyal, and not without a native cunning: it paid to be friends with the leader, didn't it? He wasn't an opportunist, but a man who had reported for the race, and wanted to win it.

Once again, Amundsen had shown his ability to choose the right man.

At Funchal, in Madeira, the dogs were given the carcass of a horse to devour. Everywhere on board there was blood, and sleeping dogs, but ashore were palm trees, a beautiful beach, air which trembled with heat. Then the Shadow came aboard. Yes, Leon from Norway was there, arriving by another ship. Here the last practical details were arranged: a few bills paid, problems discussed under the eyes of four men in the cabin, and secret telegrams sent.

Now was the moment of truth.

Even years later, when Amundsen wrote down his account, he couldn't hide his nervousness. He had prepared himself thoroughly, thought through what would happen step by step, word by word. All men on deck. Let them wait there. Not so long that they became irritable. But not too short a wait either—let the tension mount. The leader grows in stature if he lets the men wait a while. Skipper Nilsen came up on deck with a rolled map under his arm.

Then the lieutenants, close together, then Leon, up

from his cabin with a heavy document file in his hand.

As long as the dogs didn't start howling at that particular moment.

This was an important and incalculable factor. If that happened, the situation would become uncontrollable. The entire crew would have lost their tempers, and then what would happen? But the dogs had been given the last of the horse, their stomachs were now replete with flesh and blood. That was part of the plan. They would keep quiet then—God willing. At last Amundsen came on deck, and like a shock the truth was hurled at them, simple and hard, an ultimatum.

'We're sailing south.'

Everyone was officially free to refuse, but who could get back home alone from Madeira?

It worked. It worked: it was incredible. The actor had his audience in the palm of his hand and triumphed. He noted that the shock had turned into relief. He had surmounted one of the great obstacles on his way to the Pole. The palm trees wafted in the breeze, the sea bobbing to the south. Soon they'd be off.

Leon went ashore with the telegrams. One was to Scott and was eventually sent from Norway, once Leon was back there, when Scott was already in Melbourne on his way south.

The telegram was obscurely worded. It just said that Amundsen was continuing southwards, not that he was going in to assault the Pole.

A genius may be privileged to take drastic action, but we do not necessarily approve of that action.

All the men except Johansen felt a stronger devotion than ever to their leader. Maybe he had deceived them: no matter. Even the dogs love him ... and he kicks them.

The *Fram* was becalmed. Her engine was weak and they had to conserve fuel. The clumsy ship lay torpidly afloat

on a black sea. Now and again a dog got up in the heat of
the sun and howled—even the howl subdued by the heat.
A man sleeping in the shade under the canvas opened
one eye, but soon fell asleep again. You needed patience
to get through the slow hours, the hot nights, the unbear-
able days. They had to save fresh water, which had become
muddy and almost unusable as drinking water. The dogs
were thirsty and lay with their tongues hanging out, panting, their tongues no longer red, but grey.

That was when he went round from man to man saying:
'Don't worry: I'm in command.' It wasn't an order, nor
an expression of confidence, simply a friendly piece of information, intended to relieve the other men's gloomy
thoughts, and assume their burden himself. He took his
time, sitting down beside the man who was aimlessly
whittling a stick, taking out a clasp knife, scraping away
the black from under his nails, cursing a little with the
man who was cursing, being silent with the man who had
no words. He reminded them: 'I'm in command.' He had
a remarkable ability to reassure others when something
was up—far out at sea, on board a motionless ship during
the long hours of boredom.

He said nothing about his real anxiety—will we get to
the Bay of Whales before Scott? Whoever arrived last
would have to give way to the first. But this fear was his,
and his alone. He went round saying: 'I'm in command.'

On his orders, they unchained the dogs. They had to
have exercise and there was no room to walk them round
on the overfull deck on board a ship bursting with equipment. They were all freed at the same time. They had
been tied up for six weeks, and at first not one of them
noticed that they could now move about freely. Half an
hour went by. Nothing happened. But tension was mount-
ing on board. Anything could happen. The men had
emerged from their stupor and were watching when the
first of the dogs got up and took a few steps across the

deck. It stopped, astounded at what was happening. No chain to hold it back. At once all hell broke loose, and half-wild dogs hurled themselves forward to punish the one that had broken free. All of them were free. A clamour arose. Now the enemy had come. What they didn't know— because it had been done while they were asleep—was that their jaws had been bound so that they couldn't bite each other to death. Fighting was their passion. In Greenland, it had been their tradition and culture. Now they were to fight on a ship's deck.

Unable to bite, they hurled themselves forward, butting their opponents, clawing at them, kicking, rolling over and howling—a half-suppressed howl from clenched jaws. But they got their exercise, and the men emerged from their stupor.

'I'm in command.'

Then the storm broke. It caught them astern and the ship shot ahead, without so much as a splash on deck. It was true that the *Fram* was unsinkable, everybody knew that, but never had a ship rolled as she did in a storm. Amundsen knew that everything was in order on board. He had men who knew how to sail, men who could be trusted, and who in the long run would trust him. He had nothing to worry about, and went to bed, where he lay calmly, thinking: 'I'm in command.' They were now heading rapidly south.

Over the new year, 1910-11, they sailed into the pack-ice, a relief to all on board. There were seals lying on the floes, so they shot some and the fresh food cheered up both man and beast. A few penguins also appeared, dignified in their tail coats, with an expression of slight annoyance at this disturbance from the northerners, but also with a politeness which hid their curiosity, and a comical gait. Shooting a penguin was rather like shooting an elderly official. They shot several.

The *Fram* wound her way between the ice floes in waters

where she felt at home. They got through the pack-ice and into the Ross Sea, which was black and free of ice. They sailed on southwards.

And then the Great Ice Barrier itself rose up out of the sea. It was a clear day. The wall of ice was magnificent, perpendicular, blue, stern and merciless, with cold gusts of wind blowing off it. No life was visible here. A little ship— her sails furled, a few men on board, approaching the ice wall, slowly, deferentially. May we have permission. . . .

They sailed alongside the ice wall for two days. It was perhaps fifty metres high, twenty, thirty metres, but equally unapproachable everywhere. The dead ice firmly rejected both ship and men. Then a small bay opened out in the ice wall. It was the Bay of Whales.

This was an unnerving, tantalizing time for Amundsen. Was someone here before him? He clambered into the crow's nest, the sea behind him, the ice in front, and he stared through binoculars until his eyes ached. The captain called up to him, but he didn't hear. He was un-approachable now. It was his responsibility. If Scott were here, Amundsen would have exposed his treachery to the whole world—and lost. He could see nothing. . . . He rushed down, spun round on deck, and climbed up again, the sea and ice surrounding him, the men below, all silent, even the dogs silent today.

They reached the ice right inside the Bay of Whales. There was no one there. They had got there first.

Perhaps Scott wasn't planning to come here, but you couldn't count on anything. He climbed down from the crow's nest.

You've made it. You've succeeded again.

You're even a day ahead of your schedule.

Don't let anyone see that your hands are trembling.

I'm in command, aren't I? he says, and he smiles.

SCOTT

 **II**

Scott was by this time forty-two. He wasn't essentially a military man, but even so he had achieved high naval rank. The sickliness that had been so marked in his boyhood days had disappeared for ever. His shoulders bristled with strength, his body was firm and hard. He had gradually acquired the difficult art of decision-making. He had confidence in his own ability to choose rationally between alternatives which were equally unpleasant. Those who knew him shared this confidence.

Perhaps he was lacking in imagination. As a naval man, he had his timetable and he stuck to it, even if not always enthusiastically. When faced with a jubilant crowd, he assumed a cheery smile, universally popular. Not since Nelson's day had a member of the Royal Navy been met with such acclaim. But he was rather conventional, and some people found him dull. Perhaps in bad moments he had asked himself privately, 'Why am I so boring?'

The ship that was to take the expedition south was called the *Terra Nova* and had been an auxiliary ship during the *Discovery* expedition. Scott himself wasn't present when the ship sailed from England with men and cargo on board. He travelled on another ship to South Africa, where he joined the *Terra Nova*. The Empire acclaimed him, governors offering humble invitations, men in uniform standing to attention. There was strict division between officers and other ranks: a navy had its regulations. Despite the sums of money, large and small, that were still pouring in, there was a constant shortage of cash.

The ship's captain, second-in-command of the expedition, was a man called Edward Evans. He was barely thirty, handsome, black-haired, tanned, an attractive personality: women were said to faint in ecstasy as he walked by. One of his talents was raising money; with a mixture of charming impudence and strategic subtlety, he had appeared at hundreds of gatherings and brought the money in just by smiling, while Scott collected only a fraction of the amount after talking for hours. Scott admired him: he said so and meant it. Evans had qualities Scott lacked, and more besides. But maybe Evans's impetuosity made Scott over-cautious.

The *Terra Nova* sailed to Melbourne. This was the Empire too, with British tea and the Union Jack, a reception at the Governor's and a speech from Scott, a good solid one too, filled with appropriate platitudes. Filled, too, perhaps, with a certain diffidence at the sound of his own voice.

The populace hummed:

'Have you heard? The Empire is to conquer the South Pole.'

The last spot on earth not yet conquered.

Did they know that Scott was the youngest battleship commander in the Kingdom?

'Sir, a telegram....'

He hadn't time to open it. So many telegrams came, even some from women, though wagging tongues maintained that Edward Evans received more telegrams than he did. He stuffed it into his pocket. That was the advantage of a uniform with plenty of pockets. One of them was sure to be for telegrams. Papers should lie at a certain angle, and shouldn't protrude.

Back on board, he opened the telegram.

From Amundsen—which Amundsen? Oh yes, Amundsen. 'Inform you that *Fram* is setting sail for the Antarctic.'

It was like a blow in the solar plexus. The men on board were asleep. Some were on watch. He could ring—but he didn't. He remained seated, staring straight ahead. Amundsen? Wasn't he aiming for the North Pole? They hadn't been able to meet in Kristiania. Why is he going south? It doesn't say in the telegram. Is he going to explore the coastline and try to penetrate the South Pole from another angle? Surely he can't have been so insensitive as to get mixed up in the struggle for the Pole? There was a Norwegian ski-instructor on board *Terra Nova*, Tryggve Gran. Did the light dawn on Scott for a moment? Did he see something ominous about this—a ski-instructor on a polar trip, and a group of men who still hadn't learnt how to fasten a pair of skis to their boots? And what about the design of boots if skis were to be fastened to them?

He summoned Gran. Gran advised him to telegraph Nansen. Scott took his advice.

'Do you know if Amundsen is thinking of trying for the Pole?' The reply was brief: 'Not known.'

No, not known. Who did know the plans of that silent man from the North-West Passage, the man who had succeeded where great expeditions had met defeat and death? Scott recovered his self-control. He drew his own conclusions. We must stick to our original plan. Not a single change; no hurry—the apparatus is so cumbersome, the course mapped out; what more could possibly be done?

Besides, is it really our aim to reach the Pole first? Yes —but we mustn't say too much about that. That's why women swoon when Edward Evans speaks: the handsome young man who is to go to the Pole with his rocklike leader. Children broke into their piggy-banks and sent a shilling to Scott, because he was going to be the first man at the Pole, wasn't he? But keep quiet about it in case it isn't successful. The expedition was of a scientific nature. But which was the most important issue: science or the conquest of the Pole?

Both equally; who could decide such a difficult matter? It's a good thing we have a ski-instructor on board. Instructors are consoling, somehow.

He turned to Gran and said: 'No English gentleman would have behaved as Amundsen has.'

Then he had a private talk with his friend and second-in-command, Edward Evans, affectionately known as Teddy.

'Surely we should meet the challenge with greater ingenuity, sir? We want to get there first, don't we? A new rival calls for new daring.'

Scott didn't reply. It wasn't that he disliked daring, but it had to be led up to gradually and kept firmly under control. He had certain temperamental difficulties. Childhood had lasted such a long time in his life. Youth had been a period of consolidation and that had taken time, too. When he had grown up, he had achieved his one desire, to be a real man. But something was running behind him in the dark, and he had no resources to meet it, except politeness.

Port Lyttleton in New Zealand was the last port before the *Terra Nova* turned her bow southwards. Here, they stowed three tons of ice on board, which they hoped wouldn't melt until the ship was in the ice. One hundred and sixty-two sheep, three oxen and three hundred and forty barrels of pork. The supply of fresh food was a matter of life or death. Scott knew about scurvy and he also knew how reluctant many men in the polar regions were to drink the raw blood of seals or penguins. He sympathized with them. Anything coarse was deeply repugnant to him—he disliked swearing, unwashed hands and men who coughed without putting their hands in front of their mouths.

So it was agony for him to see the Siberian ponies which had come from Vladivostock. There were nineteen of them in all. They had had to change ship five times during the journey to New Zealand, and were in a wretched condition. They had been battered by the sea trip, had thirsted through the long days, given only filthy water to drink. Their fodder was disgusting. They got no exercise. Their heads hung miserably as they stood there, stowed into small stalls on board a ship bursting with equipment, dripping with ice, noisy with men bringing the last loads on board. There was no sparkle in their eyes, as if they knew they were condemned to die on the way to the Pole, in snow or sea.

There is little doubt that Robert Scott was a sensitive man. Faced with suffering animals, he himself suffered, constantly torn to shreds at the sight of their distress. It had a debilitating effect on his determination to reach his goal.

So he didn't see it as defeat when he and his men had to pull the sledges themselves across the icy wastes. By going to his own death, he was relieved of the spiritual responsibility of seeing a horse worked to death.

He stretched out his hand and tried to get one of them to lick it, but the pony didn't react. Scott told a sailor to fetch a bucket of water. The animal drank for a long time, draining the bucket, other ponies thrusting forward their muzzles, wanting some, too. They had stood like this for weeks, and would have to stand like this for weeks to come. The *Terra Nova* simply couldn't take on enough water for the animals to slake their thirst on the long journey south.

The dogs had come on board now, too: thirty-five of them from Manchuria. Too few to rely on for draw-power, and why have the animals on board otherwise? Five tons of dog-biscuits had been taken on board for them, but the dog expert, Cecil Meares, said it wasn't enough. Meares also said that he didn't want the dogs to eat the meat of either seals or penguins. Meares seemed to be almost mystically reluctant to use what the Antarctic had to offer. Scott must have known better. But he didn't use his authority at times like these: he was too courteous to set his judgment against that of the expert. The dogs looked weak already.

The man in cabin number one hadn't forgotten that he had once been one of a hundred and fifty recruits who had slept in hammocks on board the old ship *Britannia*. He had never learnt to feel happy in a crowd, but he had long ago learnt to hide his discomfort. On board the *Terra Nova*, even the officers were packed together like matches in a matchbox. They had to sleep to attention to give their neighbours room for their knees. But when it came to minimizing the discomfort of life on board, Scott was a master. He never lost his good humour. His courtesy was an example to all. And when he made a joke—which did happen occasionally—there was something polished and measured about it: a happy combination which didn't offend anyone even if it amused only a few.

Among the equipment were three motor-sledges, standing on end. They had been tested in the mountains of Norway in Scott's presence. Kathleen had been with him and Nansen had shown great interest. It had been in newspapers all over the Empire that the South Pole was to be conquered with motor-sledges. While Scott had been trying to get hold of Amundsen on the telephone—out of pure politeness, as the man was of no interest to him personally—Scott's engineer had been forced to admit with a sigh that there was always something wrong with the engines. Nothing serious. The sledges went well on smooth, firm snow. But how often was the snow smooth and firm? A runner sank, a chain snapped, a bearing overheated.

'What shall we do, sir?' Scott decided to take the sledges with him.

The land behind Port Lyttleton was green and beautiful, the distant sky light and blue. There were hundreds of people standing waving on the quays, some singing, a tugboat chugging out.

Mrs Scott was on board the *Terra Nova*, too. The two of them were below deck, together for the last time. No one knows what they said. Her ambitions for him had now become a source of grief to her. They said their goodbyes and went up on deck together.

Everyone looked at them.

The tugboat had towed the *Terra Nova* out to sea.

Kathleen disembarked and went ashore on the tug.

They waved farewell to each other.

The *Terra Nova* chugged on southwards. No one had ever seen anything like the cargo on her deck. Sacks of coal were piled up into a great mountain, and on top of the crates for the motor-sledges was a pack of dogs, howling. The engine chugged with a hollow sound, the sails helping to keep speed up. As long as the good weather held, all should go well. It didn't hold. Shortly after their departure from New Zealand, a storm blew up.

At first it was just a friendly little storm on the starboard side, and ship heeled and took water in on deck. For the time being it was only a slight test of strength between two ancient warriors: the ship and the sea, but then they were joined by the wind, with heavy skies in the west. The sea had been blue when they had sailed. At night it had twinkled with the reflected stars. Now the sea was black. It turned white with foam, spray whipping from the tops of the waves, the storm veering to port and the waves beginning to batter the ship, which chugged along deep in the water under its deck load.

But for the time being, the storm was still not a bad

one. It was bearable and as the men made their way between sacks of coal and other cargo on deck, tripping over a dog, slipping in horse dung, they still managed to joke, saying that the waves were cleaning things up on board. Then a paraffin drum was torn loose and struck one of the sailors—he lost consciousness but was grabbed just in time to stop him going over the rail. The drum crashed through some ropes securing a stack of coal sacks, pouring coal all over the deck. Coal washed away in the waves, got into every crack, each gust of wind raising a fan of coal-dust over the ship and sweeping it out to sea.

The coal-dust seeped into the cracks between the deck boards, and sank farther down, becoming a deadly hidden danger. More sacks were wrenched loose, thrown against the bulkheads, coal-dust mixing with the wash of the waves. There was coal-dust in all the gangways, coal-dust running from every stay, in every corridor, sinking down into the bunks. Then a dog was washed overboard.

It had been standing tethered on the top of a motor-sledge when a wave crashed over the deck and ripped out the metal staple. The mass of water swept the dog away. A man threw himself at it, grabbing hold of its coat; the dog twisted, the man slipped, losing his grip. The dog grabbed an iron pipe in its jaws and held on. The wave receded, then swept back again. The dog knew its life was at stake. It had hated life on board, but now it struggled to preserve it.

Its grip weakened, it was swept against the rail, lifted over; was washed back on the next wave, swam for its life in the water on deck. A man shouted. Was it Scott—the animal-lover who was making them suffer simply by having them here? He came, but it was too late. The dog was over the side, out in the open sea. It crested a wave with its head above water, was washed down, but came up again—still alive.

The ship was lying low in the water, floating heavily,

with hardly any difference in height between the sea and the deck. The dog had its chance. It had come from Manchuria and had never been trained to swim, but all the same it knew instinctively; it had once been grey and handsome, but now it was black, half-drowned, embittered in its strength. It sank.

No, it was coming up again, treading water, its nose up; they caught a glimpse of its eyes—and then wished to obliterate the sight. Then all the other dogs howled, supporting their friend, a last greeting and an expression of their own fear. The dog finally drowned.

The deck cargo had to go overboard. Orders were given and men threw the coal sacks over, cut ropes, two men to each sack as the ship lurched and waves washed icily across the deck. They had stowed these sacks on board in the hope that Our Lord would give them good weather all the way to the South Pole, but He had mocked their hope. Sack after sack was heaved out into the storm, lightening the ship a little, but more sacks split in the process, and more coal-dust sank down into the innards of the ship.

One minute the pumps were working, the next there was a message to the captain, Teddy Evans: 'Something's wrong with the pumps. . . .'

Something wrong with the pumps, was there? Evans asked what it was. An officer said that it might be the coal-dust. Perhaps it had got into the ventilators and into the filters in the pump? The pumps were working, but to little effect. The *Terra Nova* hove to. She took in more water. The water level rose in the engine-room, where the stokers were struggling to keep the fires going under the boilers.

Trickles of water mixed with coal-dust oozed through, mingling with the men's sweat. Oil dripped in, rising from the cracks; there was water everywhere, and in the middle of the water and boilers, a glow of fire was struggling to keep alive in the wet. It was stifling in the engine-room, but cold too. The stokers were sweating

above the waist, while their feet were freezing. They
hurled in the coal, but the water kept on rising. A voice
said, 'The pumps aren't working.'

Then the fire under the boiler went out.

Now the skipper shouted: 'Every man to the buckets!'
They made a chain, on slippery ladders, through narrow
enclosures, across the deck, under the relentless buffeting
of the waves; some wore oilskins, some were half-naked, all
soaked through. Here was the cook, anonymous now, here
was Scott, on his way to the Pole and his death. Here was
everybody who wasn't absolutely necessary at other posts.
The buckets flew up from the engine-room, from hand to
hand, they heaved the water over the rail, only to have
the storm hurl it back. They measured the water in
the engine-room: it was rising. Night was falling and the
Terra Nova was lying like a bird on the waves. Then the
lights went out.

So they were forced to toil on in the dark, making their
way along narrow gangways, trampling on a dog that
yelped wildly amidst the darkness and the storm. Where
were the ponies? It was rumoured that one of them was
dead. A sharp voice denied it. But soon afterwards word
went round once again from man to man. One of the
horses was dead. It sank to its knees. Then it keeled over
on its side. It had travelled so far but it had failed to
reach its destination. It faced the waves with hanging head,
soaking wet and trembling with cold; sinking down and
rolling over, it died uncomplainingly. Now it had to be
thrown overboard. But who had time or energy for a dead
pony? Every man on board was toiling with buckets of
water from the engine-room. The level of water was
measured again. It hadn't risen any more. There was a ray
of hope. Everyone knew that there was only one way down
to where the pump filters were, and that was through the
main hatch over the shaft. To open the hatch would mean

flooding the ship with water and sinking it within a few minutes.

But there had to be another way. Between the hold and the engine-room, there was a wooden bulkhead. If they could make a hole through that, it would be possible to get down to where the pump filters were.

It was a bold plan. The planks were of oak and there was very little room down there. The lanterns were out. Teddy Evans, the man whose smile could charm £100 from a group of ladies, took two men down with him. This was his first great trial; it wouldn't be his last. He had daring and courage, and it wasn't his habit to weigh up the pros and cons. Their equipment was primitive. They couldn't get to the workshop on board, so had to hunt out a makeshift chisel here and a drill there. The *Terra Nova* wasn't such a frail vessel as she was reputed to be. At least, the bulkhead they had to get through was oak, and it was solid enough.

They were standing in water up to their knees. It was something to be thankful for that the water wasn't rising, but then the ship keeled over and lay heavily in the waves. They were thrown against the bulkhead and the chisel jerked from their hands; then blood mingled with the coal-dust and sea-water. They tried to light a lamp, but it went out. So they worked in the dark, hacking away with an axe, removing a few splinters, cursing wildly, weeping, cursing again, but removing a few more splinters each time. They needed a hole large enough for a grown man to crawl through. The day went by.

A soaked cook came wading along three times with a can of something, they knew not what. He was swept off his feet by the coal-dust and water and heavy waves. He swam along with the can, and if it hadn't been full before, it was now. An hour went by. He came back again. They didn't see him as he approached in the darkness and they were hacking away with axe and chisel, testing with drills.

He made his way to them, the tea now mixed with oil and coal-dust and water. Evans drank the cold tea first, then the other two finished it. The cook had brought a chicken with him; they grinned widely and stuffed the meat into their mouths.

At last the axe-blade went through the bulkhead, but it still wasn't easy to make the hole any larger. Those three knew neither night nor day, hope nor hell; it was never-ending, bloody toil in freezing oily water. But the hole was growing larger. They could hear the buckets still going, the men bailing; the ship lurched, a pony screamed, and then the storm, millions of tons of water rising up to the sky and thundering down on to the *Terra Nova*. The hole in the bulkhead grew bigger. On the other side were the shaft and pump ventilators. Could they clear them? Eighteen hours had passed since they had begun to hack the hole in the bulkhead. Finally Evans managed to crawl through and get inside.

It was dark in here too. He found the shaft. The filters were down there. He had to dive down without even know-ing if the fault was there. He plunged into the oily water, the ship ceaselessly buffeted from side to side. He let him-self glide down, surrounded by narrow iron pipes; he held his breath; everything was slippery with oil, everything cold. He found something and tried to unscrew it. No good. He began to black out. He had to go up.

But it was a matter of life or death. He could hear through the hole in the bulkhead that the water had begun to rise again in the engine-room. So he dived again, making his way to something he could unscrew, failed to get it properly loose and had to go up again before he drowned.

But he knew what he was doing. He still had his wits about him. Someone shouted down to him and he found the strength to shout back to them to shut up. Dived for the third time.

He was glad that he had spent days getting to know

every detail of his ship: it was paying off now. The engine was not his field. But he was the captain, and as captain, everything was his field. He knew what he was doing. Up to the surface again. His stomach felt full of oily water. He vomited in the darkness. Then he started blowing the filth out of the filter, his fingers stiff, his mouth full of coal-dust. He tried blowing the coal-dust out of the mechanism, spitting the coal-dust out, blowing again, hoping it had helped—he hadn't anywhere to put the filter down while he fetched up another.

The ship lurched over and righted herself again heavily. There was a shout from the engine-room: the water was rising again. He put the little filter into his mouth, let himself slide down again into the oily water. Suddenly he had a thought: were there rats down here? The thought gave him courage. If there were rats on board, then there was still hope for his ship. They hadn't left the ship before we sailed, had they? He found the next filter, had to go up again, down again, unscrewed it and blew that one and the next one free of coal dust too. But there were always more. Had one hour gone by, or two? Someone shouted at him. He told them to shut up. Dazed, he let himself down again, finding what he was looking for, establishing when he was up again that now all the filters were in his hands and had been blown as clean of filth as it was possible to get them.

The ship was still afloat.

Now to put the filters back again.

Suddenly he went dizzy, spewing up the contents of his stomach—which was mostly coal-dust. And again he descended. Putting the filters back was worse than unscrewing them. There were some small openings which had to match up, also under the water, while he held his breath and the ship pounded on and on through the waves.

An hour went by; he went up and down, up and down, and finally there was only one filter not in place.

Then he keeled over and passed out.

He came to again. Someone had shouted at him. He knew that if one filter were out of place, he might just as well have saved himself the trouble of cleaning the others. He hunched up. It had become remarkably quiet on board, as if everybody knew what was happening and realized that it was now or never. He dived again. Then he dropped the filter.

There were cracks at the bottom of the shaft. He crawled around down there, was forced up for breath, hanging on to a pipe, noticed that he was sinking, sliding under the water, finished.

But then he felt something in his hand, a familiar shape; it was the filter. He kicked out with the last of his strength and came up.

He breathed deeply for a long time, then saying out loud that it was now or never, slipped down again, and with no misfortunes, thankfully, succeeded in getting the last filter into place.

He came up.

He groaned something unintelligible, but the man with his head through the hole they had hacked through the bulkhead understood. They could try the pumps. Eight men rushed over there. The pumps worked. The water gushed up.

The sea threw it back, but it was no longer rising in the engine-room. Soaked through, exhausted, with the water up to their necks, eight men trudged round and round, round and round, and the pump-pistons thumped and thumped. The water was brought up and thrown out. It kept coming back; but at least now they were keeping it at bay.

Then a man crawled up from the shaft, covered with oil and coal-dust. He staggered, fumbled his way over to the hole in the bulkhead, wondering for a moment whether he was going up or down. This time it was up. He

74

hoisted himself into the hole in the oak planks; someone helped him and he got his head through, but his shoulders stuck, as if they had swollen in the wet and the cold and wished to stay where they were.

So he tore off his rags and pulled himself through naked, the splinters grazing his skin. He was back with his men.

The ship was afloat. A man shouted: 'The water's going down!' The eight men on deck, pump-spikes in their sore, frozen, stiff hands, went round and round and round.

Someone threw a coat over Evans's shoulders and he went over to the pumpers. One of the eight was Scott.

Three more dogs had been washed overboard. A youth whimpered: 'Two of the ponies are dead.' The corpses were freed from the chains that still bound them and were heaved overboard.

The storm pounded relentlessly at the *Terra Nova*.

But she was still holding on. The water wasn't rising in the engine-room. Next morning it was apparent that the water was going down. The storm was abating. Almost unnoticeably, the ship began to right herself. Later on in the day—it was the third day—they got the fires going again in the engine-room.

Like a seagull with ruffled feathers, the *Terra Nova* began to recover. Soon smoke was rising from her stack: the ship was once again in motion. Not a single man on board was dry, nothing was warm, but now the fire was going again under the boilers they could set about drying a few empty sacks.

Scott had given orders that each pony was to be rubbed down thoroughly to get its circulation going. The dogs had managed better.

The animals had to be kept alive until it was time for them to die in the cold and the ice.

No human lives had been lost.

They continued the journey southwards.

*　　*　　*

The *Terra Nova* had sailed into the ice. The ship wasn't wrecked, but resembled an injured sea bird—all the men on board doing what they could to repair the damage. The icy blast from the wastelands struck them; huge icebergs drifted by, their secret deep down below the surface; icy blue in the morning light and glittering red as the sun's disc rose over open, black sea. Great albatrosses had followed the ship a long way south, like silent guards on watch above: their wings outstretched under the sky. Now even the birds had gone. The men were alone with the sea, the ice and God.

The ice closed in. The ship wriggled through the floes.

There were anguished men on deck. Shattered ponies lay on their sides and were rubbed down with warm sacks to get their circulation going. The dogs had begun to howl again. At night, the temperature fell, sharp gusts of wind blew; the stars seemed distant, alien and unreal. Day broke.

They saw their first seal. Then a dignified committee of aldermen came walking across the ice towards the ship, all dressed in black and white. They bowed politely, stood for a few minutes, staring at the *Terra Nova* with their heads on one side, and then purposefully took another step forward. They wouldn't demean themselves by coming on board before being invited. They waited with profound respect but after a while with increasingly obvious irritation. They were penguins. Now the scientists came to life. One bright spark suggested that penguins might be musical. There was a gramophone on board. No sooner said, than the music rang out over the ice. And unbelievably, the joke turned out to be true. The youngest of the penguins began to dance. The others observed his performance with condescending contempt at first, but then they seemed to warm up. Slowly, they began to sway to and fro, faltering at first, following the beat, nodding their heads cheerfully, shedding some of their dignity.

The man on board changed records and put on 'God Save the King'. This made an unmistakable impression on the penguins. They probably had their own sense of national pride and they respected the Empire's tune. They stood to attention. But the anthem created problems on board the *Terra Nova*. This was a naval expedition. Should everyone stand to attention when the national anthem is played to a flock of penguins? Some did so quite seriously, men with an inch of stubble on their chins— others did so for a joke. What example should the leader have set when he came on deck and witnessed the scene?

Scott displayed some of his natural diplomacy, tactful and controlled amusement, but human and warm nevertheless. Instead of a hearty, officer-like roar, he gave a relaxed chuckle which made the men with their hands half-way to their foreheads in honour of a distant king drop their arms and smile delightedly.

They led the ponies out on to the ice. Then the men were simply human beings, not giving or receiving orders, but brought together in their compassion for the emaciated beasts. Each pony had to be supported by four men, two on each side, rubbed down with warm sacks, persuaded to try a sugar-lump or crust of bread, and at last given the water it needed. But what a sight the ponies were in the bright sunlight against the blue ice, infested with lice and covered with sores, half-blind after standing surrounded by coal-dust in narrow stalls on board. The ponies needed help with their first steps. They slowly came back to life, whilst the *Terra Nova*, half-wrecked, rested at the edge of the ice and a dog howled with joy at the smell of snow.

They tried out the skis. For several of the men, it was the first time they had thrust their boots into straps and tried to get the apparatus fixed under their soles. It was explained to them that the skis were designed to slide along on the snow—and this was best accomplished by a pushing movement with the whole leg, from the hip downwards.

Several managed this: it looked quite hopeful. They were also shown that ski-poles were instruments of great importance, to be used in conjunction with the skis.

Scott said to Dr Wilson:

'I don't know what it is, but something's troubling me.'

Wilson was his great friend. They had been together on the first expedition south, when Shackleton had cracked up. That had been a matter of life and death for all three of them. The friendship between these two had grown into intimacy. In all his journals and letters, Scott was full of genuine admiration and even veneration for his quiet little friend, who, if slightly distant sometimes, was so wise, so warm, and became an increasing source of strength as time went by.

They could pinpoint each other's weaknesses, examine them, tolerate them; hearing the other's opinion, they learned from the advice they received. It was Scott who had most to learn. Wilson, mildly humorous, generous in his praise and discreet in his criticism, made it seem as if the fault was his, so as to guide the other more easily.

'There's something bothering me, Bill. I don't know what it is. I've searched my mind and examined my conscience. It's like an ache inside me. I think it's some wrong I have done which is weighing confusedly on my thoughts. It's painful and distracting. It stops me from concentrating on my essential tasks.'

Scott was about to hold a service. A large iceberg to port lay dark blue, the sun visible over its top, immobile against a black channel. The ponies had been taken on board again, the men were back on deck. Then his warm, slightly hoarse but clear voice was heard above the ship and crew. He was reading from the Holy Scriptures.

After this, he prayed. These men had grown up in a society founded on the twin pillars of fear of God and honour for the Empire. No one would have dreamt of sniggering at being confronted with one of these forms of power. They lived at close quarters and cursed loudly. Within them lay the universal fear of exposing their innermost thoughts and weaknesses. They were going to the Pole, just as soon as their leader had said the Lord's Prayer. A dog began to howl. But the men stood to attention.

Scott had enough sense to make the service short. He combined dignity with his customary amiability.

Later he said again to Bill:

'There's still something troubling me. I wish I knew what it was.'

'Do you want to know what I think?'

'Yes, my dear Bill, no matter how unpleasant.'

'It was our mutual friend, Teddy, who saved the ship, wasn't it? I know you've both praised him and thanked him, and he deserved it. But weren't you just a bit jealous? You, the leader.'

They faced each other.

'Yes, that's what it is. Shall I go to him and ask his forgiveness?'

'Do you really think a leader can do that? Let's think about it for a minute. Isn't it enough that you've analysed your feelings so that you can come to grips with them? He hasn't noticed your envy. You mustn't allow your conscience to undermine your position as leader.'

'Perhaps I should behave more warmly to him?'

'Maybe; but there are limits. Exaggerated warmth may seem assumed. You're in total charge. You have to decide what's best—taking everything into consideration. If you go and ask him to forgive you for being envious, wouldn't you really be doing it for your own gratification?'

'Then I'll leave it.'

'Yes, I should.'

'Bill,' he said, 'I should never have been leader of this expedition. I can't even bear to see a sick horse.'

AMUNDSEN

 III

He was now in the Antarctic. His limbs tingled with joy and he felt the strength rippling in his shoulders as he thrust forward at a brisk pace on his skis. Through all those weeks without exercise on board the *Fram*, he had felt sluggish and indolent. But after just a few days down here, he could feel his strength returning. His early morning habit of having a run in the forest while the dew still lay on the grass was paying off now. He smiled slightly to himself, enjoying the solitude, revelling in the fact that the nearest man was miles away. The days had been busy with bringing materials up to the hut, crates of provisions, struggles with the dogs, shouting, thrashing, dripping with sweat; both he and the men fell headlong into their tents and sleeping-bags when evening came. But what happy days they had been.

The morning was beautiful, the northern sky dark with the reflection from the open sea. The light was refracted in the pack-ice hummocks, but was not yet so strong that he had to wear sunglasses. There were many different kinds of snow down here: coarse-grained and sticky, fresh new snow, soft as powder, or hard drifts whipped up by a sharp wind. He let his skis glide and glide, not using his strength, as supple as a strong old wolf, knowing he had

the edge over most men down there. He went up on to
the edge of the Barrier to get a view down towards the
Fram, moored at the edge of the ice.

There were *two* ships there.

He rubbed his eyes, knowing that the light could be
deceptive, distorting things and giving them a different
shape. If you become snowblind, it's not only agonizingly
painful, it can also make you see double. Was he seeing
double now? He held a hand in front of his eyes and
turned his face away, shaking his head slightly as if to
dispel the unexpected sight from his vision. Then he
turned back towards the sea and removed his hand. There
were two ships down there. Groaning, he slipped quickly
behind a hummock of ice, like an animal taking cover
when it sees an enemy. He peered out. It was quite a large
ship, high masted, and lying moored to the edge of the ice
quite near the *Fram*. He recognized it: the *Terra Nova*,
Scott's ship.

His stomach churned, all the unpleasantness of the last
few weeks coming to the surface, having had the time to
ferment. He had stood there at home in Oppegård and
not picked up the telephone when Scott had rung, hadn't
he? He had lied to everyone; not to Leon, but he had
deceived everyone else, and had felt a shameful secret delight in doing so. It had been essential to his aim, absolutely necessary to keep totally silent. And here was Scott's
ship. They had found him.

He ripped off a mitten and spat in the snow, clenching
his fist, and cursing violently. But even while he was doing
so, he realized the futility of the gesture. What was the
use of raging—they're here! It's up to you to master the
situation. Then a thought occurred to him—you could
move on ... Well, it wasn't completely out of the question.
You could pretend you were just on a long ski-trip towards
the south, to set up a depot. A couple of men could go on
board the *Terra Nova*; bow politely and make your ex-

cuses. They'd do anything you say, wouldn't they? You could be ready to start within an hour. Then the men would be telling the truth when they went on board.

But would you lose face in front of your own men? There was something here which worried him, a basic layer of fear going deeper than the first, better hidden, a mocking laugh which cackled in an eerie voice—if you go away now will something terrible happen as a result?

Everything had gone so well up to now: they had moored the *Fram* at the edge of the ice and they had crossed the Ice Barrier. He had found the ideal place for their winter camp. The blue-ice had been hacked away about a foot down and the sectional hut set up, the equipment brought ashore, every man working, everything thought out, every man proving to be as he had anticipated. And one of them as he had feared.

He knew that the ice might break loose and drift out to sea, but he estimated it would probably hold. He had taken this calculated risk alone, necessary if they were to be one degree nearer the Pole than Scott would be if he went ashore in McMurdo Sound. Framheim was set in a little hollow with ice hummocks around it. Occasionally he woke up at night with slight traces of anxiety. Shackleton had written that the ice down here could break up into kilometre-sized floes, and be whipped out to sea in a storm. The men didn't suspect this.

Keep quiet about it.

Everything had gone so well and smoothly, not least with the dogs. The skiers, too—that was no problem, as his men were among the best skiers in the world. But he knew that they had now been trained to drive dog-teams with great mastery, throwing themselves into the dog-packs and thrashing them, one after another, until they were subdued. Sometimes the seats of their trousers were torn, and they had to use the handle of the whip, while the dogs howled like demons and never gave in; then the dogs would drool at the mouth and eat out of hands the next minute, if they were in the mood. But they had to be kept under control.

You load up, running behind the load on skis. Suddenly the dogs bolt off in the wrong direction, smelling a seal; you swear and lash out, the sweat pouring off you, even though it's twenty degrees below zero, sharp snow. So you overturn the sledge to let the dogs get their breath back. Now you're wild with fury. You thrash them, right the sledge, get them back on to course again. Then they run off.

Hour after hour, you or they, you get the technique after a while; their ancestors are wolves, they love fighting. Men who stroke cats in the yard at home in Telemark, now thrash a dog. You're in the Antarctic and you have only one idea in your head; you're going to be the first at the Pole.

You don't need a conscience. Neither do your men. Evening comes at the end of a hard day. You have kept to the plan, a painstakingly executed plan, worked out back at home, with dates and times, so many sledge-loads of equipment, so many kilos, driven from the *Fram* to the winter camp (which lies on sea-ice and might break loose—but only you know that).

And it all went according to plan. The men were up to scratch: strong, practical, a bit primitive, rather lacking in finesse. But they knew how to make their way over the icy wastelands. And their unquestioning obedience was an integral part of them. All except one.

And yet he's the most capable man of them all. He's the expert at everything. No one can drive a dog better without exhausting himself. He knows when to cajole and when to use more severe methods. He has seen more ice than any other man here: the man who headed for a distant Pole and got closer to it than anyone before him. Moreover, he followed in the shadow of a great master, the only one who can casually say: 'When Nansen and I....'

The words are like a pin-prick but you have to smile, a smile that hides a growing hatred. You couldn't refuse when Nansen offered the man's services. You had to thank him, even appear overwhelmed with gratitude. When the man came, he greeted you politely but not *deferentially*, not in the way you would have appreciated.

He knew it all.

How to put up a tent in a storm; how to get a blocked primus to work; how to patch together two old ski-straps with his back to a blizzard, and do it so it holds.

He even knew how to shit without getting his trousers full of snow. And that ability could mean the difference between reaching the Pole and dying.

There lay the ship. He looked out from behind the hummock and knew that this was his destiny. He had to go down there and confront it. The 'depot-trip' south wouldn't work. It might have been the solution, if only Hjalmar Johansen hadn't been here. He would notice cowardice. Perhaps the others would too, but he'd be the only one with the courage to point it out.

Amundsen went slowly down to the ship.

Now he'd have to listen to words he'd rather not hear: what the Englishmen thought about his change of course, perhaps what had been in the newspapers, or what Scott had said. Would there be a quarrel when he went on board? They wouldn't drive him away. But he would have preferred to do it all unhindered: either reach the Pole and return victorious, or end his life in the great wastelands to the south.

If he were victor, people would say 'He did the right thing.'

If he were dead, they'd say 'He was a hero!'

He hated meeting the Englishmen here, face to face, but he had to. He went slowly down towards the *Terra Nova*.

SCOTT

Scott was standing on the outer edge of weathered Cape Evans in McMurdo Sound. The wind was strong, tearing at his thin hair, and in the open bay, frothy waves washed towards the land. A large iceberg was drifting out there, shining blue and white, twisting heavily in the waves and revealing another facet, green colour dribbling down the steep sides, a stream of verdigris running into the dark sea and blending into it. Out there, between two skerries, was the *Terra Nova*, stranded on a shoal.

The ship had been on her way out when she had sailed too close to land and had run her bow into treacherous waters. The alarm was raised in winter quarters and Scott had run out here to the point. It was as close as he could get, but not close enough. If the ship were lost, sixty men would be helpless in McMurdo Sound.

In a year or two, some ponderous bureaucrat back home in England would perhaps write letters to another office and discuss sending out a rescue ship. The winter hut had been erected on the mainland, bolted to the mountain, and it would stand even if the stormy sea rose in all its might to crush the small creatures that had crept ashore here. Behind that hut, a volcano loomed—Mount Erebus, its top often hidden in mist, today pointing straight up into the clear air. A cap of smoke hung over the mountain, which suddenly threw up a fiery greeting, like a finger pointing at the sky, before the sparks and flames died away again in the snow. The polar wind was bitter and increasing in strength. The *Terra Nova* was aground.

The men on land had gone out in a small boat, taking ice-anchors with them. Scott had ordered the crew on board to empty the forehold of coal and take it astern. The engines were running full steam ahead, the smoke pouring darkly out of the stack. It looked as if the *Terra Nova* were crouching down in the now turbulent seas. Scott knew as he stood there on the point that this was one of those moments when he would either win or lose all. If the *Terra Nova* went down, ultimate defeat was near. It would leave desperate men, abandoned, hopeless men, their thoughts focussed on one thing only: can we hold out until they send a ship down here? Back home they don't know that we sailed into McMurdo Sound, do they? How would they find us along that endless coastline? Even if we manage to refloat the *Terra Nova* this time, similar situations would arise again and again. The thought of future accidents kept him awake at night. As he stood there and shouted with no one to hear him, he didn't notice that it was fifteen degrees below zero with a strong wind blowing. A thought crossed his mind that brought him a certain peace. Even if the *Terra Nova* does go down, will you and your men continue to the Pole? Yes, we'll do what we came here to do. Even without a ship to take us back, we shall continue southwards. He ran a hand over his face, not noticing that something was frozen on his cheeks, wishing that Wilson were here, the only man he had ever met in his life who had come really close to him. But Wilson was on board the small boat which was now trying to get the ice-anchors out to the *Terra Nova*.

You've always been dogged by misfortune, haven't you? Not great misfortunes, but persistent minor ones. They

sapped your vitality. Things weren't done as you wished.
Could it be that your plans aren't sufficiently well thought
out? You'd planned to set up winter quarters over
on Cape Crozier, where the great Emperor penguins
live. No one has seen their eggs: they hatch them out
sixty degrees below zero. Do you remember how Wilson
and you sat one evening talking about getting a whole
colony of Emperor penguins to come outside the hut door,
and giving the world a set of pictures such as they'd never
seen before? Even cautious Wilson showed a rush of enthus-
iasm. He talked about holding the great penguin eggs in his
hands, painting them, noting their colour, drawing pictures
of them, finding out everything about them, perhaps even
being there at the very moment when the penguin stuck
its head out in sixty degrees below zero and survived. We
laughed loudly then. But we didn't go ashore there.

They would have been one degree nearer the Pole if
they had, but it was impossible to come alongside with
the ship, so they had sailed westwards, then into McMurdo
Sound at Cape Evans. They had found a place for their
winter camp beneath the mighty Mount Erebus, with its
red smoke-screen of snow, a fantastic sight. He wrote in
his journal: 'It's incredible.' He added: 'The advantage
of being here is that we can study the volcano too.' But at
night he went out alone, gazed southwards and saw that
the terrain was going to be difficult to traverse. Perhaps
impossible.

The sea-ice had got in their way, and they'd had to
cross it to get the equipment ashore. All had gone well.
The ponies had had no strength, but the men had pulled
the sledges and had been in good spirits. Every man had
rubbed down his pony with hay and given it a crust, shoved
at his sledge, keeping the dogs at bay, preventing them
from attacking the ponies for a bit of raw meat. Transportation had gone well.

The motor-sledges had started, too. On even snow, they

moved forward, slowly, with great power, just as they had in distant Norway. The engines overheated very quickly. In rough terrain they needed several men to help them over bumps in the ice. More men meant more provisions and greater quantities of equipment, which in turn required more transport and therefore more fuel, which also had to be transported by men who needed food. He had now reached a decision. On the first depot trip south, the motor-sledges would remain at the winter camp. He didn't betray his disappointment to the others. Wilson, the only one he talked to, was too tactful to try to console him. But with the main thrust towards the Pole now taking place in the spring, perhaps they would have gained enough experience by then to be able to make use of the motor-sledges after all.

A terrifying thing had happened when they had gone ashore at Cape Evans. The Siberian dogs were clever beasts. They were tied up when the penguins came, as dignified as a group of priests on their way to dinner with the bishop. The dogs hurled themselves forward to attack, but were held back by their chains. The flock of polite theologians stopped, each bird making an almost imperceptible inclination of the head, probably an expression of reproof at such uncouth behaviour. The next day, the dogs had learnt. They lay there with their chains slack, starving wolves with yellow wisdom in their eyes. Again the birds came, clad in unassuming black and white, emanating a discreet sense of humour.

They too had gained experience from the day before. They knew how close they could get without incident. The dogs appeared to be sleeping, their chains in loops behind them. But suddenly they hurled themselves forward and within a few minutes had crushed the flock of birds in their jaws, tearing them to shreds; blood flowed, the dogs belched—feathers, cruelty and crushed bones everywhere.

Scott had seen it all but had been unable to stop it. Afterwards he had vomited. It destroyed his feeling of contentment. Even so, the transportation of equipment to their winter quarters had gone well. The ponies had recovered and could help by pulling. Then the ice broke up, so the *Terra Nova* could sail almost alongside where the hut was now tethered with chains against the buffeting of storms. This would ease the transfer of the remaining equipment before the ship sailed and set course back to New Zealand.

But first the *Terra Nova* was to cruise along the coast and put a party of five men ashore over on King Edward VII's Land—if possible. An additional reason—one that Scott kept buried in his unconscious; one he did not commit to paper, didn't reveal even to Wilson, who perhaps would have found a core of immorality in such a thought—was to discover if Amundsen had hidden himself somewhere in those parts. Scott would have no peace of mind until he knew.

So the *Terra Nova* sailed close to the shore and tied up at the edge of the ice. There was a piano on board, the last item to be brought ashore.

Beneath the red cap of Mount Erebus, in the middle of the snow and the wind, heavy with the smell of blood, intestines and raw meat from the flock of penguins that had been torn to shreds, surrounded by bearded men, a polar explorer sat down at the keyboard with an embarrassed smile. What should he play? Beethoven?

Yes! Yes!

And 'God Save the King'.

They doffed their caps.

Then they bade farewell to the men who were to sail on. At that point, the *Terra Nova* sailed and ran aground.

Scott shouted as he stood there on the point, but no one heard him. The men on board had begun to run from one side of the deck to the other, trying to get the ship to roll. The engine was going at full speed astern. The sea stirred. An iceberg came drifting towards the ship. If it hit her before she was afloat, she'd have been smashed to splinters and the men would go down for ever. He wondered whether to go down on his knees. Would it be hypocrisy? Are you honest or dishonest in the face of God? He cried out in anguish and threw his hands above his head. He knew that he had more than King Edward VII's Land in his thoughts when he had decided to have the *Terra Nova* sail westwards. He had been thinking about Amundsen too.

The smoke was billowing thick and black out of the stack, the engines racing at full speed astern, the men running back and forth across the deck, back and forth. It looked as if the ship were beginning to roll. Then the *Terra Nova* slid off.

He went down on his knees and thanked God.

AMUNDSEN

 **IV**

Let us take a look at the Antarctic as it lay there,
immeasurable and desolate beneath its eternal ice, surrounded by stretches of stormy sea, no wings in the skies,
no trees struggling against the wind, with winters that
never ended and a summer so short it was like a man's
last dying gasp. It was a land of mountains on which no
one had yet set foot, deep valleys and crevasses in the ice
never measured by human hands. Two small groups of
men had gone ashore here, each with a leader, one a man
with an empire behind him, the other who had left without even informing his tiny country.

Two ships had brought the expeditions here. They now
lay side by side, lashed by storms, moored to an ice-edge
that might crumble if bad weather broke out. Amundsen
knew that the man he was about to meet would think that
he'd broken the rules of the game, trying to collect the
prize when he had no right to compete. He came down
the ridge, gliding easily on his skis, slowly changing the
expression on his face from fear and bitterness to subser-
vient politeness. He had been observed. Men on board the
Terra Nova had him in their binoculars and knew that it
was the Norwegian leader who was coming. So he had
already begun the game. He had a supple hip movement

and a brilliant arm swing; he acted the great skier—and was one. His profile looked good, sharp and hard. He had a surprising, almost devastating smile; it appeared suddenly, like a flash of lightning, dangerous and ingratiating at the same time. He probably knew that they had good binoculars on board. He smiled at the snow around him.

Lieutenant Campbell came to meet him, appointed by Scott to lead the party that was to attempt to explore King Edward VII's Land. Campbell had learned his manners in British officers' clubs—which said a great deal, but not all. He didn't have his opponent's skill on skis, and wasn't at home with the snow beneath his boots. There was a stiffness about him as he went to meet Amundsen and bid him welcome.

But Campbell had spent several years in Rogaland and spoke fluent Norwegian. This disconcerted Roald Amundsen. He was proud of his good English, but it was, nevertheless, a foreign language to him, and he had to bring the tempo down, gaining time when necessary by assuming difficulties in understanding. To be confronted by a man who bade him welcome in Norwegian seemed to Amundsen a stumbling block right at the start. But the handclasp the two men exchanged was warm, firm and studied. Here were two opponents face to face. Neither betrayed his feelings, but each had some idea what was in the other's mind.

Campbell was a handsome young man, ambitious, later to marry one of Queen Maud's ladies-in-waiting, and skilled in the most intricate rules of tact and nuances of tone. He was wearing all his officer's trimmings. Amundsen had nothing to show that he was the leader of his expedition.

Campbell thought: The scoundrel. He has chosen his winter camp with great skill and is already nearer the Pole than we are.

Amundsen thought: He's here to spy on me. He thinks I'm a scoundrel.

'Herr Amundsen, it gives me great pleasure to meet you here. Captain Scott sends you his best regards. He said—they were his last words—"If you meet Captain Amundsen, do give him my regards and wish him the best of luck."'

'Sir, it is very good of you to come alongside here. I assure you that my greatest desire is that all will go well for Captain Scott and his men. He's an outstanding leader. I still regret that I wasn't able to meet him when he was in Norway last year. Tell me, sir, would you and your officers like to take the opportunity of visiting us in our winter camp up here?'

'My dear Herr Amundsen, you do me an honour which neither I nor my officers deserve. We would be delighted to visit you in your winter camp....'

So they met for lunch at Framheim, Campbell and two of his officers. Amundsen bid them welcome, pleased that the conversation was now being carried out in English, Campbell being the only Englishman who knew Norwegian. This also had the advantage that most of the Norwegians couldn't understand what Amundsen was saying. He had laid his plans, and now, with exceptional skill, he carried them out.

'Sir, I know that Captain Scott has both ponies and dogs with him, and I am sure that this dual pulling-power will be to the advantage of the British expedition. As you probably know, sir, I am relying exclusively on dogs. Would you be interested in seeing one of our dog-teams in action?'

'My dear Captain Amundsen, you are too kind...'

One of Amundsen's men, Helmer Hanssen, was from Andøya and had also been a member of the expedition through the North-West Passage. Amundsen knew that Helmer was one of the best sledge drivers in the world, though he wasn't one of the world's great thinkers. Helmer spat brown saliva and cursed roundly in Norwegian, but he knew the art of drying wet woollen socks on his body in extreme cold; in a tight spot, he could even sleep in the snow.

He had chosen the best possible team from a pack of now over a hundred first-class animals. Helmer was a highly skilled driver and a good skier; snow whirled from the dogs' paws, the sledge swept across the snow, with him skiing alongside; a shout to the dogs and they swung to the left in a great curve, circled a heap of frozen seal meat, the whip whistled, the team stopped—then started up again.

'I think you'll agree, sir, that my men are very competent when it comes to this sport—the fact is they all regard it as a sport. And as you see, they are highly skilled.'

They went inside. The cook, Lindstrøm, was clever and had wiped the soot off his hands before the guests arrived. He was no butler, but he had reversed the shirt he used as an apron and swiftly trimmed his moustache before bringing in the food. It was first-class seal meat, steaming fresh steaks, hot and strong. Campbell was not only a man who moved in court circles. He was also an adventurer on the high seas and was able to master a situation like this without difficulty.

Amundsen said in his correct, rather slow English:

'You know, sir—why try to deny it?—that we have unfortunately become rivals in the struggle for the Pole. It is my intention to reach it first. Captain Scott intends to get there before me. I respect that. I also feel, knowing his great character, that he respects me. Now I have succeeded in setting up camp here in the Bay of Whales, a few miles nearer the Pole than Captain Scott's camp at McMurdo Sound. How would it be, sir—I dare throw out the suggestion although it may seem a little bold—if we went together, struck joint camp here, agreed to go hand in hand just for the sake of science—and conquered the Pole together?'

It was such a bold stroke, in its aim to disarm the opposition, that despite his sense of the ambiguity in such exchanges, the naval officer lost his composure for a moment, and didn't know what to say. The gravy from the seal steak, heavy, sharp and red, dripped from his fork on to the table. Campbell said—taking Amundsen's measure though pretending not to—that Scott would be forced to refuse this generous offer. 'You know that he already has his own camp.' At this Amundsen bowed, and assured Campbell that he understood and respected that standpoint.

Amundsen offered his guests a ride back to the *Terra Nova* on a dog-sledge. They refused, saying that a brisk walk would do them good after so many days at sea. Amundsen went with his guests. Two of his men were doing a practice run with their dogs and swooped past. They drove well.

With a bow, Amundsen accepted an invitation to take dinner on board the *Terra Nova*. He wondered whether he should wear a dark suit and white collar, and perhaps even his bowler hat. He had brought this wardrobe with him on board the *Fram*, but decided to arrive dressed in his polar gear.

The steward on board the *Terra Nova* was immaculate. The wines were excellent, the courses plentiful; Amundsen's knowledge of gastronomy was like that of a young novice at court, and his embarrassment lent a mild warmth to the studied formality. Then he said:

'Sir, what about the motor-sledges?'

He gave himself away there—and had to, as this was his one anxiety, but he suspected that Campbell had noticed too. So he added slowly that Captain Scott was indeed pioneering a novelty in the use of motor-sledges in arctic regions.

'I do hope they are living up to your expectations.'

'I can assure you, Captain Amundsen, that up to now the

sledges have exceeded our wildest hopes and desires. I think I may be so bold as to say that the whole problem of reaching the Pole will be significantly simplified because of them. . . .'

War had now been declared across the table, every word carrying a double meaning. Campbell aimed with great skill, knowing that this was a war of nerves. Amundsen pretended not to notice that he was under fire. He asked questions of his own, casually reminding the other man that there were other forms of transport.

'What time did I tell my men to fetch me in the dog-sledge?'

So the dinner ended with a deep bow, a firm handshake and best wishes to both expeditions. Campbell considered another burst of generosity on the point of departure would increase the burden on Amundsen's guilty conscience, if he had one—'Captain Amundsen, you know that the *Terra Nova* is returning to New Zealand before the sea freezes over. It would give the crew great pleasure to take with them any mail from you and your men.'

The Norwegian stabbed back:

'I cannot thank you enough, sir, but it takes time to write letters and all our time is taken up getting the dogs and equipment in condition for the trip to the Pole. My sincerest thanks, sir.'

'I thank you, Captain Amundsen.'

'My regards to Captain Scott.'

'And mine to your men.'

So the *Terra Nova* steamed out to report to Scott as soon as possible. Amundsen went back to Framheim. He was profoundly uneasy and wished to speed up the depot trip south,

They set out on their first depot trip. It was 10 February, 1911. There were four men with three sledges and eighteen dogs, each sledge weighing three hundred kilos.

It was a mild day of swirling mists. The light was grey, with no wind across the silent ice. The skis glided easily. The dogs panted with eagerness, the sound carrying far in such weather. The land seemed to choke them with fog on that first day. But the mist was transparent in places, as if without substance, and they could see the roof of Framheim behind them. They could also see the *Fram*'s rigging. When they returned, the *Fram* would have set sail. According to plan, a ship would come to fetch them next year. Before that happened, they had to reach the Pole.

Suddenly one of the sledges stopped, and all its dogs turned their noses to the north. They howled dismally. Then the rest of the dogs stopped and howled too. But only once. The howl rose in the mist, grew and died away in the mist. It affected the men so forcefully that not one of them could lift his whip and urge the dogs on. After a while, the first team jerked and ran on, the others following in its tracks.

Prestrud went first, as he had a talent for staying on course. This was virgin territory. Never before had man set foot here. No ski-tracks, no marker stones, not a single black spot. It was easy to go round in circles, farther and farther off course, the tracks behind you growing like a vein in the skin, constant small twists or great loops. Everyone's nerves soon frayed. But Prestrud had this capacity to steer straight as long as he wasn't tired. He was given the course from the compass of the man behind, and then he kept to it as if there were a ruler across the terrain.

The light made it difficult to see unexpected features in this terrain. Suddenly a hump of ice would be right in front of you, like a person lying in wait—a madman round the corner as you're coming home in the fog, and there the madman stands. Is he smiling? You don't dare look. You go round. The land suddenly dipped. The skis took you by surprise by speeding up, and you fell over. A sudden frantic thought: are there crevasses here?

Yes, the Antarctic was criss-crossed with crevasses. And yet the ice seemed firm enough; it became a risky feat, a throw of the dice: it was an advantage to move without being roped together, but maybe it would be safer to link man to man with a long rope.

They continued into the fog.

Behind Prestrud came Helmer Hanssen. He could steer his dogs with his voice. He kept half an eye on the compass, gliding along on his skis, one hand on the load, grunting angrily at one dog, snarling a curse at another, shouting out to Prestrud: 'A little to the left!' And almost imperceptibly, Prestrud got back on course.

Behind Helmer came Hjalmar Johansen. He was the toughest in the group and the most capable. This was all familiar to him as he had accompanied Nansen. He displayed great equanimity, which masked a profound unease. One day it would break out. He had a compass, too, and kept an eye on it, checking the course of the man in front. Their course was due south.

Last came Amundsen. He had his own reasons for being last. He picked up what the others dropped, and that was important. But the real reason was that here at the back he escaped being seen. He felt most free here. A nervous twitch went unnoticed, as did a quiet word, a subdued curse. Here at the back he didn't need to play the part of the great leader. His thoughts turned to Scott: would he be able to use motor-sledges in this terrain?

In one respect, he hoped for an easy journey to the Pole, as that was when the dogs were fastest. But the more difficult the land, the worse it would be for motor-sledges. Amundsen steered the dogs just as well as the others, but he hadn't their calm. He was quicker to use the whip, bawling with rage, thrashing the team with the whip-handle, whereas the two drivers ahead were able to control their teams with a few sharp words.

The ship's rigging had vanished behind them. Prestrud was tiring. The delicate play of nerves at the back of his head, the instrument in his brain, wasn't functioning so well as when they had started. As the day went by, the shouting increased, friendly at first: 'A little to the left now.' Then angrier, containing unspoken accusations: 'Idiot! To the right, I said.' Yes, to the right, but everything was white, everything grey, not a track to follow, the body making its own demands, every man now dripping with sweat.

They struck camp. The tent went up. The dogs were given dried fish, and lay down in the snow with their tongues out, fog all round them. The men crawled into the tent, the primus making it snug inside. They had a canvas floor and a sleeping-bag between them and the snow. The pemmican tasted good. A bit of chocolate, a cup of tea.

But their bodies were sweaty, their underclothes damp. They had to dry out before they could sleep. They began to itch as the sweat dried. They crawled down into their sleeping-bags, tied up the opening, breathed slowly and deeply so that their breath would warm them up and dry the sweat. Gradually things got better. But simultaneously something else was creeping up on them, slowly, irresistibly: a chilly greeting, a reminder that they were lying on ice. No one sleeps continuously in a tent which stands on snow. They twisted and turned, dozed, heard the others snoring and dozed off again, because their bodies were tired out and demanded rest. Someone snored loudly; the others woke and cursed.

Then it was morning, up and out. This was the most difficult moment. You were lying in your sleeping-bag, peevish and unrested, but even so, it felt good lying there. You had to go out into the cold and the mist, and much of what was to be done had to be done without mittens. Get on out with you! It would take half an hour for the snow to melt in the kettle, another half an hour before tea. The dogs began to raise their voices. You could hear that a fight was building up.

Up and out! But it's better inside the sleeping-bag.

If only you were on your own here ... the others gradually became a torment. If only you could be alone at that moment of getting up. The others were constantly in the way. They stuck their arms into your things. Someone pulled at your sleeping-bag as you were crawling out. Someone else had tipped over the primus. It wasn't you. Paraffin had seeped out. It stank. You cursed and the culprit heard you, growled; so he was the one who did it, but he wouldn't admit it, the louse. He's a louse. But don't say so, not yet. Now they were all up.

Then came the pemmican, a bit of chocolate, a little seal meat, a cup of tea. Everything seemed better.

Fog today, fog every day. But the terrain was easy and they kept up their speed. The dogs worked well and everything went according to plan.

They drove through country no man had ever seen before. They didn't see it either. The fog lay like a grey cloth all round them.

They reached latitude eighty and set up the first depot there. The journey home went quickly, parts of it in their own tracks. They had marked the route with stakes and dried fish. Now it felt as if they owned this country. The men had also got to know each other better. But that could be dangerous. They'd learned one thing: it's best to keep your mouth shut.

On the last day they drove eighteen kilometres at a stretch, the sledges empty, and they held out some hope that the *Fram* hadn't yet sailed. But when the sun rose, and the fog lifted to reveal the Bay of Whales before them, the *Fram* had gone.

Down to Framheim. That was now their home.

Nose protectors.

Two men at Framheim thought nose protectors ought to be worn in severe cold. They managed to persuade a third member of the expedition over to their view. Hjalmar Johansen maintained that he'd never used nose-protectors on his trip with Fridtjof Nansen. The other three men couldn't agree on the shape of the protector and what material it should be made of. One of them, the keenest, maintained that it should be sewn of sealskin and lined with wool, made to be pushed inside one earflap so that it could be easily retrieved. The other two thought that it should be made of quite light material, perhaps cotton, but should be gathered so that it moulded itself round the ridge of the nose. There were long discussions before they agreed to disagree. Then they cut up their boots.

Amundsen had said that each man had to take a pair of thick boots with him on the trip south. What else they took with them in the way of soft shoes was up to them. But it turned out that the boots, despite their size, were too small. Everyone agreed on that point. So they had to cut up every single boot at Framheim, work that might determine the fate of the expedition. If they didn't manage to sew the boots together properly, they would have to attempt the conquest of the Pole with unsuitable, ruined footwear. Previously the boots had been shaped like a pair of long sleds forgotten in the snow after a drunken party. Now they were solidly built out, lengthened, made broader, like a fleet of barges waiting in turn on a canal. Every man had room for two pairs of loose soles inside his boots, and six pairs of thick woollen socks. It worked. And the result had its own peculiar kind of beauty.

Amundsen demonstrated his braces and reminded them of their experience on the depot trip. Remember that the tent is crowded: you should be able to slip your braces on and off without taking up too much elbow room. More important, they shouldn't slip off your shoulders. And first and foremost, they mustn't be too tight. You are more likely to freeze when something is tight. But could braces be held in place without being tight? That could be a problem.

And their function—which mustn't be entirely forgotten —is to hold your trousers up.

Don't forget: there are times when trousers have to come down. When there's a snowstorm and it's forty degrees below zero—even then trousers have to come down. You can't wear your gloves then, so the fastening mechanism must function perfectly. Pins or needles will do—it doesn't matter, but you mustn't use clips. You can't rely on a clip. You can't repair it in the cold.

Remember then: trousers have to come down. Then be pulled up again. It's a rush job.

They were ready to start on the next depot trip.

The goal for the next depot trip was latitude eighty-two. This time there were eight men with seven sledges and forty-five dogs—a migration through the wastelands. A storm blew up almost immediately, but they could probably master the storm if they put their backs into it, with chin on chest and harsh words to the dogs, in a swirl of white— a wind which slashed like a knife against your skin. Conditions deteriorated with the combination of cold and gale that met them over the barrier. Up till now, the experts had thought that when the wind blew strongly, the cold decreased, and vice versa. This turned out not to be true. The wind now came at full blast and the temperature fell. The dogs' howling seemed to freeze away the first evening, as they struck camp and had to remove their mittens to get the finely adjusted instruments and pins in their braces in order. They got themselves into the tent.

Amundsen knew what he was doing—they had to get

the provisions for men and dogs out before winter set in. Either that or fail in the spring. So he had to survive this great test of endurance whatever the cost, whether of life or death. He had no choice but to succeed. If he failed, he would stand forever in people's memories as the dishonest explorer who deceived the world. It was forty-five degrees below zero.

The dogs began to fail on the following day, and that was no joke. They had all run so easily on the previous trip, but there was one major difference now—the cold. The snow was light and powdery and carried them well, but an inch below the snow was a sharp thin crust; a heavy man in boots wouldn't notice it, but it cut the dogs' paws. They didn't howl or whine, but when a man bent over to examine the paw, he was snapped at for his pains. Two of the dogs in Amundsen's team began to limp.

This didn't bode well. They had many miles ahead of them. Next day, there was a fine, sharp, drifting snow which penetrated so far into the dogs' coats that they were soaked as soon as it melted with their body-heat. It was now forty-three below zero. The snow also found its way into the gaps in the men's clothes—not that there should have been any, but it found its way under mittens, seeped behind peaks of leather caps, forced its way through seams which should have been impervious and impenetrable to both wind and snow. It was forty-five below zero.

They weren't as resilient in severe cold. Heart, lungs, pulse—all worked more laboriously. Muscles couldn't get the oxygen they needed. They had to stop more often, turn away from the wind, every attempt at shouting like a blow on the back of the neck. The dogs had begun to lie down, so the last lingering memory of gentleness had to be suppressed. It was difficult for all of them, not least for the peasant boy from Telemark, silent and stern-eyed, Olav Bjaaland. His dog had once been their farm dog. It had wagged its tail when he came up to it. It had been his morning ritual to stand on the steps in the Morge valley and scratch it under its chin with the tip of his shoe, balancing on one leg and smiling. The sun lay over the mountains. He was young and happy. He knew he was the best skier in the world. And the dog would jump to lick his mouth.

But now you, Olav Bjaaland, a world champion skier, had to force your way ahead in a southerly gale, forty-five below, with the dogs lying down, not wanting to go on. You've got a whip: use it. Your stomach turns. You force one dog, two, three, but the leader refuses. You realize you've chosen the wrong dog as leader, but how can you change them now? Use the whip. So you become a different person, a sort of Jekyll and Hyde figure whose existence you'd never suspected. You flay the dog so that tufts of its hair loosen and blow away in the wind. Is that a tear freezing on your cheek? No one notices, not even you.

But this was where Amundsen's strength lay. He knew how to thrash a dog on. His team was the weakest, and he was driving last. Over and over again, the distance between him and the others became so great that they had to wait. Perhaps his dogs were the slackest because he couldn't slip in among them any more, stroking a dog's nose, shaking its coat, being friendly and stern at the same time. His nerves were too close to the surface. He had to stay strong and inflexible—the man urging a dog-team ahead into the storm. But he said subsequently—and we've no reason to doubt him—that it was like thrashing your own flesh and blood. When he described the trip a year later, he recalled this incident with an emotion not otherwise apparent in his words. Perhaps this goes some way towards explaining why he hardened with the years, why he lost his sensitivity, became bitter and coarse. Forty-seven below. The men crawled into the tent while the dogs lay down in the snow. They had fought over some dried fish, eaten a little snow, the cold liquid trickling down their

throats into a soaking body. The storm laid a carpet over
them.

But in the tent the temperature rose. It was now no
more than twenty-five below zero. It rose to fifteen below,
which felt almost warm. But the sweat had to dry on their
bodies, and their fingers began to stiffen. The primus sputtered. Someone knocked it with his boot and it tipped and
went out. They lit it again. More snow, more waiting.
Now was the time men had to turn their faces away to
stop themselves going for each other's throats, ripping
open arteries with predatory teeth glittering white in the
murk. Hot tea at last; then food—a bit of chocolate. Anger
sank deeper into stomachs and vanished and something
different, more gentle rose. Amundsen replaced his angry
face with a happy one. He wrote his journal without his
mittens on. He noted his observations with painful
accuracy. He kept up a conversation with his men, succeeding in praising all without offending any, even
managed a display of humour, too—surprising everyone,
a friend among friends but retaining his position as leader.

Then they had to go outside before settling down for the
night. Stomachs made demands and better now than later.
He was a master at this. A sour word, a heavy sigh, a bitter
expression would have made the operation agony at forty-
five degrees below. But taken with a light-hearted quip,
they were all men together, making himself the butt of
the joke, it was just about bearable. He knew how to do
this. Crawled out; crawled back; was happy. One by one,
all the men out, all back. They shared a kind of happiness at that moment.

Sleeping inside in a temperature of about five below,
human breath warming up the tent. The storm abated
during the night. Next day the temperature was only
thirty-five below. A hard-blown crust lay on the snow,
which the dogs could walk on, but which the men and
sledges fell through.

Some of them got out of step because of this. The three-hundred-kilo loads went down on one runner again and again, leaving the other up on the snow. Then the man had to lift—shouting at the dogs as he couldn't both lift the sledge and whip them at the same time. The others had to come and help. The whole party stopped. It again became apparent that Hjalmar Johansen was the strongest. It didn't matter that he still was, did it? Did it matter anyhow? He was strong, silent, capable, the only one apart from the leader with qualities of leadership.

The Barrier was now smooth and fine, rising slowly; nothing was visible except gusts of drifting snow, handfuls of fog, whiteness on all horizons. There was no sign of crevasses.

Then three dogs fell through into a crevasse in the snow.

They hung in their harness and howled. The dogs behind dug in their paws and held the other three up. But the snow was slippery, and slowly, slowly the dogs' paws slid nearer and nearer the crevasse. Then Johansen came up. With a mighty effort, he hauled the dogs up. A small patch of packed snow broke away from where he had just been standing, and hurtled down into eternity.

Thus they came to the land of the great crevasses. Prestrud, who was forerunner this trip too, had a rope tied round his waist, then fastened to the first dog team. But the rope sagged and hindered him. The dogs were so hungry that they began to bite through the rope, so it had to be fixed. More scolding—and abuse for the forerunner who couldn't keep on course because he was so tired, blinded by the drifting snow. Every time he swung away, the dogs got a better grip on the rope. They had to be tied together again, over and over again, and that meant taking mittens off. It was forty below zero. They reached latitude eighty-one and set up a depot. From here, Bjaaland, Hassel and Stubberud were to go back, the others to continue on to latitude eighty-two. This was part of a meticulously thought-out plan. Fewer men so far south meant less food for people and dogs. Dividing the party was very risky, but it could have its advantages too. The tracks from the first party home might be useful to the next, as long as storms and snow didn't wipe them all away.

The dog teams had to be divided too, and that was no easy task. The men going on had to have the best ones, which undeniably increased the dangers for those going back. They all knew this. There was only one man who could do it, and he was as hard as nails, dividing the dogs on a strictly utilitarian basis. Then they said farewell.

There's an art in saying goodbye at latitude eighty-one, forty-five degrees below zero. It has to be done quickly. There's not much time for thoughts. Nevertheless, thoughts were there. There was no place now for aversions that had sprung up, bitter words, half-spoken, half-suppressed, that had trembled on lips over the past two days. For if they were to freeze to death they would do so in the same tent.

Goodbye! Goodbye!

Regards to Framheim.

The five others went on southwards.

They were heading for latitude eighty-two with seal meat, pemmican and some cans of paraffin. They almost made it. Then the first dog fell. It was hit on the head with the butt of an axe and the body slung on to the load. By evening it was frozen stiff. Then Wisting cut it up, skin, fur and all, and flung the bits to the rest of the dogs, who gobbled it up. The intense cold had begun to corrode the men by now. Their physical strength dwindled and they hadn't the same powers of resistance as they had had when they had started. They were too impatient to wait until water had boiled for tea, so they drank it lukewarm, slopping it because their hands were trembling. They sat in their sleeping-bags, knowing they would freeze, half-awake through the long night.

Then Hjalmar Johansen said: 'Nansen and I shared a sleeping-bag.'

The suggestion was like a stab in the back to Amundsen. They were thousands of miles from Nansen and his journey to the north, but even so the shadow of the great master lay across them. The others soon realized that two men in a sleeping-bag would mean greater warmth and companionship, but it would also make great demands. Surely, every time one of them turned over, he'd wake the other. But the warmth! It would be worth it for the warmth.

Johansen: 'It was the only way we could survive.'

Amundsen: 'Not everyone likes the idea of two men sharing a sleeping-bag.'

'What do you mean?'

'We wouldn't all enjoy sleeping together.'

'How do you mean, *enjoy* it...?'

There was a blizzard outside; inside it was deathly still.

Johansen smoked a pipe. He took out his tobacco pouch and lit his pipe. They could see his hands shaking slightly. Only partly with cold.

'Are you suggesting we took pleasure in it...?'

He adjusted his own language, making it a shade sharper, camouflaging it behind a chilling formality.

'Herr Captain, are you really saying that Nansen and I took pleasure...?'

Amundsen demonstrated his capacity for leadership. He said nothing. But in the heavy, cold days that followed, the idea of a double sleeping-bag occupied all their thoughts.

They reached a spot close to latitude eighty-two and set up a depot there. Amundsen's dogs were exhausted, so they had to allow a couple to sit on the sledges when they turned back. But the dogs fell off and died of cold. When Wisting dismembered one of the bodies, he saw that the dog had an infected sore on its chest where the harness had rubbed. He buried the carcass so that it should not infect the others. At night they were woken by the dogs. They had found the corpse and were fighting over it. They devoured it, every last bit, and staggered away, ravenous and sore-legged.

But they got back to Framheim.

And the other three had got back safely too.

The depots were now in place.

Let winter come.

SCOTT

One of the motor-sledges was still standing on the sea-ice in windswept McMurdo Sound, a few kilometres from the mainland. The sledge sat there brooding like a small ship, covered with tarpaulins, surrounded by crates of spare parts and hundreds of cans of oil and paraffin. Now it was time to drive it into the winter quarters.

The engine was started, small, explosive sounds giving warning that a new era of mechanization had come to the Antarctic. A deputation of penguins appeared in procession across the ice to protest against so disgraceful a racket. Poisonous gas from the engine scattered in the wind, an eager young man waving his headgear to celebrate the first pollution of the Antarctic. The three motorized sledges had cost hundreds of thousands of pounds.

Then someone put a foot through the ice.

The sledge sank slowly, first a little lower on one track; then it stopped. It slipped further and overturned.

Twenty men came with ropes—seamen who knew the art of fastening a rope-end at speed. Inch by inch, they hauled the sledge up on to an even keel.

Scott came on to the scene. The sledge was ready to move, the engine started up again. Then the sledge sank. A voice yelled: 'Get away from there!' As they ran, the sledge rose up on end, went down stern first, standing for a moment like a dark fist sticking out of the water, before sinking and vanishing for ever.

They got back on to firm land. They still had two sledges.

Amundsen was having sleepless nights because of these motor-sledges.

Scott had set up winter quarters twenty-five kilometres from Hut Point, where the *Discovery* expedition and Shackleton in his time had stayed. On 24 January, 1911, he set out on his first depot trip southwards. There were eleven men in the party, with eight ponies and twenty-six dogs to draw the sleds. Some of the men were on skis.

Dogs and ponies had previously been tried separately in polar regions by the Englishmen, but the combination of the two produced additional difficulties. The dogs would try to snatch at a bit of flesh from a pony's hindquarters, so that a certain distance had to be maintained between dog and pony, dividing the expedition into two. But at the same time they had to stay together. There was another thing too: a dog-driver could ski alongside his sledge, but a pony-driver had to hold his pony at its head and because of this soon got out of step. He quickly found he had to remove his skis and wade through the snow.

The first stretch south was across sea-ice from one promontory to another. It was impossible to cross the rocky ground inland. The snow on the ice was mixed with salt and the going heavy. Nor was the ice wholly safe. The sight of the motor-sledge sinking was very much in their minds, so they urged the ponies and dogs on, sweat pouring off them. The sledges were heavily loaded. Mount Erebus was visible over to the west, the volcano protruding up through a low sea of mist and projecting its blazing pennant into the sky. It looked as if the mist were on fire.

They came unscathed across the ice and called the first camp on firm ground Camp Safety. They raised the tents. Everything was done in a military way. The officers had their ranks, the men theirs, but the cold soon forced them to live together in the same tent. The officers weren't used to this, and were afraid that it might be awkward for discipline, though it was worse for the men, who dared not talk without permission and had to get used to having officers' knees in their stomachs. The cold made sleep uneasy for all ranks, but food smoothed out their differences and the leader's bright smile was like a ray of sunlight in the tent.

One of the men on the depot trip was a captain in the Indian Army, Lawrence Oates. He was a millionaire who had given money to the expedition. Some people thought that Scott was a little too generous when it came to showing goodwill towards rich men who wished to buy their way into society. But Oates filled his place as few men could—or none. The millionaire had grown up with horses, and they had become his passion and life-study. He had followed these ponies all round the world to where they stood now, leaning against the storm.

If they were to conquer the Pole for England, they had to save as many ponies as possible, and Oates was with them at all times of the day. He studied the way they walked, looked at the angle of their necks, and noted when icicles were hanging from their muzzles, which meant that their body temperature wasn't high enough to melt the ice. At night, a wall made from blocks of ice was built round the ponies. They stood and leaned against it. The dogs let themselves be snowed under and came up from their holes steaming with warmth. But the ponies grew stiff with cold.

One day, Oates saw that two ponies were refusing their food. He knew that meant they were near collapse. Their hoofs sank deep down into the snow, but what was worse was that the driving snow got right through their thick coats and on to their skin, where it melted.

It was a difficult trip. Scott had to weigh up which was more important—saving most of the ponies or getting as far south with the depot as possible. Oates understood horses, but Scott had the final say. Wilson was ever-present, with his handsome face and good advice. They struggled on south. The weakest of the ponies had been nicknamed Weary Willy. By some mischance he'd been given the heaviest sledge and was falling behind. Alongside ran the strong young Norwegian, Tryggve Gran. Willy's weakness was clearly weakening the whole party. A blizzard broke out.

They struck camp. Even the smallest landmark had now vanished: Mount Erebus with its cloth of fire, every hillock and every slope in the terrain, all had vanished in a sea of whiteness.

The dogs buried themselves in the snow. The ponies stood behind a snow-wall with a thick layer of snow on their backs. They froze and drooped like dead things, leaning against the snow-wall but finding rest for neither head nor hoof.

The men crawled together into the largest tent. It felt as if the whole world was in there; a millimetre-thin, weather-proof tentcloth, held down with bolts and tethered with cords in the ice, shutting out the blizzard. A primus sputtered. Eleven men breathed together and the temperature rose towards zero. The tea went round and made life a little easier. Now and again, Oates crawled out, came back again, cold and snow in his wake. He said: 'They're still alive.'

After three days the blizzard was still raging. It seemed as if the Empire itself were crumbling. Scott debated inwardly whether to say the Lord's Prayer aloud. But they were sitting too close together in the tent, they could see each other's faces, hear each other's breathing. Eyes flick-

ered. A gust shook the tent. Someone leapt up, trod on
someone else, butting at the tentcloth; for a moment it
seemed as if it would collapse. Scott decided against the
Lord's Prayer.

Would the Almighty demonstrate tonight that He was
mightier than His own word? The thought troubled the
brooding Scott as he got down into his sleeping-bag and
tried to sleep.

Where was Amundsen tonight? He had telegraphed
that he was heading south, hadn't he? Scott still didn't
know that Campbell had met him in the Bay of Whales. At
last the storm was abating.

Then Weary Willy was attacked by the dogs. They were
now quite rested after sleeping through the storm, and
in better form than before. Weary Willy was wearier than
ever. He had fallen to his knees without seeing the danger.
A leash of dogs had torn themselves free, fire in their
bellies, desperate for meat. They hurled themselves at
Willy. He kicked wildly and struck one, missed the next,
and a jaw then fastened itself into the pony's belly. Willy
lay down flat, trying to crush the dog against the underlying ice, and almost succeeding. But then he was unable
to lash out. More dogs fell on him. Men shouted and
hurled themselves at the dogs. A voice yelled: 'Hit the
swine in the jaws!' So they did, with iron bars. The
dogs reeled back, came again, ripping leather trousers,
rolling back in the snow, their muzzles dripping with gore.
They were driven back. Willy was still alive, but he should
have been allowed to die. They continued southwards.
Scott wanted to go all out to reach latitude eighty and
lay down the depot there; a ton of food and equipment
was to be left for use on the journey to the Pole next
summer.

But they didn't reach latitude eighty. They could have
reached it—if they'd sacrificed Willy. Oates thought they
would manage if they drove the animal one more day

south—and then they could slaughter him. But Scott didn't agree. He had decided it was more important to get Willy back to winter quarters alive, because they would need every single animal in the spring when the journey to the Pole began.

So it was man against man, one the leader, the other an expert in his own field. It was the first and only time that Oates pitted his will against Scott's. Both were fond of animals, but this concerned more than an animal. It was a tactical assessment. Oates didn't give way. He had a strong voice, and he used it even after the decision had been made. He knew he was right. Willy couldn't survive until the spring. Only a clear, definitive order made him bow to the leader's words. The depot was laid fifteen to twenty miles short of the place originally intended. Then they turned back.

Since then, dissertations have been written about this episode. Had Oates had a premonition? Would Scott and his men have lived if Willy had been allowed to die? Willy died all the same. He couldn't manage the journey home and had to be killed.

On the spot where the depot should have been laid, according to the plan, Scott died on his journey back from the Pole—of hunger, exhaustion and cold—a few kilometres from a ton of supplies.

A few days before that, Oates had walked out of their tent, never to be seen again.

They were on their way back, retracing the tracks of their trip south. They were going in a curve, because on the journey out they'd gone off course. Scott then took a short cut across unknown terrain. One of the dog-drivers, Meares, protested, saying that a longer way could turn out to be quicker if they knew it was safe. But perhaps Scott was out of sorts: he became obstinate, peremptory and taciturn. Shrugging, Meares turned the dogs and set them off on a new course across a plateau between two walls of ice.

It was a lovely day, the sun across the snow, the brightness making their eyes smart. The men had taken off their outer clothes and put them on the sledges. The dogs had been coping well, which was something Scott hadn't expected. Perversely, he seemed put out at finding his pessimism unfounded. Then suddenly the six middle dogs in a team vanished down a crevasse.

The leader-dog, Osman, was as strong as a lion, and now had his paws thrust into firm snow, holding up the six dogs behind. They hung, swinging in their traces. The crevasse had been hidden under new snow. Two dogs were still standing on the other side of the crevasse, the sledge behind them. Then more of the edge broke away and, with a piercing howl, the last two dogs slid down. Osman was now the only one on the surface. Scott had run forward. Meares put two ski-poles down on the edge so that the snow would bear his weight better. He lay down on his stomach and edged himself forwards. At first he could see nothing, but he could hear the dogs. When his eyes had adjusted to the darkness of the crevasse, he saw the bodies of the dogs twisting and turning in their traces down below. They were trying to scramble on top of each other and were beginning to suffocate. Osman was still holding on. The sledge was still standing.

They swung the sledge round to stabilize it. That done, Scott leapt over the crevasse and helped Osman by tethering him to a ski-pole. Then Wilson came. The other men were farther back. Meares was still lying on his stomach on the edge of the crevasse. He said, 'They're still hanging there.'

Then two dogs twisted themselves free of the traces and fell. They landed on a ledge sixty feet lower down and stayed there.

The men took ropes across the crevasse and strengthened

the harness; the sledge was manoeuvred across and tethered on each side. Osman was now free. Meares was the dog expert and offered to go down to the six dogs wriggling in the traces. Scott was hesitant. Saving the dogs was important, but it was even more important not to sacrifice a man. He gave his permission.

Clouds were gathering in the north—a familiar sight. Within a few minutes, the weather could be transformed from calm to fog or blizzard. Far behind them they saw the rest of the party, but it was no use waving or shouting, as the distance was too great. They had plenty of rope on the sledges. They tried out the tethers, jumping cautiously on the edge of the crevasse, reckoning the ice would hold. Meares fastened the rope under his arms, so that both hands were free. He knew what a dog could do when it was hanging twisting on a rope. He sat down on the edge of the crevasse, drew a deep breath and said, 'Now. . . .'

They let him glide down, two men braking, the rope wound round a ski-pole so that it ran slowly. Foot by foot, they let him down the crevasse. Down below, the struggling dogs saw that the man was coming down and recognized him. They were mad with fear.

He had thrashed them so often. Now he was risking his life for their sake. When he was a few feet above them, he bellowed at them to frighten the first one. The dog stopped in the middle of a howl. With a swift thrust, Meares grabbed its jaw and clamped it shut. He had a thinner rope with him and wound it round the body of the dog, cutting the traces with a knife he had between his teeth. The dog was hoisted up.

They were clever dogs, and realized that Meares had come to help them, but they were wild with terror. The rest of the team was hanging slightly lower down the crevasse, but he couldn't get down to them because a harness strap was in the way. As his legs came level with the dogs, one of them jerked round and bit him in the shin.

He cried out, but choked back the cry and didn't kick out, because his body would have begun to swing. He hunched up and tried to get hold of the dog's head. The traces round its neck were choking it. He shouted up: 'Down!' They let him down a little. The dog and he were now level: one dog was kicked by another lower down, and attacked Meares's face. He hit it between the eyes. His body swung wildly to one side and the dog followed. They shouted something from above. As his body swung back, he managed to get the rope round the dog and the men above hoisted it up.

His strength was almost exhausted and he ought to have gone up again to rest. But could the two of them manage to get him up and then let him down again? He shouted: 'Let me hang! I must rest.' Below him were four dogs. Even farther down were two more standing on a ledge, barely discernible through the blue light. The ice walls were all around him, the crevasse apparently bottomless. There was only a six-foot gap between the ice wall at the narrowest place. Above him he could just see a fissure of white light.

Then he shouted 'Up!' They hoisted again. Now it looked as if the nearest dog had lost consciousness, half-suffocated by the traces round its neck. It was easy to get it up.

Whilst one of the two men up there hauled up the dog, the other had to hold on to Meares on his own. Now and again a few chunks of snow fell, hitting Meares on the head. The snow trickled down into his clothes and body. He was sweating profusely, yet freezing cold.

Dog after dog came up. Finally it was his turn. The two men on the edge of the crevasse hoisted him up slowly, foot by foot. There were a few metres left when he got a large lump of snow in the face. The edge above him began to creak.

They didn't seem to be pulling at all. He thought, 'If

only they would get me up!' But they hauled slowly, evenly, calmly. They shouted something—he couldn't hear what.

Then he was up.

For a moment he lay on the edge of the crevasse with his feet out and his head in Scott's arms.

The fog that had been on the way had disappeared. The sun was shining again, the light glittering across the snow. The next dog-team in the party reached them. The men still knew nothing of the incident and they waved cheerfully, asking if there was anything they could do to help. Two dogs were still down there on a ledge in the crevasse. Scott said: 'Fetch me the longest rope.' It was ninety feet long.

Meares said: 'I must have a rest first.'

'I'll go down,' replied Scott.

Wilson intervened then. He was Scott's friend, the only one who could demand a hearing in the presence of the leader. He pointed out that although they needed the dogs, they needed the men too—Scott most of all. For him to make the descent would be to put the entire expedition at risk.

'We can't leave the dogs down there, and we must get on.'

'We could shoot them.'

'I'm going down.'

They strengthened the tethers on the sledge that was standing across the crevasse. More men had now arrived. How many could approach the edge of the crevasse without it collapsing? Every man on the edge was roped to a man behind. Scott tied the ninety-foot rope round his waist. He went out on to the sledge and sat down on it. Wilson was standing on one side, Meares, who had revived, on the other. They wound the rope round ski-poles to act as a brake.

Then they let him down. It was darker down here than

he had imagined. He saw that the ice in the wall changed colour. Waves of cold struck him, the light up there slowly fading away. He shouted up: 'It's going fine....' The shout bounced from wall to wall, becoming incomprehensible, making a dog on the ledge far below him howl with fear. It sounded as if the howl descended first into the bottomless pit and then came back up with increased eeriness, becoming a hollow, ghostlike cry.

Foot by foot farther down, he hung quite calmly, but noticed with a sneaking fear that it took strength to hang like that. His ears began to buzz. The cold from the ice walls felt like branches scratching his skin.

Now he was coming to the ledge. His neck hurt when he tried to bend his head forward to see what the ledge looked like. It was about twelve feet long, and at its widest, about four feet. In two places it jutted out at an angle. He shouted up: 'Slowly!' He began jerking his body to get it swinging in towards the ice wall, so that he could reach the ledge with his feet. Otherwise they would have let him down past it. His body swayed, he hit the wall on one side and at once he felt himself drop a foot or two. Then they pulled him back up.

He got one foot on the ledge, then the other. A mitten was torn off and he hit his fingers on a projection in the ice wall. Then he hauled himself in. Two metres away from him stood the dogs, silent now.

He knew what he had to do. First loosen the rope, then whilst he was free, try to get the rope round the first dog —and wait while it was hoisted up. The dogs' eyes glowed like burning coals in the gloomy blue light.

Now it was a question of his own nerves and the dogs' intelligence. Did they understand why he had come? The ice wall behind him was slippery, snow lying here and there on the ledge. He couldn't see what was under the snow.

Then he moved closer to the dogs, inch by inch, talking

to them calmly but firmly. He had always had a way with animals. He reached the nearest dog and scratched it behind its ear. It snapped at once, fastening its teeth into his wrist. He did not jerk back, because the dog would have attacked him. He forced himself to be calm, despite the fangs in his flesh, and the dog relaxed. Then he calmly loosened the rope from his own body and fastened it round the dog's, and the dog was hauled up.

While he was standing there, with no rope, he had time to study the ice formations, the play of colours, shimmering in red above him and darkening to black below. The other dog never took its eyes off Scott's face. They stared at each other.

How deep could the crevasse be? Three hundred feet, or eighteen hundred? It was immeasurable. Perhaps it went down to bedrock here, in the coldest continent on earth, the snow of a thousand years forming the crevasse. Then they let the rope down.

Now he began to hum. He was no great singer, but he remembered hearing that a soft humming calms animals. Again, he managed to get the rope round the dog's body and again he was alone down there while the last dog was hoisted up.

This was real loneliness. While he waited, he heard a fight breaking out among the dogs up above; the situation had probably caused it: freedom, joy, the relief of being saved. He also realized that the men would have to catch the dogs first, to prevent them from falling into the crevasse again.

He waited, trying to listen, but all sounds were distorted and echoed like thunder down here. He began to fear that the waves of sound would crack the ice above him so that the crevasse would collapse. Then he saw the end of the rope slowly dangling down.

It reached him. People were shouting up there, but he couldn't hear what they were saying. He'd lost a mitten as he had been catching the last dog, and now his hand had stiffened.

When the time came to fasten the rope round his own body, he couldn't manipulate his fingers. He had to abandon the other mitten, his whole body beginning to shake. Had his mind ceased functioning? He tried to force himself to think calmly. His little finger was sticking straight out like a stiff twig. He breathed on it, managing at last to get the rope round his waist, noticing a growing darkness in his brain; was he about to freeze to death? He had got the rope round his waist. Pulled, not knowing whether it would hold. Shouted. They hauled him up.

The knot appeared to be holding. He rose. There was a smaller ledge above him. He had to get around it, pushing off with one hand. He didn't succeed, and the ice edge sliced off his leather cap, scraping his scalp, but he was too cold to notice the pain. Then he was up.

Two men were lying on the sledge that they had now dragged away from the crevasse. They placed Scott on top of them. On top of him lay Wilson. Then he was given a drink of hot tea. One of the men had brewed it while the others were struggling with the dogs.

On the way south on this first depot trip, Scott had sent back some of the men after they had completed their part of the task. The leader of this party had been Teddy Evans —the man who had saved the *Terra Nova* in the storm on the way from New Zealand. Evans and his party were to wait for Scott at Camp Safety. They were there, but two of the ponies were dead.

'They snuffed it,' said Evans, calmly. 'They were alive last night, but they weren't eating. In the morning, they collapsed and died.' Evans knew all about ships but he didn't have the same insight when it came to animals; none of Oates's feel in his fingertips as he stroked the muzzle of a pony, none of his keen sense of when to take a handful of hay and rub down the animal to get its circulation going.

The meeting at Camp Safety wasn't a pleasant one. But the leader restrained himself. He had so much to take into consideration: there was no more point in raging at Evans than at the fog which was rolling across from the open stretches of sea in the north. Scott was not in the habit of taking problems lightly as he grappled with them in solitude.

On top of the misfortune with the ponies, there was something different and much worse.

On the trip south, the doctor of the expedition, Edward Atkinson, had become snowblind and had been left behind at Camp Safety with Petty Officer Thomas Crean. Atkinson later recovered and had made his way to Hut Point, where the *Discovery* hut stood. But now Atkinson and Crean hadn't come back. Perhaps the two of them had gone on from there to the winter camp at Cape Evans. Scott was anxious about them, but he had another powerful reason for getting to Hut Point as soon as possible. They'd agreed that the men on board the *Terra Nova* would try to bring mail to Hut Point, if they had any news of Amundsen.

Scott departed, taking a few men with him. They reached the hut to find a piece of paper on the wall. 'There is a mailbag inside.'

They went in. The hut was empty.

No bag, not a soul, but there were traces of recent occupation. Maybe Atkinson and Crean had picked up the mailbag and were now on their way back to Camp Safety, but by a different route from Scott's. Scott was uneasy. The sight of the hut had also aroused memories. This was where he had stayed during the long winter months with the *Discovery* expedition. From here, he had gone south on his first polar trip.

What was in that letter? There must have been a letter, surely?

The men on board the *Terra Nova* must surely have had important news to tell if they had headed for Hut Point before setting course back to New Zealand. Scott left and hastily made tracks back to Camp Safety. From a long way away, he could see that another tent had been erected.

Atkinson and Crean were in good shape. They had the mailbag with them. It contained one single letter.

It was from Campbell on board the *Terra Nova*.

Scott was kneeling on a sleeping-bag inside the tent, open-ing the letter. He knew Campbell's handwriting. He knew the name of Amundsen would be mentioned. But he still didn't know whether it would say: 'We have found him,' or 'We haven't found him.' His hands were trembling. It was so cold inside that his breath was visible. He knew that the men were standing silently round the tent, so he wouldn't hear them. A dog began to bark, then the sound faded away, and he realized the men must have chased the animal off.

He opened the letter and read:

'We found Amundsen in the Bay of Whales. He's more than a hundred kilometres nearer the Pole than we are. He has one aim—to reach the Pole first. His men looked capable and strong; they are outstanding skiers. Amund-sen himself is a hard man, clever and strong-willed. He had over a hundred dogs with him. We saw them driving the teams ... they certainly know how....'

Scott lowered the letter; everything went black before his eyes, and he cursed, which was unusual for him. He had paid such a high price to be first man at the Pole. The expedition was to have been solely scientific. But all Eng-land knew—and the Empire demanded—that *he* should be first. The continent of the Antarctic was a British possession, wasn't it?

His head whirled and he forgot where he was. Was he

still in England? Did he still have time to decide not to make the trip at all? He pinched his leg. There were three layers of woollen clothes there, and one layer of leather. His nails scarcely penetrated through to the skin. You're kneeling on a sleeping-bag; beneath you is a thousand feet of snow and ice.

You have to make up your mind now. You're the leader. Your word is law. Can you possibly change plans and hasten the assault on the Pole, casting science aside, clearly revealing the goal, naked and sharply defined? You have to tell the men the contents of the letter. You must summon them together. But what will you say? You don't know yet....

Every minute that goes past without your going out to them is losing you their respect. They'll say: 'He didn't know what to do.'

He got up heavily, thrusting the letter into his pocket. It was written on the best quality paper and wouldn't fold easily. Cursing again, he crawled out of the tent.

Beckoning to Edward Evans, he asked him to summon the men together. They came and paraded in military order. He had insisted that they should stick to naval regulations even here. It was twenty degrees below zero and a sharp wind from the north was blowing. Above them lay low clouds.

The air of the Antarctic possessed a stillness which meant a man's voice could slice through the wastelands like a sharp knife. When the dogs were silent, a man could hear his own heart beat in the stillness; even when the dogs yelped there was a ring of discord in the sound which only served to emphasize the silence. Now everything was still.

The men had paraded and he let them wait. Then he got up on a small mound of snow which had been shovelled up and he looked at them. Rough faces, furrowed by cold, he knew them now, and liked many of them, having begun to form a picture of who was the hardest and most capable.

Those were the ones he'd take with him to the Pole.

But what should he say? 'We'll speed up our plan and take up the challenge...' or 'We'll follow our original plan. It would be beneath us to take part in a race for the Pole.'

They stared avidly at his face. He avoided those curious, demanding eyes. But now he knew what he had to do. To change the plan, which had been so carefully made, beginning again, taking new decisions, risking everything, throwing themselves into this great drama—greater than he was already in—he couldn't do it. There was security in working on a strong foundation that was already approved.

He said heavily, his voice travelling far in the stillness:

'Campbell writes that Amundsen is in the Bay of Whales, a hundred kilometres nearer than we are. He has dogs and knows how to use them. That means that he can start for the Pole earlier than we can with our ponies.

'We will continue according to our original plan. There will be no race for the Pole.

'Perhaps we can get there before him all the same.'

He dismissed the men and went back into his tent.

There was plenty of work to be done here at Camp Safety, but none of it got done that day. He heard whispers round the tent and an occasional angry voice. A fight seemed to be developing between two exasperated men. One of them misunderstood, and thought the other hadn't cursed Amundsen as roundly as he had himself. An officer's voice silenced them. Evening came.

Tempers rose in the voices outside; several men were shouting and he knew that if he went out now and said to them: 'Shall we risk everything?' then they would have gone with him and risked all. But could he? Then Wilson, Edward Evans and Atkinson came into his tent. They found him silent and unsmiling. But something had happened to their great, wise, taciturn, impassive leader that evening. He relaxed his constant dignity. He cursed and voiced his innermost thoughts: 'This was despicably done! It's our right to reach the Pole first! Amundsen told us his plan but made it deliberately ambiguous. He's dishonest!'

He got up and clenched his fists, the anger coming out. They had never seen him like this—and never would again. They had come to use strong words, thinking they would console their leader. But he was using strong words to them.

It looked as if he were going to be sick. Doctor Atkinson was there and realized what might happen. He had an old sweater ready, and held it until it was needed. Scott snatched at the sleeping-bag, tears in his eyes. There was a small spark of hope in his expression as he cried: 'Shall we go over to the Bay of Whales and beat them up? Chase them away. This is our country, isn't it?'

A kind of brotherhood grew up between the men in the tent. They were sharing in a bold plan. They could go overland to the Bay of Whales and surprise the Norwegians.

But what then? Kill them?

They had been trained in schools of war and would no doubt be able to make a plan of attack. But could they put it into action when there was no order exempting them from guilt? What would be the consequences? They were wise men. They knew that this was only a dream. And it was no time for dreams.

It was already over. Over for him too. One by one the others left the tent. Scott was alone again.

The next day he brooded even more heavily than before. They had difficulty meeting each other's eyes.

Every man had his job to do, hard work and clear, harsh orders. No shirking. We continue according to plan.

The remaining ponies had still not been taken back to

their winter quarters at Cape Evans. It wasn't possible to take them overland: they had to try out the sea-ice, which now looked firm. But the ice broke up while they were camping on it. That was a night of great fear—the worst so far for Scott and his men. Three ponies leapt into the water. Floes stood up on end, the sea breaking heavily against the ice beneath the low cloud ceiling. Then the killer whales came, and attacked the nearest pony. The animal screamed and sank, the others swimming away with their last strength. The killer whales were upon them.

The men ran to save the last two ponies still on land. The dogs were lighter of foot, managing to get across the ice and to the safety of the land. The men got there too. Two ponies were still alive. They sank down on the edge of the ice and had to be carried higher up to safety.

The sea between the ice floes was crawling with killer whales, the water red, but the heavy breakers swept in and washed the blood away.

They got under cover in the *Discovery* Hut and had to stay there for several weeks until the sea froze over again. They had nothing but seal meat to eat, and used blubber for fuel in the stove made out of an oil drum. Eleven men lay side by side on the floor, Scott among them. Behind a tarpaulin were the only two surviving ponies from the ones that had been taken on the depot journey south.

The leader said little. He seemed tired.

At last the ice settled down and they made it back to their winter quarters.

AMUNDSEN

The winter became oppressive and long for the men at
Framheim. The darkness of night lasted for twenty-four
hours, no sun sending them even a weak ray of daylight.
Southern lights flared up occasionally before blizzards
smothered them again. Sea-ice and land-ice blended together into one solid mass. In a room down in the ice, a
blizzard swirling above and black sea far below him, a
man sat turning the handle of a sewing-machine.

They had dug out a network of paths and large rooms
under Framheim. There they had stores, workshops and
a sauna. It was man's triumph over the storms and the
desolation, a building of ice. Anxiety overcame them only
rarely: what if the ice breaks and we sail away...? Amundsen went on his rounds of inspection every day. The others
didn't like it. He moved noiselessly, and they didn't hear
him coming until he was upon them. He was friendly
enough, but with a touch of coldness as he suddenly
appeared—watching them. His eyes were deep-set, black
and full of superficial smiles which concealed an inner
suspicion.

The men he had brought with him here to the Antarctic
seemed to have been made to work under the ice. The
skier from Telemark had his own carpenter's workshop.

where he was taking sledges apart and planing down every bit to make them lighter. Olav Bjaaland knew that the work he was doing would determine whether they would reach the Pole first or not. Every sledge was solid and weighed seventy-five kilos. It was his task to reduce that weight without losing any of the strength. He had good hands. They were quite familiar with wood. He appeared to have plenty of time. He would upend a runner and familiarize himself with it, then discard it, throwing it irritably away. Then he would retrieve the runner again, turn it upside-down, mutter something about the carpenter being ashamed of himself, sigh resignedly and blow a little on his fingers—it was twenty degrees below zero in the ice chamber and he had to work without mittens on. The light from the big lamp was reflected back from a thousand ice-crystals. This was one of his problems: the light came at him from all angles. He never started a day's work without sharpening his plane. He had a keen eye, and this was work he understood. He could probably fool Amundsen if he wanted to. He could hoist a sledge up on the scales and boast that it was half as light again, or more. But he couldn't deceive an ice-hummock. The wear and tear would be the test—on those hundreds of miles towards a point on the map where no human foot had yet trodden. The sledge had to stand the strain. So he had little thought for the winter darkness above him, or for the sea below—for the fragility of an ice-floe which might break one night and send Framheim out to sea. He might lie awake at nights because he couldn't get a certain runner out of his mind. It had to be planed like this, not that way. He gradually progressed, getting a trial sledge down to fifty kilos, then to thirty, and finally he whittled it down to twenty-two. Then it was as elegant as a willow branch, as slender as a naked girl, straighter than any recruit on the parade ground, but supple nevertheless—first and foremost supple, and strong. He jumped on it.

He placed it between two crates and jumped on the sledge. The crates broke. He loaded it up with many times the weight it would have to carry on the journey south. The sledge held.

Then he set about the work seriously. That had only been a trial-run. What he did now could not be redone. The sledges he was planing down were to be used on the long journey.

He breathed on his hands. Twenty-one below zero. Then the leader came. It was one of Amundsen's weaknesses that he couldn't help his suspicious nature. He was full of praise for the men and their skills, but he concealed a deep-rooted suspicion which was only too apparent in the lonely ice-chamber. The man from Telemark stood the strain best. He had some of the imperturbability of the pine forests in him. As strong as a bear, thickset across the shoulders, taciturn, difficult to get to know. The leader in his soft leather slippers slunk on. If Amundsen found himself alone on one of the ice paths, he'd sometimes start jumping up and down to test the firmness of the ice. He didn't want the men to witness this. They mustn't hear, or begin to wonder what he was doing, or it might plant a seed of unease in their minds. One night that seed could flower into the wild scream of hysteria in those confined spaces. A man could feel as if he were in a prison of ice. Above him was the blizzard, around him the desolate wastes. No way out. But worse than that was the fear that the ice was breaking up. Were they sailing out to sea? We struck camp here to be a hundred kilometres nearer to the Pole, didn't we? Amundsen had heard that wild, violent, uncontrollable scream before. No one must see him jumping.

Jumping was stupid anyway. If the ice did break, it would break without warning. A little flea-jump by one human being wouldn't produce any sign. But all the same a dull kind of peace came over him after he had done it.

It was like jumping on mountains. He saw through his own self-deception and could afford a grin. But he felt safer, even so.

As long as it lasted. Should he go out and see if he could hear the sea? No one must know.

Here was Stubberud planing away to make the provision crates lighter. That was one of the weak points in their equipment: the crates were too heavy because the boards that held them together had a lot of knots in them. The man who had built Framheim, pulling down the house and erecting it again down here, was planing away laboriously, without imagination, with an artisan's skill. Millimetre after millimetre of the twisted wood was whittled away. And the crates held.

Here was the man with the sewing-machine, sitting in his ice-room, turning the handle in almost tropical heat ... ten degrees above zero. A primus stove kept him warm. Bowls from the sides of a tent he had stretched above him caught the melting ice. This was Oscar Wisting. He was general handyman and closest to Amundsen: perhaps Wisting was the only one the leader could call a friend. Wisting was re-making tents and leather clothes, always finding the right seam, a man with no talent for leadership —the perfect companion for a great leader.

Amundsen reached Hjalmar Johansen. This was a meeting between two strange men in a room down in the ice. When there were other people present, the two of them could manoeuvre round each other in polite circles, Johansen with an ironically exaggerated use of *Herr* in his speech, Amundsen slightly terser than when he addressed the others, with a light, but noticeable emphasis on the fact that in their relationship, he was the leader. Alone, man to man, their confrontation was dangerous. It might have been possible for them to meet in mutual respect. They were both loners. Loners could hate, but they could also feel that they had more in common than most. But each was too wary to allow the other to know it. Could Amundsen afford to take the first step? What if his subordinate refused the offer of friendship? Was Johansen —who had signed a contract for a journey that obliterated his personality—to make the first move, perhaps to be rejected? There was no room for defeat on the journey to the Pole. You had to keep up a front. Put a good face on it—to the storm, to the men, to yourself.

Here, on their own down in the ice, it wasn't easy to meet. It was a large room, but there seemed little space for two pairs of eyes. Johansen was working, packing supplies. At this, as at everything else, he was a master. After all, he was the man who had saved Fridtjof Nansen's life and had brought back the nation's hero alive, wasn't he? He had received his share of glory. He was the one *essential* person on the expedition, and maybe he knew it. But he knew how to keep his knowledge to himself—in his volatile, dark, complex and rather bitter mind. He knew how to pack supplies. He discovered the minutest space, knowing how to arrange things so that they didn't rust, wouldn't come loose, would take up the least space. Perhaps that on its own wasn't too difficult, but he had also mastered the greater art—how to place each item so that it could be easily removed without destroying the system, so that there was no problem replacing it.

It was not a skill that was ever put down on paper. It was a genius in his fingertips which ceased the moment the leader came sneaking in in his silent slippers. Not a sound could be heard down here of the blizzard above them. Not a word in here—only the two men breathing.

'Is it going ... well?'

Amundsen had little imagination; he wasn't a man to find an original, amusing expression which might have softened the other.

'Shouldn't it be going well?'

'Yes, yes, of course. I know you can do it.'

'Shouldn't I be able to do it?'

'Yes, yes, better than anyone else I know.'

So he's sneaking down here meaning to imply that I can't really pack a sledge, is he? Me? A man who's packed so many sledges.... If I were to say, 'Nansen taught me,' then I'd be lying, because he didn't teach me: I taught him. But if I say it I'd be hitting him in the gut all the same—sending him away with my fist firmly planted on his one tender spot: his envy of Nansen.

But I don't even have to say anything.

He's standing there thinking about it.

Don't answer next time he speaks.

Why do they all talk so much down here in the ice? Can't they keep their mouths shut?

'What have you got the weight down to?'

No reply.

'I said what have you got the weight down to? What does that pack of pemmican weigh?'

No reply. Turn your back on him. Let him shuffle out in his leather slippers. He wears them so that he won't be heard.

Amundsen departed, trying to preserve his dignity, deeply offended, like an unmolested virgin insulted by the coarse speech of men, red in the face, yet remembering every detail of the insult; he stored up this kind of thing, having a need and a talent for revenge.

Did the man left behind chuckle?

No, he went over to the ice wall and struck it with his fists. It will be months, years, before you can be alone again—really alone, deep in the Norwegian forest or in the warmth of a crowded market place—stand there, and be alone. Are you weeping there in that ice room?

On bad days, something animal came over the men at the dining-table. There was enough food, good simple fare. They didn't have to ration anything. But at the signal for meals they sometimes dropped what they were doing and begin to run. Others pretended not to hear in the hope that the first lot would have finished by the time they got there. It was dangerous to be just behind a man. He might turn round, glaring angrily at first, without saying anything; then, his voice gathering strength, clearing his throat, standing with fists clenched above his head, he might bawl: 'Can't you keep those bloody legs of yours away from my heels?' They irritated each other constantly. One man might have put his tobacco down too close to another's plate, and suddenly the tobacco pouch would hit the wall. Lindstrøm the cook was stout and impassive, withdrawing sullenly but resolutely into the kitchen if the criticism became too strong. It was worse for the others.

Sitting here together with the same stupid, sick people day after day. The same food. Bloody coffee. Grease solidifying on the plate. Knives that weren't clean.

And in the middle of it all the leader—polite, sharp if necessary, unimaginative, with no capacity for great friendship.

Was he staring at me? Were they all staring at me? Devil take the lot of them! Week after week here at Framheim.

But the pendulum could swing just as easily over to the other side. The slightest chance of a party could make them bright as children. An attempt to bake a cake, not all that successful, but all the same ... with two poor candles because they couldn't afford any more. The seal-meat fried until it cracked like old leather, placed on a grand dish, a tin of beans around it, and knives which cut well even if they were badly cleaned. And a drink, too. The leader knew—as they did—that a drink down here had to be treated with the same respect and courtesy as a curse from the pulpit. Perhaps it cheered you up on high days and holidays, giving a fillip of life to the congregation and making them wake up. But a priest was doomed if he acquired the habit of cursing at the wrong time.

So drinks were brought to the table only rarely, but in compensation the euphoria they released was great. No one here hates anyone else, does he?

Why should he?

Thank God for all this foul weather. We're better off in here. If only the winter would last!

Now he's repeating that story again—hell, he's going to tell that same old story. He's only got one, and listen to the way he tells it, spinning it out, stealing our time. He's in love with the sound of his own voice.

Do I enjoy the sound of my own voice? But what are you doing? Is that the only story you know? Yes, it is.

You try to change the subject by mentioning the weather. You say crossly:

'It's windy.'

'Yes, it is, isn't it?'

Here, you over there—fill her up! Oh God, that's good.

It's all right here, isn't it? Winter and all, two half-empty bottles and one unopened.

Unopened ... like a virgin.

Tell us that story.

I've already told it once.

Tell it again—look, we've still got a whole bottle left.

If only winter lasts a long time.

A rumour went round that one of them was stealing aquavit. No one knew who first suspected it. It was a seed that grew from their own desire for more drink. Gradually the suspicion centred on one person, who didn't even know he was under suspicion. Two men put their heads together —both fancied a drink. They agreed that the one over there was altogether too fond of his liquor. Should they go to Amundsen and tell him? One day they saw their leader going over to the bottle store. He was conferring with Lindstrøm. Only one person had the key to the store— Amundsen. If anything had to be fetched, Lindstrøm went to him. But anyone could cut a key, couldn't he?

Of course, he could have cut a key, couldn't he?

Say what you like, he's handy—and probably uses that skill when it suits him.

Didn't you say he was staggering about yesterday?

I wouldn't go as far as that. But he looked away and ran out quickly. He was away for a long time. I think he rubbed dog-shit on his fingers.

What?

You know—you get rid of one smell when you smear yourself with another.

There were nine men sleeping together in the same room. It was too hot in the upper bunks and too cold in the lower ones. As the winter went on, it became difficult to get any sleep at all. The nights could be long. Lie there, then ... and listen ... for it must be at night that he sneaks up to the store. It wouldn't be easy, but he's clever. It's as black as pitch in here.

The wind outside. The bloody wind outside. Impossible to hear if a man is tiptoeing across the floorboards. A dog howls. Just at this very moment—of course. It should be quite quiet now. There *was* a noise....

Then one of them was so eager that in his confusion he let out an enormous belch. It sounded like a foghorn. Cries of delight rose from the three others who were also awake. They responded under blankets and in sleeping-bags like ships in choppy seas. But one of them swore: 'I can't hear a thing....'

'Didn't you hear anything? Ha, ha! That's a good one.'

'I didn't hear what I was listening for.'

No, so you must listen. Not a single one of them sounded as though he was really asleep. That snoring isn't natural, is it? It's more like a gurgling sound. Hadn't Amundsen heard that gurgling sound? Is he asleep too?

The blizzard raged over the Antarctic, over the hut in the ice, above the blackened stove pipe sticking up out of the snow. Three dogs howled. Then all the others howled in reply.

Not a single man was asleep.

But *was* someone ... the atmosphere at breakfast was hostile. It was one of the bad days. The blizzard made it impossible to go outside.

One of the men began to slop the dregs of his coffee and said: 'Listen ... it's like this....' He looked round, not daring to look at the man he suspected. Quiet, quiet round the table.

'Oh, to hell with it.'

The winter's a long one.

He went outside into the great stillness. It had been a con-solation and a tonic when he'd been with the *Belgica*. It was icy cold, the cold stinging his throat and nostrils, but he held one mitten in front of his face and had both ski-poles in the other hand. The skis didn't slide well. He just thrust his feet into the bindings and skied stiffly and slowly past the dog-tents. All was quiet in there. A southern light flared up, showering red sparks down on to his leather mittens, so that they seemed to float in front of him like small red boats. The Antarctic was illuminated for a second, then the light died, revived again, running away into a blue river beneath the horizon to the north and making an arch of green all over the sky. He skied on without thinking.

Gradually his thoughts fell into place, as they usually did when he was at peace. First they strayed to Cook, the man who was said to have cheated in the struggle for the North Pole, and probably had too. Could your destiny turn out to resemble his? If you go back without succeeding, you'll have deceived them: the people who gave you money, parliament, the Press, the whole world, Nansen and England. You'll never hear the end of it. But what if you come back victorious? For the first time he felt something like a hand squeezing his heart, unwilling to let go. It frightened him. It was some small consolation too: if that was the way it would end—with a heart attack. Then they could say what they liked about me.

Nansen would speak ... the King would come ... the newspapers would be black-edged. He played with the thought for a moment and liked it. The cold didn't feel so severe any more.... You must either win or die. Win or die. The words had a weighty ring. He liked them. He also knew that this was the truth on a knife-edge. You *must* win or die. But Scott had motor-sledges, hadn't he? You don't know the first thing about them. The Englishmen on board the *Terra Nova* boasted about the sledges, didn't they? Was that just to frighten me, or were they telling the truth?

He let his skis glide slowly, arriving at the top of a slope behind Framheim, the southern lights flaring and illuminating the view. Day after day he had been thinking about what would happen on the journey south.

He knew the name and the temperament of every single one of the hundred and ten dogs. He had made a secret study of the men; he had lifted every sledge, examined every knot, studied every crate. He had written schedules for each day's journey, considering every possible alternative, learning everything off by heart and burning the notes so that they shouldn't fall into the wrong hands. He was familiar with every aspect of the journey. He felt that his body could achieve the impossible. He was back at the dog-tents. Taking off his skis, he decided to go and see two of the bitches that had had pups. The dogs knew his smell and whined softly with pleasure. He struck a match and lit a lamp hanging in the middle of the tent. It was a large tent. The dogs were used to the cold and were comfortable in here. Snow had been shovelled up against the canvas so that the dogs couldn't rip it to shreds as they fought together.

One of the bitches had recently had five puppies. Suddenly, as he was standing there, the bitch ate one of them. It happened so quickly that he didn't have a chance to stop it. Before he knew where he was, most of the pup had vanished into her jaws. Only the tip of its tail was sticking out. It wagged cheerfully, or tragically, in farewell, then it slipped down her throat.

He almost vomited. The brown eyes of the mother changed to a yellow light. They stared at him in hatred—or scorn. Had she wished to save her young from the same toil as she had known—from the whip and the wild men blind in their desire for glory? Was that it? Or was it a grotesque joke, the dog's contempt expressed in this macabre way, to emphasize that we were all mortal—even you, a man? He stood staring into the dog's eyes and for the first time was afraid that it would go for him and tear his throat out.

He jerked back a step, stumbling over another dog, and was up in a flash, knowing that if you wavered, they could set on you like a pack of starving wolves. He had a ski-pole in his hand. He raised it ... struck.... The last vestiges of the puppy had disappeared....

He went out. It was the unpredictable that he was afraid of. That had been a glimpse of the unpredictable; the abyss you couldn't see through the blinding snow; the will that came from depths you couldn't evaluate, and which defied your own.

He had gone to Wisting that morning and asked: 'What do you know about motor-sledges?'

'Motor-sledges? Me? Nothing.'

'You must know something. You can't have travelled all the way down here without forming some opinion about motor-sledges. You know the Englishmen have them, don't you?'

'I haven't given them much thought.'

'That's just like you,' he raged. 'Not given them much

thought. Well, *I've* given them some thought; I've had to. Can't you say something, anything about motor-sledges?'

He had gripped Wisting's leather jacket and was trying to shake him, but the man was heavy, standing propped inside huge leather boots on the ice floor, his breath striking the leader full in the face. Then Wisting said slowly: 'I think perhaps they've made a mistake there. . . .'

'Where did you get that idea?'

'I've been thinking about it. They're leaving without the right experience. They've got ski-instructors with them, haven't they? They should have learned to ski before they came here. Is there any reason to think they know better about motor-sledges?'

'No!'

'No, there isn't. That kind of equipment's no good on the ice. Men, skis and dogs are what you need.'

'Yes, yes—men, skis and dogs.'

Amundsen had gone. He'd found peace of mind . . . for an hour or two. Then the anxieties came sneaking back. What do we know about motor-sledges . . . ?

They had stretched a rope from the dog-tent down to Framheim, for when they went to feed the dogs while the blizzard was raging at its worst, they needed to have something to hold on to so as not to go astray. He fastened up the tent-flap again, thrust his boots into his skis, and prepared to start back. Suddenly the blizzard was upon him.

It came, he knew, without warning, like a barrel that has sprung a leak. A storm must have been lying in wait somewhere in the dark, holding its breath so as not to betray its existence. And then suddenly . . . one ski glided away. He had had the rope; now it was gone.

He kept calm. He sat down in the snow, turning his back to the blizzard, curling up, thinking calmly—now you can't see a thing, and if you go off in the wrong direction, you're finished. The wind had been coming from the left, hadn't it? If you keep it half on your right, you'll find the rope.

But what if the wind has changed? It often veers, or blows in a whirlwind without direction. You might just as well sit here and let yourself be snowed under. You'll survive for eight or ten hours, won't you? Perhaps even a whole day.

Then you could dig yourself out. It must be fifty below zero. Maybe the others would dig you out. If you survive and are found twelve feet away from the rope, most of your face will have been eaten away by frostbite. You must find the rope now. But don't go round in circles.

You can't see a foot in front of you, but you know the storm can drop quite suddenly, and then you can save your life, if you're quick. But the wind didn't drop. He decided, thinking calmly as he sat in the storm—if the wind keeps a constant direction, the rope is *there* and Framheim is *there*. Off you go.

He was facing the blizzard now. One foot sank down and he decided to take off the other ski, but then regretted it. At once he was standing in snow halfway up his thighs, sinking into something—into a space. What was it? He was standing in snow up to his waist. All round him the blizzard was swirling. Then he shouted. His shout was torn to pieces, hurled away, a shred of the cry returning and reaching him as a hoarse whine.

He started wading slowly, stretching out his hands in the darkness and the dense snow, trying to find a rope. He didn't find it, and realized that, all things considered, it was best to try out one direction, the one he felt was the right one, rather than nose around in the snow like a blind dog. He shouted again. That would do. He didn't want to waste his strength shouting.

Suddenly he found a foot.

It was a human foot, attached to a man, and the man turned out to be holding a rope. He had been walking against the wind, from Framheim to the dog-tents, looking for his leader who was lost in the storm.

It was Johansen.

They made their way back to Framheim together.

The leader brushed himself down and rubbed his face, which was beginning to be frostbitten; he thanked Johansen and smiled. 'It was cold out—isn't it midsummer back home? I missed the rope, but I would probably have found it again.'

'Oh, would you ...?' That was Johansen.

No one replied.

A moment later the leader was sitting in the sauna. They had made themselves a steam bath in a chamber of ice, with the Antarctic blizzard above and the black sea far below. It was a little tent standing on a flagstone, under which they had lit two primus stoves; the heat rose to the man sitting above, and the ice which melted was collected up and ended in a bath.

This was one of his greatest pleasures. Here a man could be alone, here time was something that dwindled away, leaving no bitter traces behind it. Here you could think—and forgive.

He half dozed in the heat, weighing Johansen in the most delicate balance of his opinion—and decided he liked the man.

That evening they had a party in Framheim. Did anyone drink more than anyone else? No, no!

It was Midsummer Night at home. Here it was Christmas Eve.

Rough men singing Happy Christmas.

Oh, hell ... now he's going to tell that joke.

It's all right here.

Tell us that joke.

SCOTT

 **V**

Captain Robert Falcon Scott liked to sleep with an old uniform greatcoat on top of him at night. It had several red stripes and was vested with a certain dignity as it hung on a nail during the day. Alongside him he had pinned up pictures of his wife and son. His desk was a couple of old crates which he had covered with oilcloth. A Bible lay on the desk, and two other books, paper and pens. He was a man of simple habits. He folded his hands over his chest before going to sleep, and snored with the discreet dignity of a true officer. He disliked crude noises—which nevertheless reached him from the sleeping men in the rooms round about. He was content to use a cut-throat razor and always remembered to clean his teeth, but didn't attach too much importance to heel-clicking. He knew where to draw the line.

There was no chair in his room, so people who came in had to remain standing before him. The room was small, so there was no distance between the man and his captain. He himself sat on the edge of his bed, but it would have been a breach of regulations to ask a subordinate to sit down on the bed beside him. This was one of his problems during the first few weeks of overwintering at Cape Evans. How to keep appropriate order and distance and yet still show the desired friendliness in such a situation?

He never talked about Amundsen.

The hut was divided in the ratio of two to three in favour of the officers. The smallest section was allocated to other ranks and petty officers, whose number was greatest. There was no contact between the two rooms. The food was largely the same. The officers' room was dominated by a large dining-table. When they were all standing in their places, Scott would come in and sit down, then the others would sit down. The food was served by a steward in a white jacket, despite the blizzard outside. The leader picked up his knife and fork. The officers picked up theirs. The meal could begin.

Conversation was cheerful and uninhibited, but kept under control to the extent that if the leader were silent, so were the others, or they talked quietly. They were a strange bunch of men round the table, many of them very talented in their fields: doctors, zoologists and geologists, chosen to make a scientific contribution in the Antarctic. In addition, an empire demanded that they should conquer the last spot on earth where no one had hitherto set foot.

But the leader didn't mention Amundsen.

As he didn't discuss him, neither did the others—but a silent, quivering, almost dangerous question spread from man to man. He hasn't mentioned Amundsen? After the first shock of hearing that the Norwegian had gone ashore at the Bay of Whales, he hadn't said a word. What about our plans? They had been worked out on the assumption that we, and only we, were to conquer the Pole. But that was before Amundsen had come into the picture. Oughtn't we then to speed up our plans and change them?

He held a service every Sunday. It was the only time the other ranks also congregated in the officers' room. It wasn't a matter of choice. No one was allowed to absent himself. Every man clasped his hands, even though some fingers were covered in frostbite sores. A meeting with God was prescribed a sanctity here as back home in England. He read from the Bible in a clear, well-modulated voice, and prayed using ordinary, familiar words. Outside the blizzard raged. He didn't mention Amundsen in the evenings, either.

Muttering began behind his back. He was probably aware of it, but he said nothing, single-minded and stubborn. Didn't he *want* to fight ...? They would ask each other as they straightened up from shovelling snow, or forking hay for the ponies standing in their long ragged coats, miserable in the severe cold. Didn't he want to accept the challenge?

We were to be first to the Pole, weren't we? The Empire demanded it; that's why we were given money to equip an expedition.

Petty Officer Edgar Evans had also taken part in Scott's first expedition down here. Scott was fond of him, with an officer's affection for a subordinate—which was not unlike a peasant's affection for his horse. Evans was capable of anything. He had the strength of an ox and the discipline of a trained dog. He behaved perfectly when his leader was nearby; the slums had produced him and he was grateful to the Navy for having helped him get out of the slums. He was the complete man for the complete leader. But how would it affect him if the leader turned out not to be a complete man?

Evans began to mutter: 'Doesn't he want to take up the challenge?' He asked one of the others: 'Will we get our money if the Captain isn't first at the Pole?'

'Our money?'

'If he goes bankrupt for not being there first, will we still get paid?'

Word spread among officers and men alike. 'Won't he take up the challenge? It's all very well to talk about following our scientific plan. Doesn't he know what England

demands? Only a minority is interested in scientific re-
search; the Empire demands that we conquer the Pole.'

Captain Oates, cavalryman, the millionaire with experience of India, the horse expert, arrogant and silent,
with a remarkable sense of humour, one day burst out
laughing: 'Doesn't he *want* to take up the challenge?'

The expedition included a Russian groom called Anton.
Anton was a small man, almost a dwarf, thickset and strong,
whose job was to muck out the ponies—a job cavalry
officers didn't find much to their liking. Anton knew little
English, and it was a mystery to the rest of them how he
had come to be there at all. But Anton was clever and in
other circumstances might have been the one to conquer
the Pole himself. He turned to Oates, his superior officer,
and smiled: 'Scott not take up the challenge?'

Doctor Wilson was the scientific leader of the expedition. Scott and he were on christian name terms, and he
had the unquestioning loyalty of an officer to his leader.
Not a word of protest. No misplaced complaints. No suggestion of a change of plan. As a scientist—he was a zoologist—Wilson was satisfied that Scott was sticking to his
original plan, even after Amundsen had come into the
picture. He had a sense of humour which was discreet to
a degree. He turned his head to the wall after going to
bed and thought with a smile in the darkness: 'Scott won't
take up the challenge, will he?'

Teddy Evans had saved the *Terra Nova* in the storm on
their way from New Zealand. He was a bit of a barbarian,
with no limits to his courage. Ambitious to an insane
degree, clever, with a torrent of ideas that didn't always
take into account the possible effects of his actions. The
art of moderation was not part of his make-up. He had
assumed it was self-evident that Scott would accelerate
and modify his plans from the moment he knew that
Amundsen was in the Bay of Whales. No longer a careful,
step-by-step advance southwards, but a mighty thrust—

with but one view in mind, to get there first, whatever the cost in animals, sledges, or men. But Scott didn't want to.

Evans wanted to. He wanted to bring Scott round to share his view, if that were possible, but as an officer, he knew that he couldn't. The iron-clad naval regulations hold good even in the Antarctic, so Evans was left with the problem of surreptitiously influencing his leader, not confronting him directly, but stealthily igniting a spark where there seemed to be nothing but ash. Evans didn't understand. Didn't Scott want to take up the challenge?

One day Evans was sent for. The leader wants you.

Evans went, certain that at last Scott wished to discuss a new, better and swifter plan with his second-in-command. He clicked his heels quietly and stood to attention. It was crowded in the room and he was standing so close to Scott that he had to look down on him. The captain was sitting on the edge of his bed, but couldn't—according to regulations—ask his second-in-command to sit down beside him.

'My dear Evans, I have asked you to come because there's something we must look into together.'

'Sir.'

'As far as possible I want the actual polar party to be composed of men from all branches of the armed forces. True, we ourselves are in the Navy, and naturally that lies closest to our hearts. But wouldn't England want the Army represented too?'

Evans was silent.

At Cape Evans, men crawled into their sleeping-bags head first to get as far away from the others as possible. Away from humanity—men who surrounded them with insufferable chatter, snores, spitting and silly stories, smoke from their sour pipes and jokes they'd all heard before. Men went outside to throw up. Their vomit froze to ice. Others slipped on the frozen vomit, hating the man responsible, cursing him, hating the whole world, Scott and his ideals;

they would pick up the deep-frozen, iron-hard vomit and hurl it at the hut wall, running away so that no one would know what they had done.

They were sometimes on the edge of insanity. They would sneak out at night with the thought of suicide their only consolation, but their courage failed them—men on whom an Empire depended. Some of them broke into the stores to steal drink; they found only fruit juice, but drank it all the same. The juice stained, the break-in was exposed, and there was a private reprimand from the leader. Scott thought about the problem. Perhaps we need a detention centre? But there's no room for one. We could dig a room out of the ice, but the person inside might freeze to death. That would be an inhuman punishment. And in any case, we'd have to consider the consequences very carefully. We'll just have to hope that a private reprimand will suffice. The next step, if necessary, would have to be a reprimand in front of everyone.

Blizzards day and night, crawling into hibernation, trying to sleep, but who could sleep days and nights in a blizzard? Military discipline was a great help then. Everyone remained standing until the leader had sat down. Subdued, correct conversations round the table.

Sunday services. Gymnastics every morning.

One day some crates had to be brought indoors. They had been forgotten outside and no one knew what they contained. There was equipment all over the snow slopes, but slowly things were brought under control. It turned out that the crates had been brought ashore when the *Terra Nova* returned after Campbell and his men had seen Amundsen. Scott had been on the depot trip south then.

There turned out to be some maps in the crates, perhaps important ones, perhaps not. The blizzard was raging for the third day running; a weak little shimmer of light in the middle of the day—just enough to enable you to recognize the man beside you—revealed a piece of paper fluttering about.

It had been thrust into one of the crates—perhaps it wasn't all that important. A hand stretched out for the paper: it was a letter. In the biting cold, the fingers of that hand stiffened up and the letter blew away.

It was probably only a greeting from Campbell but even so ... if the leader heard about it, or the second-in-command, who was coming now, raising his voice into a familiar roar.... The men started searching. The letter reappeared. A man stamped on something, was just about to bend down and pick it up when suddenly a squall appeared and the man could see neither his hand nor the letter.

That was the first evening.

Next morning, a further search was instituted. Scott wasn't yet in the picture, but Evans swore that he'd find the letter, if it was a letter. It might contain an important message from Campbell. He cursed his friend, now back in New Zealand. Wasn't there a safer way of handing over a letter than putting it in a crate with a lot of maps?

Men shovelled, men cursed, but what use was it all with the blizzard swirling round them?

That was the second evening.

Next morning was fine.

The ponies were taken out for exercise.

Evans issued a command: 'That letter must be found.'

'Sir, one of the ponies is eating something.'

That 'something' turned out to be a letter. They saved it in the nick of time.

The letter was addressed to Lieutenant Evans. It was from Campbell.

Campbell wrote to say that he had made some observations during his meeting with Roald Amundsen in the Bay of Whales. The Norwegian seemed tough and clever. His men were taciturn and knew the art of driving a dog-team. Their skis seemed to be welded to their own bodies. Worse than that, the Norwegians had erected a row of large tents for their dogs. From this, one could draw the conclusion that Amundsen was considering starting very early in the spring, and was protecting the dogs from the cold by letting them sleep in tents. With this plan, the likelihood of Amundsen being first at the Pole was great.

This was a bitter pill for Evans. His mind was full of explosive ideas and he met every difficulty with a wealth of quick counter-moves. The information about Amundsen's dog-tent made him think that they themselves could use a tent as night-quarters for the ponies. In the course of a few hours, he had sketched out a different and bolder plan of attack. If they put it into action, the Norwegians could be beaten in the race for the Pole.

Scott's plan consisted of advancing slowly, with three parties together, but each organized independently: one dog party, one pony party and a party with motor-sledges. When they reached Beardmore Glacier—the great, inhumanly difficult slope up to the Pole plateau itself—then only five men would continue, on foot, to the Pole, being their own beasts of burden into the unknown.

Evans now sketched out a plan which was based on an early start in the spring. A party with ponies, dogs and tents would advance to Beardmore Glacier and strike camp there before the winter was over. There they would make preparations for the climb, find a route, risk everything, sacrifice dogs and ponies, perhaps even men if that were unavoidable. The polar party would then leave winter quarters well-rested, and advance along a marked route, be helped up Beardmore Glacier and be ready to start on the last lap when summer set in.

But at this point in Evans's plan, naval regulations became more of a problem than the blizzards of the Antarctic. Campbell was his subordinate. He had written to another subordinate in a language and form which—it had to be admitted—constituted a criticism of the leader and his plan. Such criticism should eventually be directed to the leader personally; a courteous submission that he reconsider his excellent plan and eventually accept the information that one of his men had a different concept from his own of the plan of attack and its details. A letter from one subordinate to another must be considered private. As a naval lieutenant, Evans had no right to reveal the contents of his private correspondence to the leader of a British expedition, unless that leader personally expressed a wish that he should do so.

On the other hand, Evans couldn't put his plan to Scott without revealing his source of information. To conceal the actual starting point of his reflections would mean deceiving the leader, and if he deceived Scott, it would mean that he could face a court martial. This was a complex problem which gave him a headache for several days. He thought out his own plan, compared it with Scott's, saw all the advantages of his own, and incidentally lost some of his respect for the leader—though desisted from giving expression to that.

He contemplated going to Wilson and putting the plan to him. This had advantages and disadvantages. Wilson was a wise man, with a great capacity for listening, whether the matter was of personal interest to him or not. He would no doubt throw back his large, handsome head, nod with satisfaction, declare himself largely in agreement with Campbell, praise Evans's plan—and then say they should let Scott know.

But what about Scott?

The leader would then have to acknowledge that not only had Campbell gone behind Scott's back, but that Evans had done the same by going first to Wilson. It looked as if the whole of the alternative plan for the British conquest of the Pole would go by the board because of naval protocol. But Evans was in no mood to be stopped.

Delicate manoeuvres weren't his speciality. The idea that the human mind has its labyrinths—and that it may therefore be necessary to tread softly when venturing there —was one that he had little experience of. Though this time, he chose wisely. He decided that the only way which would meet with Scott's approval was to put all his cards on the table. He would hand over Campbell's letter with a polite, formal request for the leader to read it—a military tone of voice, with slight emphasis on the fact that Campbell must have had very little time in which to write the letter, because *Terra Nova* was being made ready to sail: 'Hence these grossly informal pages, but the letter has one important point, which I'd like to direct your attention to, sir. Despite my lack of experience in polar exploration, I personally have worked out what I have light-heartedly called an alternative plan for the conquest of the Pole.'

He went to see Scott.

Heels together, not too hard because it irritated Scott if done too ostentatiously, reminding him how unpleasant it could be to be the leader—but necessary all the same, because Scott *was* the leader, and had carefully considered the consequences of allowing any naval regulation to be ignored.

Not much room here in Scott's place. He was sitting on the edge of his bed, but Evans was not permitted to join him there. He handed over the letter, explaining briefly and straightforwardly, remaining standing, as he had not been dismissed. Scott read slowly. He read the letter again even more slowly, having learnt to perfection the art of impassivity. Not a flicker in his expression.

Evans didn't show any sign of emotion either, as he stood at ease, a foot or so from Scott's sloping shoulders and an old uniform greatcoat on a nail which was so close to his head that one sleeve was scratching his ear.

Scott finished reading. He looked up.

Their eyes met.

They were both strong men—the leader and his second-in-command. The latter had saved the *Terra Nova* during the storm, and they were both aware of this. The one man had wide experience from his previous trip, the other was a sailor and nothing more—but with an inflexible will, an imagination that Scott lacked, a hardness which came naturally to him, Evans, and which at best the leader could imitate with inner revulsion. Both knew what they were doing.

The Empire would make its demands and Amundsen would demand the Pole. The Norwegian attack could only be met by counter-attack. But was the leader capable of approving a plan which originated from his second-in-command—could he adopt it, set his stamp on it, taking the responsibility and eventually harvesting the glory? Scott was not a man to throw out both arms and cry: 'You have found the solution, well done!' That would be against regulations.

So he sat there, an ember smouldering inside him. He was capable of jealousy—when he had time. It wasn't in his nature to be rash. His strength lay in his slow obstinacy, which could look like an inability to act.

He had disliked Evans ever since that time in the storm, when his second-in-command had shown ingenuity and courage which would become legendary.

Here he was again—his bold self-confidence almost amounting to insolence, his plan prepared, a glint in his eyes, a leader of men.

He'd probably sacrifice them, too, granted. His own victory might be won at the expense of others. But the leader had to evaluate. Scott had a unique capacity for that, and he could conceal his weakness behind his duty. Did he suspect that Evans had the capacity to hate? He himself had the capacity for resignation.

'My dear Evans,' he began, his tone of voice telling Evans all he needed to know. 'My dear Evans, Campbell's good will is beyond doubt, and yours too. But the letter and your understanding of the matter will not alter my plans. This is a scientific expedition. We shall continue as if the Norwegians didn't exist. To change the subject, I have given the good Wilson permission to go out and collect eggs.

'Thank you, Evans.'

He was to collect Emperor penguin eggs. That would be of great interest.

The Emperor penguins laid their eggs at Cape Crozier. Earlier expeditions had established that. But up to now the eggs had not been seen by man. Cape Crozier was one of the most weather-torn places on the map, a hell-hole even by Antarctic standards. The eggs could be collected only in winter, as that was when the Emperor penguins hatched them out.

Wilson wanted to go there. He was a zoologist and despite his wisdom was single-minded in this respect. He was willing to risk his life to be able to hold such an egg in his hands. It was a nobler ambition than that of his fellow-men on the trip to the Pole. They were ready to risk their lives to be able to stand on a spot on the map called The Pole, which would no doubt turn out to be no different from any other spot.

Wilson took with him Henry Bowers, a lieutenant in the British Navy. He was a man with an unusually large nose and a profile which, once seen, was never forgotten. Not a specialist in anything, except that of being Jack-of-all-trades, he had the impassiveness of a stone and a remarkable, instinctive ability to find his way about in fog and snow.

In addition, Wilson took with him the young zoology student, Cherry-Garrard, a handsome young man, apparently created to conquer fair maidens—had there been any there to conquer. He might appear weak, but he wasn't, though he never lost his intense dislike of the cold. It was an unfortunate characteristic in a polar explorer. Scott probably had an ulterior motive in sending these three out. If their trip succeeded in midwinter, then perhaps starting out earlier than his original plan would also be possible. The terrain from Cape Evans to Cape Crozier was wild and dangerous, high mountains and crevasses, passes through which the wind swept more forcefully than out in the open.

The snow was like sand. They hauled the sledges along with ropes over their shoulders. The temperature was at first average—about forty below—and the evenings in the tent were tolerable when the primus was alight.

But the temperature fell. It fell to sixty-three below zero. Their sleeping-bags were frozen stiff and couldn't be spread out when they crawled into the tent. A man whose clothes got damp when the swirling snow was melted by his body-heat ran the risk of being bow-shaped when he left the tent, because the moisture soon froze and his clothes couldn't be straightened out.

But they reached Cape Crozier. They built a stone hut in a pass below Mount Terror. From there, they made their way to the hatching grounds. The story of Edward Wilson collecting twelve penguin eggs in a blizzard, at sixty degrees below zero, packing them up, carrying them carefully with him to be able to study them later—is one of the greatest in scientific history.

Then a hurricane broke. Their tent, which had been lying folded outside the stone hut, blew away. When night fell, the tarpaulin they were using as a roof was also swept away by the storm.

This meant death. They hadn't eaten for two days. When the hurricane finally abated, they got the primus going. They sat in the snow between the stone walls and ate. The roof had gone now.

They had to find the tent or die. They knew that. So they moved out on a three-line course and each followed a route in the direction the hurricane had blown. They had a few hours before night fell in which to do it.

One of them stumbled on the tent. It was lying under the snow, wedged under a stone which had been wrenched away by the storm....

They got back to Cape Evans and their winter quarters. They had been away for five weeks.

Wilson had saved the eggs.

All three were confined to their bunks with frostbite.

Scott was sitting on the edge of Wilson's bunk.

'My dear Bill, I am filled with admiration for you and your achievements. I'm delighted you got the eggs back. There's no doubt that your expedition was a complete success. I know your sufferings were great, but the results are even greater.

'Nevertheless, my dear friend, let us be quite clear on one point. Your expedition has shown that it's not possible to make a start to the south before winter is over. That would cost us dogs and ponies, and presumably human lives too. We can't afford that. The dogs are to be used for other expeditions I am planning. Nor can we take any unnecessary risks with the ponies. Let's establish here and now that our expedition continues to be what it set out to be, a scientific one.

'So we'll follow our original plan.

'I expect we'll be criticized for this. It's part of our job to be able to take criticism.'

Wilson nodded.

'But I think that one day soon we should discuss the actual composition of the polar party, so that all branches of the armed forces are represented if possible.'

THE RACE

Wilson offered no expression of gratitude.
Evans wasn't present.
The winter passed. Soon spring would come.

CONVERSATION

'I am very grateful to you, Mr Amundsen, for giving me the pleasure of meeting you in private. You know that there's no one I respect more than yourself: both you personally and your polar expertise.'

'You are too kind, Herr Scott. I can only reply that the pleasure is all mine on this occasion.'

'Then I'd like to suggest, Mr Amundsen, that we both try to find out the truth about each other—as far as possible. Nothing would be nicer than to maintain that level of exquisite courtesy which comes so naturally to you, but strictly speaking, courtesy alone is immaterial. It is of primary importance that we attempt to achieve a deeper understanding of our situation—and of ourselves.'

'Again, I'm in complete agreement with you, Herr Scott. In private I too can acknowledge the bitterest truths about myself. And about others.'

'I tried to telephone you when I was in Kristiania.'

'I heard the telephone, but deliberately didn't answer. I was standing beside the apparatus, knowing that you were ringing. I was too cowardly. I couldn't meet you face to face and conceal the fact that I'd just decided to become your rival here. It would—quite rightly—have been construed as dishonesty, face to face. On the other hand, I didn't want to tell you the truth at such an early stage.

That would have reduced the shock effect on you that I wished to achieve. Also—and I think this is important—I might have had difficulties with my government. You probably know that because of Norway's dependence on England, the Norwegian authorities might have demanded that I didn't announce myself as your rival.'

'I realize that I am now revealing my small-mindedness, Mr Amundsen, but I wish your authorities *had* stopped you. Not because I think they would have been justified in doing so. But you, because of your boundless ambition, which even allows you to keep silent to the point of dishonesty, will no doubt understand how your ambition torments me.'

'I quite understand that, Herr Scott. If we are talking about wishes, then perhaps I may be granted one of my own. For instance, those motor-sledges ... I wish them in hell.'

'I often share your wish on that particular point. The first one is already there—it went through the ice to the bottom.'

'I feel bound to account more clearly for my motives and tactics in switching from north to south, Herr Scott. You will understand, I'm no scientist. My one aim is to set the record. I want it to be said that Amundsen got there first, and although even I have my doubts when it comes to Cook and Peary—especially the latter: I think one day there'll be evidence that he didn't reach the Pole either—even so, the conquest of the North Pole would always have a shadow hanging over it for me. After all, they'd say, he wasn't the *first* there. That's what drove me to join in the struggle for the South Pole, which is your primary goal. It is, isn't it? Isn't it true that you are deceiving yourself and everyone else when you maintain that the Pole itself is merely a subsidiary aim of your expedition? You daren't admit that it's the Pole you are after—and you want to reach it first. You think that's a crude motive. There's also a touch of cowardice in you, Herr Scott. Not when it comes to physical danger: I think your sense of duty would drive you to the greatest daring if necessary. But would you dare take on something that smacks of dishonour? *I* dare. I can freely admit that I have one aim: to get to the Pole first.'

'And I'm sure you'll succeed, Mr Amundsen. You're shameless enough, and although I *do* think your fool-hardiness deplorable, I must concede it's also immensely effective. You know only too well that Shackleton said the ice in the Bay of Whales is drifting. That was no more than a couple of winters ago, and yet you've set up your winter quarters there.'

'That was a calculated risk. I must win or die, quite literally. After revealing my little dishonesty to you, I can save my honour only by winning. In the Bay of Whales I'm a hundred kilometres nearer the Pole.'

'That will probably turn out to be enough.'

'You're a bit of a pessimist by nature, aren't you, Herr Scott?'

'Yes. Strictly speaking, I think it comes from my having a more active mind than yours—forgive my bluntness, but we did promise not to keep anything back.'

'I'll gladly forgive you. Go on.'

'I have a more fertile imagination than you have. But this can be a disadvantage in a man who has to lead other men in desperate situations. A general who gives the order to shell a town can't afford to have too many scruples about killing his fellow human beings. It is probably a help if he has the backing of an empire, but only if he is one of those simple beings who can believe in the rights of that empire. Then perhaps he can also believe in his own rights. You are such a man, but without the empire. I have the empire, but am not the man.'

'It seems to me that the man who lacks the goal will never find the means to achieve it. Can you really claim,

Herr Scott, that you are down here to conquer the Pole
when you don't thrust aside every obstacle to try to get
there first?'

'Have you ever seen a penguin egg, Mr Amundsen?'

'I don't understand. . . .'

'You have the advantage of not always understanding.
My good friend, Dr Wilson, came back from Cape Crozier
with twelve Emperor penguin eggs. They've never before
been seen by man. It was my men who fetched those eggs.
They're being studied under a microscope already. Man's
knowledge will take a slight step forward, and it's thanks
to me. It gives me great pleasure to know that.'

'It gives me pleasure too, Herr Scott. But I think you
are missing the point. What do you want most? Even you
presumably put the Pole before these eggs? I'm quite convinced I'd find it ludicrous if people said of me, "He was
after the Pole—he didn't succeed, but at least he came
home with a dozen eggs." '

'Which no one has ever seen before.'

'And which no one really needed to see.'

'Mr Amundsen, I gladly admit that you possess a number of characteristics that I lack. If my character is nobler,
it might well turn out to be a weakness. But forgive me
for asking—are you really as calm as you appear? I'm not
referring to your ability to conceal your inner anxiety—
may I ask if you are an hysteric?'

'I think there's an element of truth in that suggestion,
Herr Scott. There is a streak of hysteria in me. It might
be to do with the fact that I have never lived what I would
call a normal life. For instance, sexual relations are of no
interest to me. Naturally, I conceal this lack of interest
as best I can, which may mean that now and again I make
a show of bad taste in this respect, to pretend that I'm as
much of a man as the rest. I have asked myself whether
my tendencies lie in the direction of my own sex. Possibly.
But you see, I am too wise to allow myself to be tempted.

I am also too much of a coward. We all have our weaknesses. This stern asceticism in my nature strengthens an ambition which was strong enough already. I keep profound forces within me constantly under control—so hysteria is never far away.'

'Does it ever break out?'

'Sometimes, when small things go against me. For instance, if a dog team runs off course, not once—I can cope with that—but time and time again. Then I'm not just angry. Then I scream and rage. My men mustn't see it, so I immediately bend over and bite my glove if I feel an attack coming on. Also I don't have any finer feelings when it comes to thrashing the dogs.'

'I have.'

'I know. Believe me—I wish I had too.'

'Wouldn't this hysteria be dangerous if it broke loose one crucial day?'

'Undoubtedly. My anxiety is increased, not only by the possibility of my own hysterical outbursts, but also by the realization that hysteria is something quite lacking in your make-up.'

'I think you're right there. In exchange—to speak of my own weaknesses—I have a very rigid nature. All my years in the Navy have intensified this. Orders are orders. To give a counter-order is no laughing matter. A navy has to have regulations. Do you know, my men click their heels when they come into the little room which is both my bedroom and my office? I sit there in an old uniform greatcoat.'

'We all sleep in the same room at our place. I know all my men's ways of farting and belching—and they know mine. It's an intimacy I loathe. But I learn as they learn. I think it's one of my stronger points.'

'You undoubtedly have many strong points, Mr Amundsen, but if I may say so—forgive me again—I can't say I like you.'

'I know. I've thought a great deal about that. The strange thing is that I think it's to my advantage. My awareness of your dislike makes me spiteful and drives me on. But your antipathy has a paralysing influence on you because you feel it is an unworthy emotion.'

'Have any of your men discovered your hysterical inclinations?'

'One, the best and most dangerous of all. He was Nansen's man before he was mine.'

'Why do you say he's the most dangerous?'

'Because he's the only one who has qualities of leadership in him. The others I chose myself. They are practical men, marvellous skiers, they can tolerate the cold— tolerate anything. But they are insignificant, and it was my wish that they should be. There must be no doubt that I am the leader. But Nansen ordered me to take his man with me, and I had no choice.'

'Has Nansen not been your patron and your friend?'

'Outwardly, yes. Naturally, I've had to support that impression. But inwardly, he probably had his doubts about my own ability to manage an expedition to the south at his age. So it was easier for him to lend me the *Fram*, while at the same time taking some of the glory by reminding me that the plans for an expedition to the South Pole had been worked out by him while he was up in the Arctic. It wasn't a bad idea. To land me with Hjalmar Johansen was a master-stroke. He's much too independent to be my subordinate.'

'And he's noticed your inclination to hysteria.'

'He suspects it. And if the hysteria breaks out one day, and I lose control, I'm afraid it will be in his presence.'

'You've no great talent for making friends, have you, Mr Amundsen?'

'I've only one friend, really, and that's myself. My brother, Leon, perhaps, but I think I can say (it's a prophecy that I think will turn out true) that a brother who has done me so much service, seen so far down into my ambitious soul, with whom I have discussed things so openly—and who therefore knows all my deceptions, to-wards you, for instance—a brother like that won't always be able to be my brother. I foresee that there will be a split between us.'

'I'm proud to be able to say, Mr Amundsen, that when my father and brother died, I supported my whole family.'

'I agree wholeheartedly that your pride is justified. But hasn't that developed your sense of duty to such an extent that you are hardly able to behave immorally, even if it were necessary to achieve your goal? Tell me, Herr Scott, is it quite honest of you to portray yourself as a man totally without moral failings?'

'I am not that. For instance, I've noticed myself showing an increasing tendency to envy. When Mr Evans, my second-in-command, clearly saved the *Terra Nova* by his courageous behaviour in the storm south of New Zealand, I envied him with all my heart. You see, that's the kind of deed that's always remembered. One man saves a ship and crew. Perhaps deep down that was my motive for rejecting his plan for conquering the Pole before you.'

'In my opinion, Evans's plan had a chance of succeeding, Herr Scott. A swift, bold thrust would be necessary to beat me and my men.'

'I know. But that also means risking the lives of men and animals. This is no laughing matter for a nature such as mine. And anyway, do I want to emerge as the victor due to a plan which I didn't originate? Wouldn't Evans be the real victor?'

'Excuse me, Herr Scott, but now I must smile. This is something I can understand. I can't help liking you better and better.'

'Unfortunately, I can't pretend to feel the same about you.'

'I think you're going to die, Herr Scott.'

'I think so too. But I also think—I know—I'm going to die an honest man and a proud one.'

'And I know if I die, death will give me a glory that will conceal my personal failings.'

'So, strictly speaking, you don't mind dying?'

'I would prefer to live as the victor. As the loser, I'd rather die. I think that if I get to the Pole and find your flag there, then I'll play my last card—it will be difficult, leading my men on the way back, keeping a journal that will tell posterity what a great man I was ... and then finding a crevasse in the ice one night when everyone is asleep.'

'If I find your flag at the Pole—and I'm afraid that's to be my destiny—I'll bring my men back as well. I would feel it my duty to survive. But if I die, I think my reputation for greatness will be a valid one.'

'Proud words, Herr Scott. And you have every right to say them.'

'I think, Mr Amundsen, that there is little left to add to our interesting conversation. May I ask just one more question? What do you think is the greatest weakness in my expedition?'

'Herr Scott, in my country we have a famous ski-race called the Holmenkoll Run. It would seem strange if one of the competitors appeared in the race with a ski-instructor. It would be said—and with some justification—that the man should have taken the necessary instruction before appearing at the starting line.'

'I see what you mean. My race will probably be even harder than this one in Holmenkoll. I've heard rumours that your men are first-class skiers.'

'They're among the best in the world. But tell me now ... what's the truth about those motor-sledges of yours? You wished them in hell, but they may well be of some assistance to you.'

'It's understandable that you are worried on this point.

The motor-sledges are a novelty, and may reverse all your calculations. Will you allow me one small evasion—even though it is a form of dishonesty? I must decline to give you any further information about those sledges. When are you leaving?'

'Unfortunately I must also decline from giving you any further information. But I wish you and your men well, Herr Scott!

'I know your aim. Now you know mine.'

'Mr Amundsen, may I once again thank you for your great kindness in allowing this conference so far apart from our men?'

'It is I who should be grateful, Herr Scott. We're in agreement in not allowing this frank conversation of ours to go any further?'

'In absolute agreement. Goodbye.'

'Goodbye.'

AMUNDSEN

 **VI**

The leader was sullen. At breakfast, they could see his hands trembling. He never had been much good at carrying on a quick and amusing conversation. Either he contented himself with brief answers, or reiterated what he'd said in his speech on 17 May. He was up at half past three every morning. It was now August. Spring had started, but sluggishly, the blizzards still tottering in from the sea like gruff old women. Everything should have been ready for the start: the sledges had been hauled out and loaded, the harness examined, every piece of clothing checked. But time and time again a weakness was revealed, corrected, some small thing changed. At breakfast, they noticed that his hands were trembling.

They had often discussed the Englishmen's motor-sledges. Most of the men had little faith in the machines. But now Amundsen glowered at anyone who expressed an opinion when they were mentioned. So they dropped the subject and talked about dogs instead. They had over a hundred of them, ninety of which were to be taken on the great journey to the south. The dogs were bursting with strength, fighting and biting each other's ears in the instinctive knowledge that their victims couldn't lick themselves there. The cold made the sores swell and inflammation set in. But if a dog were bitten, then the others visited it and stood patiently in line to slip in and lick the sick one. The one that had done the biting joined in too, begging patiently to be allowed to atone for its crime with a soft wet lick. The thermometer stood at forty-five below.

It ought to rise to thirty before they could start. The blizzards had to blow themselves out. Hjalmar had said this, without reminding them of what he had experienced before. Helmer, who had driven dogs under northern skies and perhaps knew more than anyone else about dogs and their reactions, also advised against an early start. But something told them that if any one of them had mentioned motor-sledges, the leader would have gone for his throat. He was like a fierce, powerful dog on a leash—a dog which snarls, its teeth shining white in savage jaws.

But it made the men uneasy that Amundsen was so sullen and tight-lipped just now, when for once they could have done with a few friendly words. Everyone had his own stomach-ache to struggle with before the departure. The last letters had to be written home. If the men didn't return from the Pole, at least the *Fram* would come to fetch the mail. They were not all equally good at writing, and they were better with ski-poles than they were with pens. They scratched down a few halting words. The ink had frozen several times during the course of the winter, and had to be thawed again. Gentle, humane words didn't come easily to these men, but they were put down nevertheless. You know I'm fond of you....

Forty-five below.

Blizzard after blizzard, and it was now into September. A man waking early at Framheim saw the leader sitting for a while with his head in his hands, having been out at dawn to look at the weather. But not a word.

Then, on 7 September, the weather looked good. They agreed to leave on the 8th. Everything was ready: the dogs were bursting with strength. One of the bitches was on heat. The leader slept little on the night before the 8th. He woke all the men at break of dawn. They turned out.

The weather was passable, the temperature thirty below, a bitter wind blowing from behind them. The final preparations took time and it was far into the morning before they were all ready. Eight men were leaving. The ninth, Lindstrøm, the cook, would be alone again.

They were ready by their sledges. There was a sense of celebration in the air and no one could bear to wait a moment longer. One man went behind an ice hummock and vomited. Lindstrøm came with steaming hot coffee and offered each one of them half a cup in farewell. Then Helmer Hanssen's dogs bolted. The load on his sledge was four hundred kilos. He was in no position to stop them. Perhaps it was the bitch on heat making the dogs wild, their excess strength throbbing like a wound beneath their coats and urging them on. Helmer raced after them. He brandished his whip—and let fly a good many oaths. He was a good skier, but the dog team vanished in a swirl of snow.

Then bitter fog rolled in from the sea.

Wisting's dog team bolted too. He had to throw himself on to the sledge to tip it over. The dogs dragged him along, forcing snow inside his clothes and down his neck, snow soon melted by his own warmth. They raced on with the loaded sledge on its side, toiling on but unable to get up to the speed of Helmer's team, going onwards despite the whip slashing down on them. Wisting had to relinquish the load. Raging, dispirited, with the trace of a tear in the corner of his eye, he set about slogging after them, following their tracks. They would have to stop somewhere, then he would have them again.

The rest of the men had by this time scattered the dogs and tethered them. As the fog swirled in from the sea, making the air bitterly cold, two men happened to be

standing beside each other: Hjalmar Johansen and the
leader. They were walking up and down, stamping in the
snow to keep warm. There was a narrow opening here
between a hummock of ice and a sledge. If they were to go
off the track they'd have to wade in loose snow, and neither
of them wished to do that. It was so narrow that they
brushed against each other each time they met. They had
always found it difficult to talk to each other when alone
together. It was easier if others were there, especially when
the conversation was about concrete facts in a field where
both were knowledgeable. Small talk, face to face, made
them both clam up.

The leader knew what the other man was thinking. 'We
set out too early.' But Hjalmar was no angel, either. He
had other thoughts. 'I could have led this expedition as
well as he has. . . .'

There was a hidden resentment in him because he had
never had the courage to achieve his potential—to be
leader of his own expedition. You were too mindful of
your own pleasures, weren't you? You chose the fleeting
delights of the moment. This man who's now your leader
was ambitious enough to be awake when you were asleep.
Hjalmar betrayed his disappointment in his own achievements by small jibes aimed at the other man's most vulnerable points. As now: 'At least a motor-sledge can't bolt.'

Then a penguin came along. It was a sign of spring.
Both of them stood, staring open-mouthed. Clad in black-
and-white like a priest, a young bird moving at a dignified
pace, with small apologetic bows of its head, nodding to
the right, nodding to the left, passing between them, turning round and nodding in farewell, then disappearing into
the mist.

The two men remained standing for a moment, staring
at each other. Then Amundsen pulled off one of his mittens and hunted out his watch: 'They've been gone half
an hour,' he barked.

That incident united them, the leader and Hjalmar Johansen. Johansen fished out his watch too, peered at it, established that Amundsen was right, growled his criticism as an addendum to the leader's, both thinking they could have fetched the dogs back in a shorter time.

At last they were all collected up again. They set off south.

The temperature had now fallen five degrees in an hour. Fog was drifting in great billows across the snow. They had brief glimpses of clear skies and saw distant mountains in the west, but then the fog rolled in again and they heard nothing but angry shouts at the dogs. The tracks from their depot trip had vanished. But they found the flags and had no difficulty with the route. The dogs were wild, streaking quickly southwards.

Then one of the bitches began to dance about on her hind legs, getting entangled in the traces and unable to free herself. She lay like a bundle in the snow and the other dogs dragged her along until Wisting disentangled her. The team behind had to stop. The man ahead had too long a start. As soon as the dog was free, it began dancing on its hind legs again. Then the man driving at the back shouted: 'There's something coming up behind us.'

The bitch Camilla had had pups back at Framheim, three of them, who should have stayed with Lindstrøm. They must have escaped and were following the tracks.

At that moment a rift appeared in the clouds, the fog apparently drifting back to sea. The temperature was falling, the men's breath clouded voluminously white in front of their mouths. The view had cleared. And there behind them three small bundles were scampering along for all they were worth, their faint yelps reaching the men and the bitch, who was again up on her hindlegs. One of the teams was about to bolt again.

The men tried to throw themselves on the sledge, tip

it over, one runner cutting down into the snow. Tried to get the load on the cross, so that the dogs couldn't escape. The man ahead shouted, wanting to know what was going on. The man behind ploughed into his team. Then cursing and shouting, dogs howling—and behind the racket the huge stillness, strange and sickly.

The pups caught up with them. Then the men struck their first camp. The eight men had two tents: Amundsen the leader in one, Hjalmar in the other. Both men knew that if their team were hungry, and there was little food, there had to be strict justice in the tent. The temperature had fallen to forty-five below. There was an eerie light over the snow and inside the tent the light hurt their eyes. The damp breath of the four men made the tentcloth wet on the inside, and the dampness froze, creating sparkling ice droplets everywhere.

The dogs had now calmed down and they dug themselves into the snow. Now and again, a bark was heard, but it was soon quite quiet outside. The mother was feeding her pups. Tomorrow they would have to die.

They all knew it. They couldn't advance on the Pole with three pups in tow. Today the pups had been frisking around in the harness and had got entangled in the traces. They'd tried to chew through the traces as they ran free and happy alongside. Hjalmar was afraid that the dogs wouldn't want to eat the pups so early on the trip. They wouldn't be hungry enough. So the pups were superfluous. Not to mention the dull, sullen pain inside him at the thought of having to kill them. No one wanted to do it, but someone had to. He was the toughest.

The temperature dropped further.

When morning came, it was fifty below.

Amundsen had hoped that the temperature would rise once they were over the Barrier. Shackleton's experience had indicated that it would. Here the opposite was true. Leather clothes had stiffened during the course of the night, damp from the breath of four men in the tent. It was like crawling into bark casings, which had to be softened before you could move properly. The warmth to soften them came from your own body, and that body had to work at fifty below. The dogs had to be kicked up. Three small pups tumbled round in the snow, snapping at each other's heels. They were allowed to live another day. It was too cold for the men to think clearly.

As the party moved on south, ninety dogs and eight men, a balloon of frozen breath developed round them. It was like a cloud of fog following them in the midst of a clear sky. Inside that cloud of breath their own breathing became laboured. It was a strange, eerie sound. Warm air hit air already dense with frozen droplets from their previous breath. Even the dogs had begun to lie down. They had to be thrashed to get up. The three pups were still running behind in the tracks.

They struck camp after only nine miles. Then Johansen did the deed. He strangled two pups, but the third ran back towards home. He threw the two corpses away into the snow. The dogs weren't hungry enough yet to eat fellow dog.

That night Camilla tore herself free and by morning she'd disappeared. It was fifty-two below. They knew which way the bitch had gone, and didn't even discuss the matter. They were still human. Prestrud and Bjaaland went back along the track, alone together. They went without tent or food, and if a blizzard blew up, it would obliterate their tracks. It was slow going. They felt their bodies getting soaked with sweat and they knew that if they stopped the sweat would freeze and make their clothes so stiff that it would be difficult to bend to fix their ski-bindings.

They found the bitch. She was lying with her pup in the snow; the puppy had frozen to death. She didn't want to return to the pack. They shot her and turned back.

That same day the compasses froze. At first Amundsen's

compass-needle began to go wrong. It wouldn't float freely. Shortly afterwards, Wisting shouted: 'My compass has frozen too!' This meant that they had no means of finding their way in unknown territory. They would still be able to find the latitude eighty depot they had laid down the previous autumn and there they could unload the sledges and return in their own tracks to Framheim.

The decision rested with one man. It was hard for him to take it. If his mind had been on motor-sledges, he didn't mention it.

He gave the order curtly, harshly, gruffly: 'As soon as we've found the depot, we'll turn back.' In the tent that evening, he brought out a bottle of gin. It was the first time he'd ever allowed alcohol on a trip. The gin was frozen, and the bottle cracked when they tried to thaw it out. He picked up the pieces of glass without betraying his disappointment—and threw the frozen gin out of the tent.

That night all the dogs began to sneeze. There were ninety dogs in a circle round the tents, sneezing and sneezing. No one got a wink of sleep. It was fifty-five below. The next day they found the depot and unloaded the sledges. The return trip began.

He knew it was his fault that they'd started too early, but he wasn't big enough to admit it. He couldn't bring himself to say: 'You were right, Hjalmar.' Fifty-five below didn't exactly soften a man's disposition. Three dogs fell in their traces and refused to be whipped to their feet. One of them was dead. The other two hadn't an ounce of strength left. They had to disperse one team and let some of the dogs sit on the load. Others had to run loose behind the sledges on the way home.

Fifty-six below zero. Now the snow was in their faces. The sledges were lighter for the dogs to haul, but no one knew whether they would get back alive to Framheim.

Then their watches began to freeze. First Hjalmar's,

although it was wrapped in wool, between his leather jacket and his underclothes. He fished it out with numb fingers and held it up to the vanishing light over the plain; a few stars were out, casting down a glimpse of hope. He shook the watch. It was frozen.

He shouted in despair, and the others replied, one after another, eight in all. They took out their watches, pulling off their mittens, turning their faces away from the wind. They risked their fingers to find out if their watches were still going. They weren't. Time was standing still. Without knowing the time, they'd never be able to get back to Framheim. Then a dog howled. At the same moment, the clouds above them were torn apart and a wild glitter of stars leapt out before the raw fog swirled together again above their heads, covering everything.

The snow began to settle. Huge patches of snow—perhaps ten kilometres or more across—sinking down on to a substratum of older snow. It sometimes happened with a bang, sometimes with a whimper, like the sigh of resignation made by a dying man. The dogs howled. One of the men screamed. He was surrounded by fog, the nearest dog like a grey wisp, and suddenly the surface cracked all around him as the snow sank a foot or two straight down. They never found out who had screamed.

It was now sixty degrees below zero. As long as it was just their cheeks and noses that were frostbitten, in one respect there was nothing to prevent them going on. They were terrified of getting frostbite in their feet. If your toes went, it was bad enough. If a heel went, it would be difficult for a skier to keep going.

One of Prestrud's dogs dropped dead. It had kept going until it was stiff as a board, but when it could go on no longer, it sank to the ground and was was cold before the man from the sledge reached it. He freed the traces. If he had had the strength, he would have dismembered the dog and let the others eat their friend. But as soon as he stopped the team, dog after dog curled up in the snow. Most of them whined softly, sticking their noses down into the snow, unable to go on.

They had to take Prestrud's team out of harness. Two dogs shuffled behind; if they had the energy to go on, they might be saved. If not, the great white darkness, the deathly cold here on the Barrier would embrace them for ever. Prestrud was skiing behind Hjalmar Johansen's team. The two of them were the last in the party. It was daytime now, and a cowl of light hung above them. But their watches had stopped and all they had to rely on were their tracks. If the tracks filled in, they were lost. Their compass needles had stuck fast with the cold and wouldn't budge. There was a large cloud of frozen breath round the party. Inside that cloud, they had to keep going.

Amundsen's team was also dispersed now. Then the incident occurred which he later tried to cover, and which did not become known until many years afterwards. Hjalmar Johansen's journals were found half a generation later in a hotel cellar in Kristiania. Then the truth about the leader's desertion came to light. Olav Bjaaland also wrote curt, hard words in his notebook. They revealed something of the same truth.

But do we *really* know what happened to him? It appears that he suddenly broke down. He was sitting on Wisting's sledge. The dogs in his team were the most vigorous. Suddenly they put on a spurt; the nearest team tried to follow, but soon fell behind. In the course of half an hour, the party had spread itself out in freezing fog and all contact between teams was lost. Their compasses were frozen. Their watches were frozen. They had a track to follow, but what if a blizzard came and filled it up again?

He had pulled right away from them. We don't know if it was some kind of aberration. The pressure on his nerves had been colossal and had increased by their having to turn back. Later on in his life he was to show signs of being

mentally unbalanced, though up until now he had overcome every difficulty. Now he, the skipper, was abandoning
a sinking ship. If it were panic, then he had no excuse for
what he did. It could have been—which is even more
reprehensible but still demonstrates that streak of brutality
in him—the realization that everything was at stake. Let
the weakest fall behind. The strongest would survive. If
they all got back, all well and good. If they didn't, that was
that. In either case, the survivors would fight for the Pole
and try to get there before Scott. He might have been in
a position to rationalize in this way. His ice-cold mind
might have been able to grasp more clearly than the others
could what the task really involved. He had a general's
sense of duty in the face of an inhuman aim. His egotism
was boundless. Or maybe he was simply afraid.

This last is probably the most likely explanation, as it
followed from the fact that he would never admit to fear.
All his relationships, his public image, his aura of greatness—all would demand that he deny fear. But he couldn't
have been afraid of death itself, even if the fear of a slow
death in the cold must have frightened him more than a
sudden, abrupt, possibly wished-for death. What he was
afraid of was dying under precisely *these* circumstances—
during a return trip, in the middle of defeat, before he'd
had a chance to make another attempt. Fear had gripped
him. He had fled.

It was no use shouting after the leader; it was no use
waving from man to man; it was useless to urge on the
dogs: their limits had been reached. The dogs kept plodding on, but they couldn't increase their pace. Hjalmar
Johansen knew that he had to let them maintain their
own pace, otherwise the whole team would break down.

He was the last in the party. Behind, Prestrud was trudg-
ing along on his skis. Prestrud groaned: 'Hjalmar, I
think my heel's frozen.'

Prestrud was limping now, though still able to move

his foot. He should have been wrapped up and laid on a sledge, so that his boot wouldn't wear his frostbitten foot away. But the dogs couldn't haul the man as well.

They could, however, still maintain a faster pace than the man behind. They drew away. It wasn't much use for the dog-driver to regulate the speed. They had to be allowed to maintain their own pace or they would stop altogether and lie down in the snow. Then it would require superhuman strength and brutality to get them up and going again.

Prestrud still had some contact with the man in front, but with every stride, his boot was wearing into his heel. Was the same thing beginning to happen to the other heel? Prestrud tried to shout. The man in front replied. But neither could make out what the other was saying.

The first stirrings of anger were beginning deep down inside Hjalmar Johansen. At first he wanted to believe that the men in front hadn't been able to stop the dogs, that they thought they would maintain a natural pace then stop and wait for those coming up behind. But no one waited. He began to realize the bitter truth—they'd been left behind. It was sixty below, and they had no tent. They had neither tent nor cooking vessels. With fresh dogs, they could have reached Framheim in twelve hours—with working compasses and good watches. They had none of these.

He tried to hold the dogs back, but it was no use. They had set their noses in the snow and were hauling away for all they were worth. They were more vigorous than before, as if they knew they were on their way home, and they seemed to realize that if they used the last of their strength, there was still some hope for them. But behind them was Prestrud, groaning with pain: no one heard him.

Johansen had to stop the dogs by overturning the sledge. Then in the stillness he heard the laboured panting of a single dog. He went up to it, but by then it was dead.

He extricated it from the traces and threw it aside. He

felt like screaming, but couldn't. He noticed that he was
the only person in the world—just him, miles away from
humanity, a solitary skier behind him somewhere and
someone ahead of him who was already out of sight. But
not a sound; profound stillness. Darkness was falling. This
was the ultimate stillness singing in his ears. He leant over
to listen to his own wrist. It felt as if his pulse had
frozen.

Then Prestrud came, still toiling on. Both feet had now
lost all feeling. He had little strength left. He rested on his
ski-poles and said quietly: 'You must go on. I'll follow.'

'I won't go on without you.'

'But I can't keep up with the dogs.'

Again they set off northwards. It was dark now. They
could just see the tracks. Now and again, the fog and clouds
drifted away. A half-moon was sitting at an angle over the
Antarctic. Then they saw the landscape around them.
White—with gentle slopes of snow, heaps of ice, a blue
track their only contact with the world of human beings.
Almost immediately, the fog swirled back.

Again Prestrud lagged behind. Johansen had to tip the
sledge, stop the dogs, let them rest, while he waited for
the man. The wait became longer and longer each time.
It occurred to him that at midnight, those in front might
stop, put up the tent, get the primus going and send a
couple of men back to meet him. That would be proof
that Amundsen could behave like a leader. But no one
came to meet them.

Suddenly he saw something dark in front of him in the
track.

So they were there at last; he put on a spurt, the dogs
getting wind of something and increasing the pace. But it
wasn't the rest of the party. It was four dogs that had been
left behind. They were still alive. As he went on, they
staggered to their feet and followed him. The severe cold
had eaten away the hair on the dogs' paws, and they were

leaving blood-stained tracks in the snow.

Then he had to wait for Prestrud.

The man behind was still managing to haul himself along. Johansen got him up on to the sledge, took off his outer garment and spread it over him. But it was dangerous to sleep and anyway, the dogs couldn't manage the extra load, so Prestrud had to get off again. He fell in the snow, hauled himself up, and once more the party began to stagger northwards.

During the night, Johansen overtook Hassel, who had been abandoned by those in front. He was bitter—both about the men who had left him behind and the ones he had waited for. Hjalmar Johansen said they had to wait for Prestrud. Hassel and Johansen found each other in their criticism of Amundsen. What kind of an expedition was this at sixty below and in the dark, with frozen watches and no compass? Then Hassel grew impatient, and both men lost their tempers. Johansen made sure he kept the tent that Hassel had on his sledge. Hassel set off alone in the tracks northwards.

Johansen waited two hours before Prestrud came. This could have been the end. But Prestrud was tough. He was rigid with cold but didn't collapse. He couldn't speak, but nodded that he would still try to use the last of his strength. As night slowly turned into day, they made their way down from the inland ice on to the sea-ice. It was an area full of 'crevasses. Prestrud fell down, but luckily the fissure was a shallow one. Johansen found him in the dark, had to remove his mittens and tie two dog harnesses round the man, then use his gigantic strength to haul his frozen companion up. By this time, the dogs had entangled themselves completely in the traces and couldn't pull. It was too dark to disentangle them. He had to cut them free, losing his knife, finding it again, cutting himself, noticing that there was still some mild warmth in his blood. Inflammation soon affected open sores in severe cold. The dogs were loose. If they were to take the sledge with them Johansen would have to pull it himself. Prestrud sat on it. But he mustn't be allowed to sleep.

Those dogs that were still alive struggled along behind the man; two were left lying in the tracks. It couldn't be very many more kilometres to Framheim. Not a soul in sight. The track was a weak, dark colour which made it stand out from the surrounding snow.

He knew that this could be the end. Again and again he went back to Prestrud and shook him. The man groaned, but was indomitable, tough-willed, and he staggered up, got his feet moving, kept going behind the sledge that Johansen was pulling, falling several times, but still alive. A dog managed to jump on to the sledge. Johansen let it sit there, the champion of the ice hauling one of his dogs home. Then they lost the track. It was only a few hours until daylight, but perhaps only minutes till they lost the last degrees of body-heat. They either had to get under cover soon or die. Suddenly they heard a dog bark in the distance. They set off on a different course. Again there were cracks in the ice. They wouldn't have been so dangerous if the men could have seen them and had had the strength to go on. This might have been the end, just as they were on the point of rescue. Johansen was now staggering on ahead on his own, cautiously testing the way, retracing his own tracks, hoisting the sledge-rope over his shoulder, Prestrud riding on the sledge. Then he followed the track through the snow and the darkness, stopping the sledge again, starting off to make another track and turning back to the sledge.

He was not immortal. Later he took his own life. But that night he saved both his own life and Prestrud's.

They found Framheim and staggered inside. Lindstrøm was brewing hot coffee:

'Ssh,' he said. 'The leader is asleep.'

*　　*　　*

Trouble broke out at the breakfast table. Amundsen got up, but the two of them didn't exchange greetings. They were sitting shoulder to shoulder, their woollen sweaters rubbing against each other. They were slurping hot coffee and irritating each other with the noise. Most of them had slept little that night, some not at all. Then Johansen turned to Amundsen; nine inches between the two weather-beaten faces. Neither was a newcomer to the Antarctic or the Arctic. But the man who had gone with Nansen felt coldly at ease, while the other was visibly quivering with apprehension. They stared at each other for a long time.

The leader's mouth was open, but he said nothing. Johansen was tight-lipped, clearing his throat as a warning that speech was on its way. Then Amundsen slammed down his cup and said: 'What do you think you were doing last night, dawdling like that?'

Silence crept from man to man round the table, while a dog outside howled an audible greeting from the bitter reality of the previous night. The man to whom the question had been directed took his time answering. Everyone was staring at him.

He stared steadily back at the leader. Was he remembering the time he'd been flat on his back with a polar bear on top of him, his hands round its throat, the moment before Nansen shot?

'That was,' said Johansen, 'a peculiar thing to do: travelling on ahead when it was sixty below. . . .'

Amundsen leapt to his feet, his stool falling over behind him, and they saw his hand fumbling for the cup as if he were going to throw it. He didn't find it. It was so cramped round the table that it seemed almost laughable to stand upright with eight men in such close proximity. But it was difficult to sit down without manoeuvring through all those woollen sweaters and those elbows on the table.

Johansen repeated:

'That was a peculiar thing to do. It could have meant life or death to Prestrud and me. I demand an explanation.'

Johansen was not ignorant of people, and years in the ice had sharpened his perception, but he had failed to master one point. He recognized Amundsen's ambition and his unwillingness to face a man on equal terms. He knew Amundsen had a higher opinion of his own qualities of leadership than Johansen did. But although the subordinate was cleverer than his leader in most respects, that vicious streak of self-esteem in Amundsen hadn't dawned on him. Johansen knew how to choose his words, and was meticulous at finding the right ones. They hit home like barbed arrows.

'It was behaviour unworthy of a leader.'

At the same moment, Prestrud cried: 'My legs hurt!'

He hadn't spoken soon enough. It was a diversionary manoeuvre that failed. Perhaps Johansen's doom was sealed by Prestrud's failure to intervene sooner. They saw Amundsen go pale. His face aged suddenly. He had coarse working hands and grease in the furrows of his skin; he was unshaven, his eyes red-rimmed from the cold of the trip south. His profile would have frightened off a pack of robbers. It didn't frighten Johansen.

Johansen got up, squaring his shoulders. The two of them had been sitting beside each other, and now they stood chest to chest. The man from the North Pole hurled his words in the teeth of the man who would have sacrificed any life—including his own—to be first at the opposite Pole: 'I repeat, it was behaviour unworthy of a leader.'

Then Johansen cursed. It was an indication of his feelings, if such a thing were necessary after what had already happened. He didn't often swear, and when he did it was a fairly unimaginative process, but this time the oaths came from the heart.

Then Amundsen began to stammer. They'd never heard him like this before. He spewed out obscenities they had no idea he would dream of allowing past his lips. Amundsen was a bit of an old maid and had to force himself to smile at others' risqué stories. His own contributions on those topics were as arid as desert sand. Now he was standing there spitting out words they hadn't realized he knew.

He slid out from his cramped position between Johansen and Hassel. The former couldn't now turn round; slowly he began to explain, thinking perhaps that by laying the cold facts on the table, he would force the leader to bring himself under control. He reminded him that Prestrud and he had fallen behind, that their dogs had dropped dead, and where had the others got to? 'We had no tent, we had no primus. It was a matter of life or death. Prestrud's heels were both frostbitten. I demand an explanation.'

'My heels were frostbitten!' echoed Prestrud.

Amundsen replied: 'So were Stubberud's and Hassel's, weren't they?'

'Yes, yes,' the two of them confirmed.

It was the truth, but they knew he was lying too. When an honest word could have made him more human and more of a leader than before, he spurned the truth and chose to tell a half-truth which amounted to a lie. Hassel's and Stubberud's feet had been frostbitten. But were the leader's? Why had he been the first man home? Johansen could have remained silent at this stage. Perhaps that would have changed the course of his life. But he didn't. Like many calm people, when he was angry he could be uncontrollable. He made the same mistake again. He underestimated the extent of his opponent's need to be greatest.

He asked in an icy voice: 'Who got home first, you or them?'

Now it was time for the coffee cups to fly. There was little room for fists, but the table was narrow enough for men on both sides to join the great battle. Stubberud had been silent up to now. The man who spoke seldom, but who had built Framheim, now slapped a foot up on the table among the pancakes and rancid butter and shouted: 'Look at that!'

A naked foot, the heel looking like kohlrabi, blue, swollen and painful. Prestrud raised his foot without a word, easing it out of his slipper and showing it. His foot was worse. It helped a bit. They turned their attention to treating the feet. They quickly packed cold rags round them, aware that they had to apply hot poultices before washing with a solution of boric acid. 'Off to bed with you!' said Amundsen. 'Yes, to bed,' commanded Johansen. It was a wise remark, a tactful appeal for negotiations, a wave across the trenches from men on the point of digging themselves in. Wisting said that people with frostbitten heels should keep them high up. So they rigged up a cradle for each bad foot and fastened them to nails in the roof. Amundsen found a hammer. Johansen banged in the nails.

Then they parted. There was a blizzard outside and very little room inside. Everyone suspected that the following few hours might be decisive in what would happen later. Let every man make his way to a place of solitude—a dog-tent, an ice-bin below Framheim, a corner of an untidy kitchen. No one was to be disturbed. Three men lay in bed resting their ruined feet, Hassel, Stubberud and Prestrud. The conquest of the Pole had receded further into the distance.

The leader's place of solitude was a tiny room in the ice where no one ever sat for long, free from smells because of the cold, the seat covered in sealskin. Others on their way there saw that it was occupied and left again. He stayed there for a long time.

Alone, he had a strength that everyone else lacked. Now he had the peace and quiet to think through what had happened. He was both afraid and unafraid: afraid of revealing himself, but courageous in his will and ability to prevent it. He had not learned how to give way to someone who called his greatness into question; but he could plan strategy by instinct, just as telling half-truths was part of his nature. There were now two alternatives. A generous soul might have chosen one way: he chose another, and his choice was a master-stroke.

Dinner. There was more room round the table than usual as the three men with frostbitten feet were lying in great pain in their bunks. They had their food taken up to them—pea soup and seal steaks. They ate slowly. Amundsen cleared his throat. This was the moment. He was leader and had to act. They all put down their knives and forks. Eight faces stared into his.

He said slowly: 'I've changed my mind.'

They hadn't expected this. Changing his mind involved admitting his own faults, didn't it? He went on: 'I've changed my plans for the trip to the Pole. Eight men will be too many. Five will be sufficient. The other three will go east and explore King Edward VII's Land.'

The three were Prestrud, Stubberud and Johansen.

Then the man from the Arctic rose. This personal vengeance was a mortal thrust. So the truth had been too hard to bear, and now he was being rejected for having had the courage to speak.

'What if I refuse?'

He might have got the support of the others then, if he had wanted to, ignoring their averted eyes, standing up and banging the table, getting out his contract and ripping it in two. The other men would have done the same— perhaps.

But in this situation Amundsen showed himself in complete command. He had foreseen this and cried: 'Bjaaland, come with me!'

The two men went into the kitchen together; what was said was inaudible to the others. Wisting was called in when Bjaaland came back. 'I've sworn I'll say nothing,' he said, dispiritedly.

Man after man went out there and man after man came back. Finally it was Johansen's turn. Amundsen handed him a letter. It was a written order relieving Johansen of his part in the journey to the Pole. Instead, he was to go eastwards with Prestrud, under Prestrud's leadership.

Johansen was a professional soldier. To be angry was one thing. To refuse to obey a written order, correctly formulated, based on a contract which he had signed, was another matter. He said nothing.

The nine men never forgot the following days and weeks at Framheim. Outside, blizzards alternated with severe cold, some days the fog and raw weather drifting in from Ross Sea. Spring was approaching. Had the English already started? Were the motor-sledges working?

The nine men tried to avoid each other. Before, they had always eaten together, but now they gulped down a little food in the kitchen with Lindstrøm and didn't come in to dinner. The ruined dog-traces from the first trip were repaired. Seven men circled round Johansen, trying to show their sympathy. They regretted their lack of support for him, and felt like traitors. But he was not a man to thaw at a pleasant word.

Amundsen was polite to Johansen, not exaggeratedly so, but always correct. They still sat side by side as they worked on the equipment. They still ate together sometimes. If the one man were hoping that the other would give way and take back his words, it was a forlorn hope.

The three men whose heels were frostbitten spent most of their time in bed. Slowly, very slowly, a new skin grew beneath the old one. Prestrud was leafing through a medical textbook one evening when he said: 'There's something here about frostbite. What we did was probably wrong....'

Amundsen leaped up, grabbed something and hurled it. An awl stuck in the wall. He wrenched it out, his hands trembling, and put it down on the table.

'Play solitaire!' he cried. 'Play solitaire! When I say your foot will heal, it will heal.'

'But will it heal fast enough?' asked Prestrud.

Johansen said quietly, but pointedly: 'After all, we still don't know if the motor-sledges are working, do we?'

Amundsen rushed out.

There were still blizzards over the Antarctic; the days passed, then everything was ready once again for a new start. It was cramped, untidy and unpleasant at Framheim.

At last, on 19 October, the day came for the five to leave—Amundsen, Wisting, Hassel, Bjaaland and Hanssen. The dogs were in good shape.

Everyone shook hands and wished them good luck. Amundsen and Johansen stood face to face. It was a beautiful day in the Antarctic.

They shook hands too.

'I wish you the best for the trip to the Pole.'

Amundsen thanked him and wished him the same for the trip east.

SCOTT

It was a solitary expedition that departed for the south. The first troop received its starting orders on 24 October, 1911, and consisted of two motor-sledges with trailers and four men, the leader Edward Evans. Day, Lashly and Hooper had been allocated to him as crew. The engines had to be started with soldering lamps and it took a good hour to warm them up. This had to be done with infinite caution, or a bearing would go. But then the engines ran with short, staccato bursts, the machinery trembling—the mechanic, too, as at any time something might start smoking and the parts would have to be unscrewed in the cold and blizzard. The motor-sledges were very powerful. If they held out for a few weeks on the way south, Scott and his men would get the heavy equipment transported far more quickly than anyone had imagined.

There was a great farewell scene when the first troop departed. The leader remained behind by the hut wall in McMurdo Sound, watching the sledges through binoculars. They moved fifteen hundred metres forward on that first surge, the mechanic running alongside, holding an icy cold finger on the accelerator to keep it in the right position. When the man slipped, his finger slipped too, and the accelerator jerked out, making the engine stop with a groan. Or the regulator would get stuck while the man was lying in the snow; the sledge would begin to lurch, its speed increasing, the man running after it; an ice hummock loomed ahead, at the last minute the man threw himself at the sledge with an oath—grasping the wheel, yanking the sledge away, the trailer tipping over and the tracks slithering in the snow. Now the engine was running hot. There was nothing to do but switch it off. Then the sledge had to be righted, the engine started—it was warm now, and so was the mechanic. The engine started. The man ran alongside again, his finger on the accelerator.

The first real test for the motor-sledges was the slope up from the sea-ice on to the land-ice. They surmounted this obstacle superbly. Indeed, they appeared to improve as the difficulties increased—and Scott, still able to follow their progress through his binoculars, felt his spirits rising. He had staked a great deal on the use of motor-sledges. The Empire had spent thousands of pounds on the three the expedition had brought with them. He himself was pessimistic about their usefulness; optimistic too, in the long term; he just didn't think he would be the one to succeed thanks to the use of motor-sledges. This was his modesty showing through again—his insistence on being prepared for every contingency was a hindrance. He was always filled with anxiety, but now, as he stood looking through his binoculars, for once fortune was on his side.

A few days later, the second troop set out. This main troop was led by Scott himself. The sledges were drawn by ponies, in fine form after a hard winter, driven according to rules worked out back on English country estates with a horse-specialist, Captain Oates, in charge of the stables. Scott loved ponies because they couldn't eat each other. It made him physically sick when dog ate dog. He knew that starving men in the ice had eaten their dogs. A pony was an affectionate animal and there was something very English about the way it behaved. It might nibble at its reins, but in principle it didn't eat as a dog did. A pony was also big enough for a man to pat it without having to bend down! A dog wasn't a natural draught-animal, and was made to hunt or to lie by the fire. Wilson and Scott had discussed the pros and cons of dogs and horses and, half-jokingly, they had come down on the side of the horse, while at the same time realizing the defects in their own arguments. The leader had decided to take dogs too, just so that justice was seen to be done on that point, but neither he nor the others had any faith in them.

Then the third division set off after an interval of a few days, the dog-expert, Meares, leading the troop, the Russian, Demetri, as his assistant, each driving a team. They had light loads, for the plan was that they should travel at high speed. They were really included to show that the Empire's scepticism over the use of dogs in Arctic regions was justified.

The great expedition spread out across the Antarctic, men with strong profiles, nerves of steel and a wealth of experience led by one constantly filled with anxiety—not so much over whether he would be first at the Pole, although that was a matter of interest, but more over each of his men, and over his own inadequacies. Every evening when he wrote his journal, he worried over the latest problem, and always came to the same conclusion: perhaps I'm capable enough in this group, but nevertheless I'm not capable enough.

The advance party with the two motor-sledges zig-zagged on between ice hummocks and deep crevasses. Edward Evans, the man who had wanted to start earlier to win the race with Amundsen, urged the sledges and his three men forward. The engines got hot and had to be stopped so that the bearings didn't crack. Cooling down couldn't be too fast or too slow, so they packed woollen blankets round the engines and ran up and down alongside, stamping on the ice to keep their toes from freezing. But the woollen blankets blew away; lash them down. The rope was frozen stiff. Lie face down on top of the blanket, to anchor it on the engine. It was red-hot. The blanket caught fire. Jump off, swear, curse, shake your fists in the air, nearly hitting your companion, spit in the snow, saying: 'It's all Amundsen's fault.'

On to the south.

The first party had to get to latitude eighty-one-thirty, with or without the motor-sledges, where they were to wait for the next team. It was a military order, and Evans had sworn that no one, no one would overtake his men. He pressed the sledges and men to their utmost, flinging an empty petrol can into the tracks with a note: 'Everything's going fine.'

Behind them came the ponies in troop two. Here was Petty Officer Edgar Evans, a master at all practical work—welding metal, repairing harness in severe cold, lighting a primus in a blizzard. The power of the Empire rested on him. He was supposed to have enough brainpower to transmit an order from an officer to the men in the ranks. But the problem with Edgar Evans was that no one knew what he was thinking. No one had any idea that there was one question gnawing away at him: 'Will I get my money if Scott isn't first at the Pole?'

Edgar Evans was the one man in the troop whom Scott admired most and he expressed this admiration often and gladly, though always as an officer to a subordinate, friendly, slightly lofty, not condescending, but in confirmation of the fact that the testimonial was well earned.

The ponies had begun to rear up on their hind legs. This hadn't been part of the calculations. According to the plans worked out in detail, partly back in England and partly in a hut in McMurdo Sound, a pony simply didn't stand on its hind legs. If they did so back in England, that was another matter. There it was decorative, and in that situation, the rider would learn to control his horse. Rear-ing up in the ice, in a bitter wind and driving snow, just wasn't right.

Oates had no explanation to offer. Scott always accepted information from the expert in the troop, and now Oates had no solution. It was wearing for the driver when a pony, which looked exhausted and hung its head, suddenly got up on its hind legs. The driver behind had to stop. The man ahead heard the fuss, got out of step, and in a very few minutes the whole caravan had come to a halt. There were many episodes of this kind. A thousand minor, day-to-day worries were wrecking the march. They were already three days behind schedule.

The weather was passable, but Wilson went snowblind. He held on to the sledge and plodded on, in great pain, saying that it didn't matter all that much: 'It would have been rather nice if I'd been able to see. I want to write my diary this evening in my sleeping-bag.' It was a half-hearted joke. He kept a light touch. He knew that in a few days the pain would go and he would be able to see again. If he could be left in peace in a dark room, every-thing would soon be better. But it was a thousand kilo-metres to the Pole and a thousand back. The day was good —or bad—clear, with the sky high over the ice and the sun pouring down.

Behind the ponies came the dogs. They were getting closer, they recognized the smell of meat ahead and were running wildly along in the tracks. They had only been included to show that they were superfluous. Meares was slightly bitter, for he knew that he'd be given orders to turn back before they reached the Pole, and he'd have liked to have been included.

Everyone knew that the party which would try to reach the Pole would consist of five men only. One would be Scott. Who would the other four be?

They didn't realize that this very decision was Scott's greatest worry. The moral aspect of the question occupied him most. How can I assess the men objectively so that I can justify my choice? If I can't, how can I in all conscience give orders to the rest of them to turn back? He studied them intently on the quiet. This man or that man was no good on skis. This man or that man was clumsy when it came to loading a sledge. But who was the easiest to get on with? Who had that one characteristic which made it possible to bear the considerable strains? I watched them all through a long winter. But we were indoors then.

They found an empty petrol can with a piece of paper under its lid. All was well. Spirits rose among the members of the pony team, and the good news filtered back to the men racing behind with the dogs. If the motor-sledges were holding out—which no one had really expected—the route to the Pole would be easier. They were now four days behind schedule.

They found another petrol can, dark and beautiful in the snow. Wilson, with his sore eyes, tore aside the cloth he had put over his face to revel in the sight of something black. It probably contained a message of reassurance that everything was all right. Scott snatched the note. A cylinder had cracked.

It was a bitter disappointment which wrenched his heart, and his first lucid thought was that if the engines were constructed in the same way, surely now that one had gone the other would go too. They could see the abandoned motor-sledge ahead of them, shipwrecked in the snow. Evans and his men had loaded the equipment on to the other sledge and raced on.

As leader, Scott couldn't afford to show his disappointment, or at least, he had to keep it under control. If he were seen to be visibly disappointed, his despair would rebound on the men and become an additional burden to them. He managed this in a masterly way. It was one of the things they'd learnt in the Navy. Moreover, it was a quality he had been born with, and partly explained his

moral strength. He slapped his friend Wilson on the back
and smiled: 'Here's something else black to look at! See
how black the engine is with grease and oil!' He skied
back to the dog-party to inform the men personally, hoping
to make their disappointment easier to bear. The pony
party had now struck camp.

They left early next morning. Soon they saw another
can in the snow. It could contain one of two things. Scott
stopped to read the note and said to the man nearest to
him: 'I think we should take it easy.' They did. The last
motor-sledge had gone wrong.

They found it a kilometre farther on.

Evans and his men had put the sledge straps over their
own shoulders and were continuing on foot. Their orders
were to get to latitude eighty-one-thirty with or without
engines. No one, absolutely no one, was going to overtake
them. Then a blizzard broke out. It was a big one. They
crawled into their tents, the ponies standing outside with
their backs to the storm, trembling in the cold and wind.
The wet ate its way in through their coats. The men tried
to build a snow wall round the animals, but it wasn't much
help against a storm which obliterated all boundaries and
knocked a man over in the snow if he had nothing to hold
on to. The dogs let themselves be snowed under; they were
born to this life and were glad of a day off. Inside the tents
the men lay in their sleeping-bags; Wilson, whose eyes
were better, Scott, with his pipe alight, his pencil, his diary
and a worried expression. They couldn't all sleep at once:
someone had to keep watch in case the blizzard should rip
away the tent-ropes. They didn't know that a few miles
ahead of them, Evans was still urging his men on.

No one was going to overtake *him*. Hadn't he saved the
Terra Nova? Wouldn't he have set out in the depths of
winter if it increased their chances of beating Amundsen
to the Pole? The leader had rejected him, refused even
to consider his plan seriously. So he had urged on the

motor-sledges until they had both broken down, and now four men were hauling the sledges with inhuman toil, the blizzard raging around them. He had decided not to strike camp until evening. Evans had limitless courage, matchless strength, and he could be brutal face to face, man to man. He was the officer. He urged on the three others and himself alike.

Daylight came and the weather was slightly better. The main party was five days behind schedule. Scott said to Oates: 'Would it be reasonable to drive the horses a little harder so that we can make up some of the time we've lost? I would like us to tackle this problem together, considering the fact that we have to be back in winter quarters before the autumn storms set in. But Amundsen's existence mustn't influence our decision.'

'I think, sir, it would be all right to drive the horses a bit harder.'

'Then we'll do so, even though tormenting animals is painful to us all.'

The dogs had overtaken the ponies, and together, the second and third troops continued southwards. At latitude eighty-one-thirty, they found Edward Evans and his three men, who had built a huge snow cairn to pass the time during the six days they had been waiting. Evans had driven himself and the others to extremes—across crevasses and through blizzards, exhausting the men and himself, freezing their feet, wearing out their equipment, all so as not to be overtaken by those behind. The meeting between him and Scott was not a friendly one.

On the one side was Scott, obstinate, advancing slowly, conserving his strength: we're heading for the Pole, but only according to the plan I've so carefully worked out; Evans on the other, the hero of the *Terra Nova*, determined to throw everything—even his own life—into the struggle against Amundsen. He had now demonstrated the possibility of travelling to the Pole at a greater speed than Scott thought wise.

Once they'd been friends, and outwardly they still were. They spoke a little more briskly than when they'd last met, but with an undertone of heat which made them forget the cold around them. Both were officers. Evans knew his duty to the leader of the expedition, but they had both lost the admiration they'd once felt for each other.

There was one way to lessen their dissatisfaction; pressing on further south. As they stood there in the fog, shouts from the men and howls from the dogs coming at them from all directions, tents being erected, primuses sputtering, Evans suppressing everything he'd decided to say—suddenly the weather cleared. It was an absorbing experience. In a few moments the fog was driven away and the sun was beating down on the snow. The shadows darkened, a dog raised its nose and howled at the light. Men's voices died away. Then they saw the mountains— due south, on their course to the Pole. They had to climb those mountainsides: their sweat would pour and their muscles tense; they'd have to thrash the dogs and use every ounce of strength—either that or die. They were on the Barrier now, and had to get up to the plateau, a climb of two thousand metres or more—through narrow clefts, across deep crevasses, across a wilderness where only Shackleton had been before them. That was their route. Then the antagonism Scott had felt towards his second-in-command vanished, and Evans half-turned towards Scott with an apologetic smile. Both had a sense of larger dimensions, both felt a need to doff their leather caps to the mountains in the south.

All at once, a blizzard appeared on the horizon, taking half an hour to reach them. They knew from Scott's previous journey that a storm could slide over into good weather, and clear weather over into fog, from one moment to the next. As now. A wall of fog was approaching from the north. The tents were up and as yet the sunlight was still round them like a chilly, beautiful curtain. The men were smiling. The dogs were eating. But the wall of fog was drifting closer and closer, until it enveloped the nearest tent.

The wall was so thick that the rest of the party stood in bright light and couldn't see the nearest man fifty metres away. It was a blanket being drawn round them. They noticed with surprise and discomfort that the temperature was beginning to rise. They didn't like the temperature to drop, though they were used to that: it could drop to forty, which was all right, then fifty, and that meant danger ahead for dogs and men. But they hadn't anticipated that it might rise above the freezing point, the cold changing to warmth. That was what happened now.

The men had crawled into their tents, which were covered with drops of ice inside, a pretty pattern, a beautiful sight to see as the light from a match flared up, or the little blue flame of the primus transformed the tent into a fairy-tale cave, half buried in the ice. But now the drops of ice began to thaw.

Previously, they had been able to find some kind of peace in their sleeping-bags at night. A man on the ice, bundled up in clothes and sleeping-bag, seldom slept all through the night. He woke feeling cold, rubbed his feet against each other, dozed off again, finding rest in dreams which came and went. He was relatively at ease, because this was the best part of the day. But now water began to drip from the tentcloth.

It could never have happened before in this country of low temperatures, and it made them feel as if God had finally abandoned them. When the first drop fell and hit a sleeping-bag, they didn't realize what it was. All at once, the dogs began to howl, not the howl that heralded a fight, nor a fierce growl, but a dismal wailing from the depths of the wet snow, echoing through the fog.

Scott was half-lying on his sleeping-bag, entering the day's events in his diary. A drop of water fell on to the paper. He had decided to write in ink today; because of the cold it had been impossible for many days, so he'd been using a pencil. Then a drop hit the word he'd just written in his strong, loose handwriting, and the word dissolved into a nasty illegible blue blob. He wondered: 'Is that a symbol of my destiny ... to become a blob that no one can read?'

Unpleasant. If only they could have stood up, then the drops from the canvas wouldn't have tormented them so much. But they had to lie where they were, as it began to rain more and more heavily inside. They pulled their leather hoods over their heads; some crawled right down into their sleeping-bags and tied up the opening, usually the last resort when the nights were too cold. But now the clammy wetness seeped right into the sleeping-bags and they felt cold in the one place they had been able to keep warm.

One man said: 'Let's go outside.'

But outside the snow was falling in thick white flakes, turning to rain, becoming snow again, lying in a soaking wet layer on sledges, dogs and ponies. The tents were like small white pyramids, the snow not sliding off the cloth, but melting from the heat within. It dripped on and on.

This continued for a long time. The night was a long one and when morning came, no one had slept. Oates had been out over and over again to see the ponies, who stood with their heads hanging as if the strength were dripping from them like the rain off their coats. Then suddenly a pony reared up on its hind legs and screamed into the grey, impenetrable world around it, before collapsing. Oates tried to find a dry bunch of hay to rub it down, but by now everything was soaking. He would have liked to use some of his clothing, but all his clothes were wet. He shivered from the cold and, standing in the snow, used the

inside of a woollen sweater to dry the prostrate pony. The
day went by. Another night fell. They had realized that
they might freeze to death in the polar wilderness, but
they'd never imagined they might die in mild weather.
On the second day, Scott gathered the men together to
hold a service. They crowded into his tent. Not all of them
could get in, so some stood hunched in the tent-opening.
It was as cold and wet inside as out. Some lay in their
sleeping-bags, others knelt. With the nearest face a bare
few inches from his own, Scott spoke the Lord's Prayer in
a strong, clerical voice. The service was over.

The mild weather continued.

The dogs had vanished. They were lying somewhere
down inside the slush, with an almost invisible opening
letting air in and out. They did this in cold weather and
seemed to be comfortable enough, but now they were
soaked through and freezing. It was even worse for the
ponies. The men worked with them for hours on end,
constantly rubbing them down with hay. Two ponies had
already collapsed.

When it cleared, the fine weather came as rapidly as the
fog. The men crept out of their tents, tore off their wet
clothes, helped the ponies to their feet. The first dog-
muzzle peeped out, pointing south and looking at the un-
changed wilderness of snow. But then—it was a scene they
never forgot—in the blue sky far away, like huge white
columns in the sky, rose two steep mountain tops, a cleft
behind them, which must have been what Shackleton called
The Portal.

They were to go through that cleft.

They dug themselves out of the wet snow and took
down the tents. There was no point in drying anything yet,
as the temperature was dropping. They noticed their wet
clothes stiffening, the tentcloth crackling as they rolled it
up. They had to get moving now. They also had to get
the dogs and ponies moving as only motion would save

them all from freezing to death if the temperature continued to drop.

It did. But by now they were fuelled with strength and suppressed resentment. If the Pole dared to try and thwart them with wet weather, then they would show the Pole that they were indomitable. Again the great party was under way, men hauling sledges, ponies hauling, feet sinking deep into the snow. The dogs panted, up to their stomachs in the new snow, no grip for their paws; the men went ahead to make a track. A sledge overturned and a man had to go back and yank it up on to an even keel. The dogs panted and heaved. Then the fog came down.

No, it wasn't settling in after all. The Deity was playing tricks on them. He allowed the fog to approach and they saw wet patches drifting across the endless white frozen land. But then the fog was held back as if by an invisible hand. They had begun to climb the mountain, up into the sunshine. They could see the crevasses and circumvent them. But a few hundred metres behind them, the fog was creeping nearer—then drifting away again. It was as if God wished to remind them that they weren't the masters here in the south.

Step by step up. In some places, the mountainside was a gentle gradient, and then the men ahead could take a breather and look down at those behind. But often there were steep slopes and then they had to unload and lift the equipment up, or find ways round, clinging on with crampons, steadying the ponies so that they didn't slide backwards. They knew that this was as far as a horse could go.

It was part of the plan that the horses should die here. The dogs were to go on a bit farther and then turn back to winter quarters. Scott had deferred the inevitable decision about slaughtering the ponies. He should have given orders for it to be done the day before, but it was an order he dreaded most of all—except for the decision as to which

men were to turn back soon and which to go on with him
to the Pole.

He stood with his back to Oates and said casually:
'You'll have to do it this evening. . . .'

Oates knew what he meant.

Scott went out to study the route for the next day. Oates
threw a biscuit down on the snow; a pony bent down and
nibbled at it, then got a bullet through its head. The
dogs smelt the blood and went wild in their chains, pulling and dragging at them to get free, and as the shots rang
out, pony after pony sank to its knees. Soon the dogs got
the great meal of flesh and blood they had been craving,
and needed so badly. Some of the men were able to eat a
horse steak. Others couldn't. Scott returned.

The tents had been set up at the foot of the mountains.
A new moon shone beautifully over the camp and the land
round about; the temperature was mild, twenty degrees
below; it was almost warm in the tents—men sleeping, the
dogs heavy with all that food, groaning with repletion.

But Scott wasn't asleep.

The next day they crawled farther up. As usual, Wilson
found time to sketch the mountains. The dogs were
managing better in the climb than anyone had imagined
they would.

Teddy Evans casually approached Scott. Briefly, without showing undue deference, but with open friendliness,
a tacit indication that he accepted Scott's leadership even
while disagreeing with his strategy, Evans made it clear
that he would very much like to be included in the party
going to the Pole.

Scott met this courtesy with courtesy, responding
pleasantly to the man who had made this move towards
him. But he didn't say a word about which men he wanted
to take with him to the Pole.

The other Evans in the party, Edgar, was a stronger
character than his namesake. He kept his own counsel,

didn't oppose his leader and always made himself useful
—a dog who managed better than the dogs.

He too wanted to go to the Pole. He looked across at his
namesake and smiled. Scott's digestion was upset, and
now and again he had to find an isolated place behind an
ice hummock. He disliked letting the others see him—
privacy was impossible here. He was embarrassed, a hundred kilometres or so from the Pole, his strength dwindling
as he squatted, thinking: 'Who shall I take with me?'

A cold wind had begun to blow from the north, thirty-
five below, and his trousers filled with fine snow, which
melted as he fastened his clothes. Where was Amundsen
now? But you're not competing with Amundsen, are you?
That was your secret aim, though, wasn't it, the aim you
hadn't the guts to admit to, that you would reach the Pole
before him after all? But if you don't get there first, even
if you haven't admitted what the race really involved,
have you the inner strength to go on if you get to the Pole
and see that you've lost?

His stomach improved during the night.

The next day the dogs were to go back to the base camp.
He told Meares. Being a civilian, Meares felt he had the
right to protest loudly and heatedly: 'It's obvious, sir,
that the dogs can still be very useful—maybe they could
even hold out as far as the Pole. Are we out to beat Amundsen or aren't we?'

'My plan, my dear Meares, is to use the dogs for other
expeditions during our second overwintering. So they must
be sent back from here. Thank you for all your help. You
will return with Demetri today.' Not another word. But his
stomach was bad again.

Slowly they made their way up the slope to the plateau.
The men hauled their own sledges and often had to work
together, eight to each sledge, which meant they had to
leave one sledge and return to fetch the next, making the

route twice as long. Scott experimented one day to see whether it was more effective to joke with the men or whether he should keep quiet, turning an impassive face to everyone. Did the others find his attempt to transmit his good humour a nuisance? He spent a whole night awake in his sleeping-bag, thinking about it and coming to no very definite conclusion. He would have liked to discuss it with Wilson. When they got back to England—at this stage he probably thought they would; for a moment he folded his hands across his stomach—he wanted to discuss this question thoroughly with Wilson: is one person's attempt to transmit his good humour to another a help or a hindrance?

Outside it was now sunny both day and night, making the tent warm inside. The light flowed over them and there were no dark spots, no point on which to rest the eyes. Far horizons seemed to float above the snow and wilderness. White peaks on which no human foot would ever tread, were outlined against blue sky, causing human thoughts to roam far and wide. Was he right to keep quiet about the composition of the polar party?

He hadn't even chosen the men yet, a fact that troubled him. He found himself shirking his job, which was to haul sledges like the others. He was distracted and fell down a crevasse. He hung in the rope and harness for half an hour, dangling there and telling himself that this had happened before, that he'd doubtless survive this time too. The men fastened the sledges into the snow, anchored each other down and hauled up their leader.

But he still didn't know who to take with him to the Pole.

He assessed them. He knew his own limitations: he wasn't man enough to say: 'I'm just not good enough, so I'm handing over the leadership to you, Evans my friend.' Yet he wondered whether his age, forty-three, didn't disqualify him from taking part in this last great thrust to the

Pole. Would his strength hold out on the way back? Such doubts were humbug, he decided. He had already got himself so far, and he would lead the team which would conquer the Pole, even if he knew his own strength might not measure up to the others'. He hadn't shown himself to be less strong so far, had he?

He had to have Wilson with him. Wilson was his only friend, and the tent was desolate without him. Wilson knew all the answers, could put up with everything, found all the things the others lost, and he could keep his mouth shut even though he was the only one with the right to speak. An hour without a few words with Wilson was an hour lost. So Wilson had to come. He *had* to, even if it turned out that he wasn't as tough as the others.

For the time being, there was no evidence that he was inadequate, was there? He had to have Edgar Evans as well. Evans could solve any practical problem, patch a ski-binding in severe cold, erect a tent that was frozen stiff. Evans could sew a mitten together in the evening, while the others lay in their sleeping-bags. He was the dog and the horse, now that the dogs and horses had been either slaughtered or sent back to winter quarters. So Evans had to come too.

The team was to consist of five men—that left two vacancies. It had often worried Scott, a naval man, that perhaps his branch of the Forces would gain more honour than the other branches. So he wanted to have an army officer with him, too. That was where Oates fitted in. All England's returned officers would be pleased to hear that one of their men from the Indian Army had been included in the assault on the Pole. Oates was as strong as a bear. Scott chose him, but said nothing about it. He had one space left.

That vacancy could go to his second-in-command, Teddy Evans. It was a disadvantage that Evans was a naval officer, as there were already several Navy men in the team. When he assessed the problem he came to the conclusion that he might just as well choose Bowers, also a naval lieutenant. Bowers would walk to the Pole; he hated skis. He sank to knee- and then thigh-level in the snow, despising the use of skis and preferring to continue on foot. Bowers was immortal. Or at least, Scott corrected himself silently, Bowers appeared to be immortal.

Should he take Bowers? He wanted to be included. An anonymous kind of chap—his face didn't stand out in a crowd; his features were rather wintry, as though the snow had etched itself deep into the furrows round his eyes and nose. We see him in retrospect as a dead man in a tent—but he wasn't dead then: he was alive, a half-smile on his face, taciturn, a good friend of Edgar Evans, impersonal, aloof, but always there when help was needed.

But that would leave no place for Edward Evans.

This was Scott's most difficult choice. He said: 'I haven't decided,' and 'It's my right as leader of the expedition to choose the best men, and nothing but the best.' He repeated to himself a number of platitudes to camouflage the truth he was unwilling to see, but he saw through them—he just didn't want to take Teddy Evans with him.

'Remember how Evans can project himself to a crowd. That wide smile, whiter than the Antarctic snow, that deep, slightly staccato voice, that glint in the eyes—all the qualities that made him indispensable when we were collecting money for this trip. Women couldn't resist him. Must he come with me to the Pole? Is he destined to be the conqueror of the Pole, coming back the darling of the journalists? Without being obviously disloyal to me on a single point, he will nevertheless succeed in betraying me on every point. Must he come too? He'll step up the pace on the way to the Pole, always one step ahead, looking back, smiling, my subordinate, who manages to remind me without saying a word that I should be subordinate to him. He was the man who saved the *Terra Nova*. He'll wring every drop out of that episode—and he deserves to: without him we'd be drowned corpses by now, drifting somewhere south of New Zealand. Must he come too? He's capable of reaching the Pole. Perhaps we'd be first if he came too. He would squeeze every last drop from his body to be first man there. He would burst his lungs, risk his sight in the polar light, let his skin grow blotchy in the strong sunlight, allow the storms to slash his face and every limb be frostbitten. Perhaps he'd die on the way back. But can you rely on that? What am I saying...? He may survive. He's not a thief. He doesn't want to steal my glory, but he's the kind of man who gets his just deserts because he is the strongest, the wildest, the most dangerous, the fastest thinker—and perhaps the most vulnerable too, the man who one day must lose everything—but before that happens he'll want to win most. You, on the other hand, have your plans and will stick to them.'

They had struggled up the mountainside towards the plateau now, and the plain lay in front of them, the Pole in the middle of it. They put up the tent. The men had crawled inside. Then he asked them to leave it for a minute.

'Evans, my friend, I'd like a word with you.' The two of them were left alone. Inside, one man was shouting, tearing his hair, throwing himself down on the sleeping-bag and whimpering, leaping up and down, almost forgetting that the other man was a captain in the British Navy and he a lieutenant. There was less than a few feet between them. Both were distraught. Both were right. They couldn't fight. They were subjected to an iron-hard discipline. If Evans hit out, he'd be put under arrest as soon as he returned to England—even if he returned as a hero from the Pole. But now he hadn't the strength to control himself. He spoke in a low voice, spitting specks of saliva into Scott's face. 'Your motives are very dubious....'

He knew how to aim—and how to score a hit. Scott now had two alternatives. He could either reason with the man, patiently explaining the military situation, the superior officer inviting his subordinate to discuss the problem, presenting the argument—including his own pettiness—making a clean breast of it, and finally reminding him of one irrefutable factor: 'I am your superior officer. It is my duty to take that decision, and I've taken it.'

Either that or cut the conversation short, saying briefly: 'You may go now.' One man was sitting hunched up on a sleeping-bag. The other was speechless. Then Edward Evans shook Scott by the hand, got up and crawled out of the tent. The next day, the men who weren't going on to the Pole turned back. It was a painful farewell. Everyone had his own thoughts, but no one said a word about his own troubles. The party turning back helped to push the sledges for half an hour, then they shook hands and wished each other well. Scott said goodbye to Evans last of all. They stood a little apart from the others. It was a lovely day.

'I've always admired you, Evans.'

'Sir, you're the best officer England could wish for.'

Then they parted. But Evans had not forgiven or forgotten his bitterness. He wanted to get back to winter quarters in record time. Even when the fog came, he didn't strike camp, forcing the men to go on. They soon went off course. He drove them into inhuman territory, where there was crevasse upon crevasse and they could hardly find room to erect their tent. They couldn't take a step away from it without risking falling into the depths. Then—in the midst of catastrophe, as when the *Terra Nova* had been about to sink—he scrambled on alone and discovered that the crevasses weren't so deep after all, nor so steep, but more like frozen waves. He climbed over the crest of a wave and hung one arm over a chasm: he had left the men behind, so if he fell now it would be his last fall. He found a way out. Then he fell on his knees and wept.

His strength had been sapped: victory was denied him.

He cursed Scott and scrambled back in his own tracks, letting no one see that he was the loser; the man who more than anyone had deserved to win. He led his men through the crevasses, across chasms and down on to firm ice.

But he got scurvy before they reached winter quarters. His teeth fell out and blood streamed from his nose and mouth. He spasmodically lost his senses, rushing out of the tent and crying that he wanted to go back to Scott. The men had to drag him back into the tent. They held him down while a man set off on skis to their winter quarters in McMurdo Sound. The doctor, Atkinson, came back with him and Evans's life was saved.

Far down south, five men were on their way to the Pole. Their leader was more taciturn than ever. He looked at Wilson now and again and smiled wanly, as if apologizing for something he didn't even wish to mention. Blizzard followed blizzard. They lost hours every day and days every week. They slept little at night.

At this time, when the pressure on Scott was greater and his strength wasn't what it had been when they set out, we notice that there is a warmer, more intense note in what he wrote in his journal. He grew in stature as the danger grew. His words contained a proud grandeur as he began to suspect destruction.

At last they had a few good days, and quickly advanced south. They had passed the point where Shackleton had had to turn back. The terrain was easy now, the going good. Tomorrow or the next day the Pole would be theirs. None of them was snowblind now. But Bowers had the best eyes. 'Sir?' he said, pointing.

AMUNDSEN

VII

Bjaaland was driving ahead, down a gentle slope. The weather was good, misty, almost mild, only twenty below, with light snow coming from the northwest. The dogs weren't practised yet, but with every hour their teamwork improved. They had no one ahead now and the dogs were keeping up a good speed. Amundsen was last, on skis, and had his hands full keeping the party together.

Bjaaland had a natural tendency to veer constantly to the right. They could see his efforts to keep on course. Almost imperceptibly, he would turn the dogs' noses and the tips of his skis slightly to the left so that they wouldn't cheat him by slipping back to the right, but a few minutes later the man behind would shout: 'You're pulling to the right!' It happened time and time again. The going was easy at the moment, as they knew the route from last autumn's depot trip. They knew that greater difficulties lay ahead but they daydreamed that perhaps they could find the perfect way south—over gentle inclines and slanting slopes, between unknown mountains to the Pole. But it was only a fantasy. Then one of the runners on Bjaaland's sledge cut through the snow and the sledge tipped over.

It sank slowly, accompanied by the howling of a dog which was abruptly terminated. Helmer Hanssen, who was

behind Bjaaland, braked rapidly. Bjaaland's sledge sank
even deeper. He slipped out of his skis and, like lightning,
grabbed a dog by its harness and helped it pull, but the
sledge went on sinking. Bjaaland tore off one mitt with his
teeth, then the other, leaving himself bare-handed, with a
better grip on the rope, his feet thrust into the snow and
his powerful body hunched to hold the sledge up. The
dogs dug their claws down into the snow—an instinctively
wise reaction. They understood the situation as well as the
man did; if the sledge slid down, so would they. Bjaaland
had a knife. He could unsheath it, cut the rope and sacrifice sledge and equipment. Then they would have to go
back to Framheim and their whole schedule would fall
apart. Now the leader's attitude, all or nothing, overcame
the skier from Telemark. He would rather go down than
give up being first to the Pole.

Helmer had tipped his sledge over, so that his dogs
couldn't bolt. He put on a spurt and leapt over the
crevasse, only guessing that it was beneath Bjaaland's
sledge. As he leapt, he heard the snow and ice hurtling
down behind him. Now there was a huge black hole to
his left. He landed safely at Bjaaland's feet, grasped the
harness, and the two of them hung on until their vision
swam, but together they slid, foot by foot, towards the
crevasse as the sledge slowly sank down.

They could still see the crates. Now the dogs were howling. Then Amundsen came and spanned the crevasse on
his skis. Suddenly the fog rolled over them. A minute
before, visibility had been good, but now they could see
only the outline of Wisting's team. The crevasse seemed to
be a little narrower to the left. Wisting took the chance that
it was. Or was the fog creating an illusion?—they didn't
know, but clung on to the rope, the dogs hunched in
desperation, their claws in the snow. The men could still
see the crates. Hassel shouted: 'We're in a filthy hole!'
Wisting got his team over the crevasse, his sledge standing

with one end on each side, apparently firm. Swiftly, Hassel grabbed the rope from his sledge and they anchored Wisting's sledge at both ends so that now they had a firm point to work from.

Amundsen again crossed the crevasse on skis. Something rustled beneath him. He got another rope from Hanssen's sledge. They anchored Bjaaland's sledge to Wisting's. Just as they had done so, Bjaaland's sledge sank another foot, the back held by one rope, the front by the dogs and two men. Bjaaland yelled: 'I can't hold on any longer.' Hassel: 'We're in the devil of a mess.'

They got the front of the sledge anchored too, then let the dogs free. Now they had to get their breath back, but the ground was creaking all round them. Bjaaland threw himself down in the snow, lay there for a second, then leapt up and cried: 'We must tether the dogs. There are crevasses everywhere.'

They leapt up and got the dogs tethered, patches of snow hurtling down round them. Amundsen noticed that one of his skis sank into the snow whenever he turned quickly. The sledge was still hanging by ropes, but then it tipped. Wisting and Amundsen lay on their stomachs, one on each side of the crevasse, peering down. As they watched, the crates came loose, dangling now by the ropes alone. The crate of cooking equipment was swinging about under the sledge, the tethers still holding. Hassel moaned: 'We're in a filthy hole.'

They couldn't get the cargo up without letting a man down, so Amundsen had to make a quick decision. They all looked at him. He noticed it. He had their total obedience. Everyone volunteered, before he had even said a word: they knew what he'd say because he had always insisted on all or nothing. If they returned to Framheim for more cooking equipment they'd lose the race. He was prepared to die, even to allow others to die, but he couldn't lose.

So he made the decision. All four were willing to go down. No one asked him to go. One of the others would be more dispensable. He felt a warm glow inside him—and a joy which gave him strength. He noted in a quick flash of intuition that he'd chosen the right men. He said curtly that someone would have to go down to rescue the things. 'I think you're the lightest, Wisting. You'll have to do it without mittens—your hands look hard.' They tied a rope round Wisting's waist, fastened it to Hassel's sledge, two men lay down on the edge of the crevasse, and then they let Wisting down.

He had taken his leather cap off. They asked later why he had done so. 'Perhaps so I could see better,' he answered then; the leather peak obscured the view. Perhaps—or perhaps it was because he wished to go bareheaded into the last great stillness if he didn't return. He dangled down there. The rope cut under his armpits. Hanging like this, he had to get another rope round the cooking crate, tie it, loosen the knots in the rope holding it, steer the crate round himself and the sledge, while the four of them hauled it up, and then he'd be left hanging down there until they could hoist him up again.

There was no bottom visible beneath him; not a sound from the chasm below. The noise of the men breathing and groaning reached him from above; an occasional suppressed oath, a faint grunt from one of the dogs, as if even they knew what was at stake and were helping by keeping quiet. They let the rope down to him again. He fastened it round the next crate.

His hands were stiff. He couldn't remember whether he had lost his cap, as it had become difficult to breathe with the rope squeezing his chest. A lump of ice broke away from the crevasse edge and hit him on the head. He jerked involuntarily away and the rope began to swing. Suddenly —it was a close thing—the crate he was working on started loosening. He was hanging half under it. It began to slip out of its rope. He got a hand into the lashings, slipped the loose rope round it, shouted, half suffocating, 'Pull!'

Hassel's voice from above: 'God, what a mess!'

They got the cases up; they got the sledge up. Then they hauled up Wisting. They noticed that Amundsen was kneeling beside a little dome-shaped hillock of ice and had got the primus going. He was making cocoa—warming to the stomach. The temperature had risen to fifteen below, but the fog had come rolling in too. They could see only what was directly in front of them. The leader's voice rang out: 'Here, drink up now.' Bjaaland sat down on the ice-dome. It collapsed under him. They realized then that all those beautiful little domes of ice the sun had been playing on were hollow inside, and beneath them lay the ultimate great depths. There were thousands of similar domes all round them. The fog became thicker. They realized there were crevasses running from dome to dome, a network of nerves under the skin of the snow.

They drank the cocoa.

They agreed that it would be best to set up the tent right where they were. The dogs were fed and tethered. The men inched forward, poking in front of them with ski-poles, following their own tracks back again. It was difficult to find a safe place for the tent. One peg vanished. They heard it hurtling down below them. They hauled the tent-rope one foot to the left, where they found a firm hold, then crawled inside.

All the dogs began to howl, perhaps because they felt abandoned with the men no longer round them. The fog was now as thick as porridge. Or maybe the dogs were howling because the damp had soaked through their coats and they were beginning to freeze. The men sat close together inside the tent, listening to each other's breathing. Hassel said, by way of explanation: 'We're in a filthy hole.'

'But we're ahead of schedule,' replied Wisting calmly.

Bjaaland: 'We must get out of this hell-hole.'

The four of them slept little. Amundsen stayed awake. He was half-sitting, half-lying, pondering on the sudden realization that the whole tent could hurtle down into the depths at any moment. Surely if it did, it would be best to be asleep? He decided that he could check the equipment to help make the time pass. He carried an inventory in his head. Crate number one contained five thousand three hundred dog biscuits and weighed 50.38 kilos. Crate number two contained a hundred and twelve rations of dog-pemmican, eleven of dried milk, cocoa and biscuits, altogether 80.4 kilos. Haven't you brought the medical equipment? What use was that? We could hardly treat each other on the way to the Pole. A little first-aid kit and the old dentist's tongs—they hadn't been used this winter —those were the things to bring with you. Toothache could finish a man off. We could probably pull a tooth out at a pinch, but we couldn't heal a sick man. You took a razor with you, too, and that was deliberate.

Beard or no beard was a matter of some importance: long beards meant icicles; the snow got into them and everything froze solid. A short beard was best, as it protected the face. Hence the razor.

But no medical equipment.

He felt cheered as he thought about his men. His courage returned and he knew the tent wouldn't sink that night. You picked them: Helmer Julius Hanssen, forty-one; he was with you on the *Gjøa*, a skilled dog-driver, you know what he's worth. Sverre Helge Hassel, thirty-five; he was on the second *Fram* expedition and he had skied round the Ringnes Islands in the Arctic Ocean. He had been in the Arctic before he even met you.

Olav Bjaaland, thirty-seven, one of the best skiers in Norway and in the world, quiet, but never unfriendly. He's a great lad with a fighting spirit—the first in every ski-track and indispensable on this, the longest ski-trip the world had ever seen. Oscar Wisting, forty, naval officer. A new man when he was taken on, but now your closest friend—probably your only friend—a man capable of being a leader, who never actually pushed himself into the rôle—so a man after your own heart, fundamentally sound, heavy-shouldered, not stupid, though perhaps lacking in imagination, not gifted with great spirit; born to be close to you.

Are you thinking about Johansen tonight? Yes, as the other four sleep, each snoring in a different key, dreaming on the ice. You know you've made the right choice. You can't change your nature, can you? Perhaps you can admit that, here in the tent, among the crevasses, the dogs no longer howling. Was that a creaking noise out there? Is this the moment before we all go down? You admit it tonight: there was a man on the team who could compete with you. So you didn't take him. Could you deny your true self? Don't you know better than anyone what you're doing, what you want, what it will cost? You've thought it out down to the last detail, haven't you? A thousand times you had to choose between different alternatives— and you know you made the right choice. Only a real stroke of bad luck can snatch your victory from you now. You had to take Johansen with you from Norway because Nansen insisted. Do you already anticipate a day of reckoning between Johansen and yourself? You made the right decision. If he'd come too there would have been suppressed defiance, silent criticism, a man who ate like a maggot into your self-esteem, your apparently superior assurance. Then you would have lost your self-confidence. You wouldn't have been completely justified in feeling yourself a leader. You might have made a wrong decision today.

Are we sinking now? If we are, we won't be in a position to hear the criticism; we'll die far away from the glory. But as we go down, it would be nice to know that the world would acclaim us, silent courageous men, under their immortal leader—who met death on the greatest ski-trip the world had ever seen.

They didn't sink. The next day they found a way out of the filthy hole.

They had to kill the first of the dogs—Jala. She was pregnant and couldn't carry on with them. They had built snow cairns on the way south to make the return trip easier. So they stacked her pups, eight of them, dead before birth, on top of one of the cairns. They would provide food for the rest of the dogs on the way home. Their mother lay alongside them.

But as they moved south, one man sobbed; just which man was never established. They were moving inside a blanket of fog. They might be explorers, but they didn't explore each other's weaknesses. A dog turned in its traces and howled. It was lashed.

Onwards to the south.

Had anyone heard the stillness? There was no point in talking about it. To talk about stillness, where everything was stillness, would have been like pointing it out, enticing it closer, making it into a creature that would eat its way into you, become part of you, making you look back when you crawled out of the tent and left the others in there—you were alone in the stillness and you knew you would die here.

Don't talk about the stillness.

The next day, three dogs broke loose and ran back along their own tracks. They had probably been Jala's lovers. Now the male dogs wanted to find her again. They would probably find her ... and then they would eat her and her puppies. Onwards to the south.

The fog lifted. Then—it was a breathtaking sight—two great birds came flying from the north, cruising above them, continuing on south as if hoping to reach the Pole before them. Perhaps they were crossing the continent.

The fog rolled in again, as thick as soup, but they made good progress, thirty kilometres a day. The dogs were now on top form, but they would soon grow thinner and weaker, and then the day would come when they would have to be whipped on.

They themselves would still have enough food, but they knew that they too would get weaker as the going got tougher—then it would be a matter of willpower; then they'd see whether they were destined to reach the Pole or not.

The fog thinned and one morning the sky was high, clear and blue. Then they saw the mountains, huge and distant, yet so close in this strange clear air. They had to cross those mountains: behind them was the Pole. They stopped and looked. Yes, behind there was the Pole.

Never had they seen such high mountains, never such huge, such craggy ones, with caps of ice on which the sun was burning, a glittering sky above.

They carried on south.

They hadn't known the mountains would be so *solid*. Up to now, most of the journey had been across flat ice; they'd wriggled round ice hummocks, scrambled across crevasses, smiling at each other to gain courage as they looked down at death. They had crossed the immeasurable cap of ice which enclosed the Antarctic, with its secrets and storms that no man could face without a sense of desolation. But this was the actual mainland—until now unseen except by Shackleton and his few brave men; mountains without names or faces, cold and unexplored, with steep precipices shining blue-black in the sun, rocky outcrops where the snow had been unable to stick. Mountains in the moonlight—like queens as they shyly disrobe, wild in their loveliness, inconceivable to the human mind, inaccessible to the human foot. But that was where they were to go.

They had not imagined they'd be so *solid*. They had

covered all those miles in good weather, watery sunlight through thin clouds. Now the mountains lay brooding ahead of them. One or two of them seemed to sneeze in indignation at the sight of the intruders, throwing huge avalanches down the mountainside, sending boulders and chunks of ice scattering down. The massiveness of the mountains weighed on a man's chest, clamping him down, fastening him to the ground, making wonder and fear trickle from the corners of his eyes, so that each of the five men looked away rather than face each other. These were the ruthless, powerful, unconquerable mountains of the Antarctic.

That was where they were going. But don't talk about it now. You have come through fog, among bottomless crevasses. It was all a bit of a joke ... though it could prove a fatal one ... you'd probably use up your strength; you had wriggled between victory and defeat. But there had been a touch of innocence about it all. Now you had to climb up there. Don't mention it to anyone. Not even to the dogs—they often lay down and stared up there, then turned their heads with questioning eyes towards their driver. Don't voice your fears. Don't let the problem weigh you down before you begin. Put up the tent.

Your last night on the Ice Barrier—if God willed it and fortune was with you—before the return journey. Have you doffed your cap to the Pole in reverence, and would you—the thought was painful—perhaps not be the first there after all? Would you come back if that were the case? He *knew*—and so did the others, probably—that if they reached the Pole and found another flag there, they would have no desire to come back alive. But don't go out of the tent and look up at the mountains.

They are waiting for you in the moonlight, swelling in the ghostly light that runs from their snow-white sides down to here. Don't talk about them! It's as if the mountains were lying on top of your sleeping-bag and pressing on your heart. You know how to drive a dog, how to ski, how to wend your way between crevasses. But can you find your way through mountain passes, pass upon pass, bottomless abysses—find the way there, as well as the way back?

They gave the mountains names. It gave him a marvellous sense of power to be able to point out a mountain and say: 'We'll call that one Mount Nansen.' The other four in the party didn't share their leader's sensitivity and had no inkling of the underlying currents that were making him happy and proud, even giving him an inexplicable feeling of revenge. Revenge on whom? And why? Mount Nansen was inaccessible. Perhaps it wasn't quite the right name for that particular mountain. For shouldn't you climb up there—never mind the sweat, even if it takes a day to do it—just to say you'd stood on the top and thought; 'This is Fridtjof Nansen's mountain. I found it. I named it. I'm standing on the summit of it.'

But the mountain was inaccessible. Amundsen generously dispensed names to the others. Each and every one who had given money to the expedition had a mountain in the Antarctic named after him. He scratched with strange spelling and firm handwriting on to a piece of paper. The four men he had with him also had the mountain tops round about named after them. They didn't attempt to conceal their pride. They had all the human failings, as well as man's uncontrollable delight in climbing mountains.

Now they had to find their way through a narrow pass, turn and find other ways, climb screes, slide down again, knowing that half the day had been wasted. But despondency wasn't allowed to get a grip on them. God and the weather both showed mercy as they crossed the mountains to the south. There was a slightly misty sun above them, which stung their skin but didn't scorch their faces. No fog. No blizzards. They came to a chasm of immeasurable depth. Over it stretched a bridge of snow—narrow but strong, which might bear two men at a time, and if they were lucky, the dogs could get across it too. They just might escape with their lives. They had to choose. *He* had to choose. They might well hurtle down and disappear for ever—one man or all of them, but if it worked, it worked and they'd have saved time. Or they could make a detour through other mountains, perhaps finding the way barred by more precipices, more screes and overhangs, which no dog-driver could force. It might take days. Weeks of delay might be the result. One man went over the bridge.

Olav Bjaaland didn't feel giddy, but a nerve quivered a little in the back of his head and in his thigh muscles; he was not a romantic, so he didn't wave his cap when he was across; on the contrary, he had put crampons on his boots so as not to slip, and now he bent down and tightened one of the straps. But the bridge held. He returned.

It might be several hundred metres down into that gaping chasm on one side, where the light seeped down. It was an interesting sight, as Bjaaland said nonchalantly, but only later, when he was at a safe distance from the abyss. Two men were sent over next—Hassel and Hanssen.

Hassel stopped and jumped on the bridge. It held.

There were three mountain peaks up here, two on one side and one on the other. A little wisp of cloud was floating up there, and then the stillness, the stillness which could drive a man insane. Only the sound of Hassel jumping. The bridge held.

So they unhitched the dogs and the men all pulled. The sledges weighed four hundred kilos each, so they pulled slowly, two by two over first, dividing the weight. At one place the bridge creaked under them, but it held, and they got the sledge over on to firm ground. After that they hauled the other sledge across. Then came the rest of the sledges, and finally the dogs, who were clever enough to know that it was foolish to hasten over a bridge with no rail, flanked by precipices and with edges which were so slippery that they had to dig their claws in. All of them got over safely.

Then one of the team—no matter which—was overcome by giddiness. He threw himself down in the snow, everything swirling round his head. The leader, who had thought of everything and had heard about these giddy attacks from the experiences of mountaineers, went over to the man and talked calmly to him. 'There, it's nothing to worry about. It'll soon be over. Don't take it as anything more than it is. Anyone can have an attack of giddiness. Be thankful it didn't happen sooner. *I* didn't feel too good coming over the bridge either.'

The others had turned away by this time. No one had suspected Amundsen of having that particular skill. He could calm a man down, joke with him, play the gentle mother when a tough, adult man lay in the snow biting his mitten—crushed by the mountains and by fear, while something indefinable buzzed in his head and he wished he were back in the green fields he had once known.

They had to go on.

As they sweated up the slopes, the dogs were thrashed and the men began to be ravaged by thirst. Their bodies had lost so much liquid and had been given so little back. Some swallowed cocoa, a little tea, a mouthful or two of water melted from snow, but there was no great torrent of water. Now, as their bodies screamed for moisture, they began to indulge in fantasies about water. They sucked pieces of ice. That helped a little, but it was no more than sticking your tongue out and licking a little coldness, a few drops which cheered you up momentarily. As they were getting their breath back on the ascents, they talked about water, about the streams at home, about deep draughts of cold water, simply pouring it down, putting your head back and ... then one of them shouted furiously: 'Can't you shut up! Must you drive me mad with all this talk of water!' All the dogs had their tongues hanging out; they ate snow, they circled around sniffing for something to drink but finding nothing. The dogs had grown thin. They were eating everything in sight by now; a ski-binding vanished down a voracious throat; the dogs gobbled up their own excrement. The men noticed that as the thirst afflicted them, their thoughts became more basic, and they grew more brutal, angrier, coarser in their language, no longer moving some distance away from the tent when they pulled down their trousers and did what had to be done. They took a few steps to one side and didn't care who saw them.

They dreamed about water.

They couldn't sleep at night for their watery thoughts.

They sought out passes and crossings, they found them or thought they had found them, they slipped on the steep slopes, wound ropes round the sledge-runners to prevent them from sliding downwards, and then suddenly they could slake their thirst. They found a mountain which was sufficiently accessible for them to climb up to the snow-free stony scree and stand on bare ground ... it was so long since they ... it felt so strange. They took off their mittens and felt the rock. It was as hard as at home in Norway. They would take home a few stones from here. If they got home—if these mountains let them through and they found their way back alive. They laid the rocks in a depot. They had no need to take them to the Pole. One man said: 'If someone's got there before us....'

One anxiety afflicted them all; what happens if we get there at the same time? Do we greet the others politely and have a chat? Take a cup of cocoa together? Is that what we'd do? Or would we do something else?

Man against man, stick against stick, sort it out and let the snow cover the tracks? Wouldn't we be justified in keeping the victory to ourselves now we've got this far?

But they knew these were the fantasies of thirsty men and nothing more. They hurried on. They surmounted the last mountain and saw the landscape spreading out before them. It was the beginning of the great wide plain to the south. Shackleton had seen this and had had to turn back. They had known that if they reached this spot, victory would be within their grasp. Now they were here. It was a moment they had not mentioned until now. It had been easier to talk about it at Framheim ... while it was still a long way in the future. There the dogs had been out in the snow, keeping the men awake with their eternal fights. But now the men had toiled over the Barrier and up the mountainsides together with the dogs, lashing wildly out at them, patting them the next moment, and almost imperceptibly they had picked out the strongest, noted the weakest, knowing that the latter would have to go first. Though the weakest might be the ones they'd got most work out of.

We whipped them, didn't we? We yelled and cursed, we devised new ways of punishing them. We wept together in driving blizzards, we froze together when the temperature dropped, we rolled round in the snow with bare hands fixing the traces on to a reluctant dog, but we were pleased with them, all the same.

Now twenty-four of the dogs had to die, and after that, they had to eat the meat. The rest of them will go with us to the Pole, to be worn down and worn out, some slaughtered on the way back. According to the plan, twelve dogs will return with us to Framheim. But here twenty-four are to die.

There was a steep mountain to the right, a rocky scree where there were constant small avalanches, the sounds sharp, like blows from a clenched fist on their eardrums. The dogs had toiled bravely all day, and it was as if they knew that the day was coming to an end—they hastened towards it, gathering their strength and putting their last ounce of energy into it.

Put up the tent here on the edge of a precipice.

No rash step to one side. Don't let your thirst get you down this evening. That would be ignoble. You have to live with your thirst: they have to die with theirs.

Amundsen went into the tent. He couldn't face this. If he chose to go into the tent, it was his right as leader. They understood and respected the fact that he was showing them his weakness, his humility at this moment. He lit the primus and it hissed sharply. Then the first shot went off.

He had something in his eye and rubbed it out. You're going to the Pole, aren't you? This is part of the price. Another shot. The very thought gripped his heart and squeezed—was Hjalmar doing the shooting this evening? Shot after shot, and the rest of the dogs huddled together, whimpering. Then they had to tear the entrails out.

What happened next was revolting; they didn't like talking about it, even later. The acrid, suffocating smell of warm blood, intestines, liver and lungs. A pack of dogs screaming with hunger, suffering from their toils, scrambling for something to eat, dogs which were nevertheless held back by some primitive emotion they didn't understand, squeezed there between the precipice and the mountain, tethered by chains, but still free enough to hurl themselves on to the food.

But they didn't do it.

One man vomited. Another cried out for water.

Then the first dog leapt forward, then the others, suddenly all of them revelling in the food with bloody jaws, thrusting their muzzles into the meat, eating and swelling, rolling in the blood and snow, with no energy for fighting —there was enough food for them all.

But a man vomited.

Moonlight over the mountain peaks which now rose

behind them, stillness creeping up on tiptoe, circling round inside the tent, stealing every word from their mouths and robbing them of speech this evening.

Cutlets, cooked on the primus; time to eat.

Help yourselves.

They chewed in silence.

One man said in a low voice: 'I'm so thirsty. If only we had a little water.'

They called the place The Butcher's Shop. They didn't want to stay there long. A smell of blood hung in the air; gorged dogs lurched around, gobbling entrails, intestines hanging from their jaws; men woke with the taste of dog in their mouths, then went out of the tent to spew. They broke camp. Suddenly a blizzard was over them, but they couldn't face erecting the tent again. They had to get away. Moisture had stiffened the canvas, so they had to roll it up with the greatest care to avoid splitting it. The dogs wanted to get away too, and bolted when they were put in harness. They were going downhill now, but hadn't got the ropes fastened to the runners. Bjaaland went ahead and vanished. They heard him shouting. He and the dogs were hanging in the rope—across something which could have been a chasm, or just a shallow hollow, how could they know? They couldn't see the bottom. The blizzard was blowing from the north. They had to haul the dogs up, then the man. They continued.

The blizzard was coming at them from the right: that became apparent when evening fell and they struck camp. The wind and the snow had eaten away the skin on their right cheeks. The skin had been half eroded before, by cold and wind. Now it vanished altogether. Everyone had his right cheek flayed free of skin, bare, raw flesh exposed to the wind, pus oozing out of it. They forced themselves on, step by step, steering by compass, occasionally disappearing into steep hollows, entangling themselves round blocks of ice, hour after hour, dripping with sweat and freezing in the bitter wind.

The blizzard lasted three days. For three days they forced themselves to leave the tent each morning, get the dogs into harness, urging them to move; for three days they tramped onwards, step by step towards the Pole. They said: 'It was better to get away from The Butcher's Shop.' But now that wasn't the only reason that they defied the blizzard. They were getting closer. Up till now, they had been able to brush aside the last great excitement—it was still days and weeks away—we couldn't meet anyone ... not yet. We won't have any evidence for a long time ... it's just a matter of going on ... for the time being. But now they knew that at any moment they might catch sight of alien sledge-tracks in the snow, or footmarks from men who had walked here before them, perhaps only a few hours earlier. And then...?

They concealed their thoughts, but their very silence betrayed them, as did their bitter, scornful, harsh, sour way of answering when anyone spoke. Man followed man; the dogs suspected something was up. They had learnt on this trip to listen to men's voices and knew when they could take liberties, and when it was dangerous to risk the whiplash. These days it was dangerous. But they went on south. Mountain terrain had changed now to open plain, inclining slightly towards the Pole, but the going had become as sticky as tar. A peculiar, hard, tough snow took all the slide from their skis and runners, forcing them to tramp on, helping the dogs to pull. And then the insuffer-able tension—what would they see when the fog lifted? Patches of fog came and went, drifting away in great wisps, revealing the wilderness to the south, then rolling back again. Not a track to be seen, no alien smells noted by the dogs.

Amundsen was silent: his men knew him now. He could act the good angel—perhaps overdoing it; he could help

anyone who needed a helping hand. He wasn't too grand
for the dirtiest work. He wouldn't spare himself, whatever
happened. But they had learnt to read the signs. He over-
did the omniscient, understanding leader when he was
heading for a spell of bad temper. Slowly he stiffened like
a block of ice, and after the period of amicability came
the day he refused to answer when anyone spoke to him.
And when they didn't speak to him, he might ask bitingly:
'Why don't you talk? What plots are you hatching now?'
Plots—thus were his most deep-rooted suspicions revealed.
Perhaps, now they were getting closer and he had deceived
the world, staked his life, both his own and theirs—perhaps the thought occurred to him that the others were
plotting against him. Perhaps they'd let him slip down
into a crevasse, leaving him shouting down there while
they danced on the edge, grinning mockingly, getting the
little brandy bottle out, the only one they had with them,
drinking to victory, going back to life and stealing his
triumph? His nerve broke ... he went off. . . .

Was that what was in his mind? Was he wondering
whether one of the men had slipped a note to Scott's men
when they had been guests at Framheim? Just a short
note: Our leader is insane. We won't get to the Pole.
We're doomed to lose. . . .

He didn't really believe it. He knew it wasn't like that.
But in the nightmare of uncertainty, aggravated by his
physical condition—emaciated, scabs on his right cheek,
hands trembling slightly as he raised his cup of hot cocoa
in the tent in the evenings, his shaky handwriting revealing signs of cold and exhaustion—in that situation he
might look at his companions and think they had secret
plans to stick a knife in his back.

No, no, I know I can rely on each and every one of them,
but at night I leap up and go out of the tent, at thirty
degrees below, in my underclothes ... no, not in my underclothes; none of us takes his clothes off; we get dressed to

crawl into our sleeping-bags. I smell of filth. No, filth freezes
solid, sweat freezes, crusts of filth freeze, but they thaw
from your body-warmth. I just don't feel it. I get sores on
my body from chafing woollen underclothes which are stiff
with stale sweat. Leap up and go out. Moonlight over the
wilderness towards the Pole.

In the stillness, a dog comes sniffing at me, wagging its
tail. I can hear it breathing, hear the stillness, mile after
mile of stillness. No sign of Scott's tracks...? No sound of
human breathing to the south?

You deceived the entire world. If you go home as victor,
will the verdict be that you deceived the world?

He stood trembling, not wishing to be seen. Were the
others in the tent awake? Were they lying there wondering
about him, putting their heads together, making plans he
wasn't allowed to share? He didn't even know what they
had in their private packs. He had said: 'Take what you
like with you, provided it doesn't weigh more than three
kilos.' But he should have demanded to see, shouldn't he?
They had secrets, had they? He crawled into the tent and
routed them out in his mind.

The primus hissed. A cup of hot soup, a pemmican
ration for each of the dogs—and then off.

On that day they got farther south than any other human
being had ever been before. Shackleton had got this far.
No one had been any farther. This was their official standpoint: they were duty-bound to believe it. Once that belief
had gone, chaos would ensue. But what if someone else
had got here first—we don't know yet, do we? Perhaps
it was many kilometres ahead, perhaps only five hundred
metres. But the blizzard had covered up their tracks. They
raised the flag. They stood to attention. Then they went
on, urging on the dogs, the wilderness white and wide. One
of the dogs began to sniff to the south. For days and weeks
the dogs had sniffed towards both north and south, and the
men had simply paid no attention. Now Amundsen flew

into a rage. He couldn't control it, screaming at the dog. He hadn't got a whip, nor could he reach it with his ski-pole, but he almost threw himself on the animal and stamped on it. The dogs went on sniffing to the south.

Several other dogs did the same. The men exchanged glances. The leader had hidden his face in a scarf. One of the others hiccoughed. It was Bjaaland. He went over to the dog that had been sniffing, scratched it behind its ear and said quietly: 'Don't do that ... don't do that ... otherwise I'll kill you!' he bellowed.

They had wheels on each sledge which measured the distance they'd travelled. They had calculated over and over again, and they knew the time would come about three o'clock.

The leader shouted.

They were at the Pole.

There was no one there, nothing there but stillness—not a track, not a cairn, not a tent.

He should have laughed or cried, or jumped about waving his arms. The others, bursting with anxiety, should have done the same. But they did nothing. They just clasped each other warmly by the hand. They flapped their arms. They said that was a good job well done. But they didn't dance. They put up the tent. They fed the dogs, and lit the primus. Now they were men on their travels once more. They had their duties. They had reached their goal and used few words.

But he knew what he wanted. He sent three men out in three directions, one to the north, one to the east, one to the west—Bjaaland, Hassel and Wisting. They went on skis and took no equipment with them. Twenty kilometres out, they turned and skied the twenty kilometres back. If a blizzard came, they'd have no tracks to follow. They had no tent, they had no sleeping-bags ... they knew they were risking their lives but they didn't even bother to raise a hand in farewell as they left.

Small dots that disappeared into the grey mist, white wastelands without end, nothing to fix the eye on. Each had a compass. They set off . . . and they returned.

Now no one could say they hadn't reached the Pole, and just as well! They took observations every hour to get the point of the Pole fixed as mathematically accurately as possible. They put up a little tent on the actual spot. Inside it, Amundsen placed a letter.

This was a diabolical triumph, a brilliant way of celebrating his victory. The letter was to Scott. He requested Captain Scott, who would no doubt be the next man there, he wrote, to take the letter back to King Haakon of Norway. So much could happen on their journey back.

May all go well for you!

This was the victor's wily greeting to the man who was now doomed to failure, exquisitely formulated, irreproachable in that it involved the King, the surprising little twist in the moment of victory which would find its place in all subsequent accounts of the journey. But something gnawed at him. What are we hanging around here for? They had to set about going back.

They had a good journey back to Framheim.

SCOTT

Bowers had good eyesight. He was shading his eyes with
one hand and staring. 'Sir?' he said. All night there had
been a boyish, subdued excitement in the tent, and conse-
quently no one had had much sleep. The leader had felt
compelled to calm them down, like a teacher in a class of
small boys, but the excitement was infectious. He had
joked with Edgar Evans about who would win if the two
of them put on their skis and raced to the Pole. That day
they had been rushing south. The weather had been misty,
occasional fog in the north, a bitter, sour wind, but at least
it was behind them.

Tension lay like a lump on their chests, a dormant cancer
liable to dissolve at any moment into wild, uncontrollable
joy, or to swell into a malignancy—as now. Bowers remained standing for a long time, staring into the distance.
The others stared too, but there was nothing to see.

'Only a shadow,' he said.

But they began to hate Bowers, throwing sour looks at
him, though he was more than willing to admit he was
wrong at the slightest sign. The shadow he thought he had
seen lay slightly to the east of their course. Imperceptibly,
they headed towards it. Evans felt the tips of his fingers
tingling.

He had been careless with his mittens lately, tearing them off, holding them in his mouth as he fixed ski-bindings and tent-ropes with his bare hands. Now his fingers were tingling.

Bowers stopped abruptly, pointed again, saying in a deep gruff voice: 'Look, sir.' They gathered round him and then the others saw what he had seen. It *could* have been a shadow and for one more minute they believed it was. If the sun had been out, there would have been a thousand opportunities for dark shadows across the snow. But wasn't the shadow fluttering...? Wasn't it on a pole?

It was a flag, put up by human hands. Suddenly, hand clasping his stomach, heaving, choking, a man left the group and vomited. It was Evans.

Scott's voice, sharply: 'We'll go on over there.' Emotion flooded him, disorderly and unworthy, not the reasoned reaction he had always adhered to. Now it all poured out: We've lost. What will they say at home? They'll make us pay for being last. How will we make it back to winter quarters? Could it be something else ... but what? It is a flag; and it must be Amundsen's. If only I had him here, I'd take off my cap and greet him politely ... before sticking a knife into his heart. He cheated me. He isn't here ... or is he? Dear God, now we'll never get home. What the hell are we doing here anyway?

Evans is behaving so oddly. I should have stopped him going about barehanded so much. He was only showing off in front of the others.

There's the flag.

Scott had known it for a long time, felt it in his gut, deep down inside like a festering sore, the knowledge that it would end like this. Hadn't I seen it in the others' faces, their fear, their false hope; didn't I say to myself in the tent at night, You *could* be first, but you know you won't be, don't you? You prepared yourself for defeat, you steeled yourself for defeat. But you didn't fight hard enough to avoid it. My second-in-command, Ted Evans, had another plan, didn't he? And I sent him back. There's the flag.

They had stopped in a silent circle round it. A black flag on a high pole. Ski-tracks all round, dog-tracks, sledge tracks pointing in a southerly direction. No snow had fallen since the Norwegians had been here. There were yellow patches from the dogs, and another patch where a man had relieved himself before leaving. Again Evans vomited. Under different circumstances he would have choked it back, so to speak, swallowing, forcing himself under control when the leader had shouted. Now he turned to Scott, his mouth open, grinning, lifting his hand, grimacing, spewing again and weeping. They had lost. They weren't men to waste words. The leader said it was time to put the tent up.

But they didn't want to spend the night there. Not so close to that black flag, not among the tracks of the other men and their dogs. They continued for a kilometre or so and then erected the tent.

It was heavy going that day. They were men of few words. Evans had sat down on the sledge, appearing not to hear when spoken to. According to the plan, they were to have had a celebration meal when they reached the Pole. Scott gave orders that it should be served anyway. They used extra paraffin—tea and pemmican, double rations of cocoa.

A dull, animal contentment settled over them as they sat huddled together in the tent, feeling that their stomachs once again had something to work on. Their thoughts clarified. They could begin to arrange things in their minds. So it had happened. But they could forget it. They were here now. They sat in their sleeping-bags. They weren't cold. They ate. They felt good for the moment. But they didn't talk to each other.

Scott wrote his diary as night fell. He knew the others were still awake. His handwriting was clear and strong still, and tonight he tried to give it an extra stroke of dignity. His words were subdued, but vibrated with suppressed pain. He forced his troubles under control.

When daylight came, they would measure the height of the sun. This was Bowers's thankless task, but suddenly he cried: 'What's the point? We know where we are, don't we?' Normally he was an officer who behaved impeccably towards superiors and subordinates alike. He knew his duty. It was a brief outburst. He seemed to turn and crawl back, retreating into the shell of his own dignity. Scott had noticed the outburst.

When Bowers pointed in the direction he thought the Pole must be, they caught sight of a tent. They walked slowly over to it. It was a small, elegant, impudent tent, held up by a single pole. It had a Norwegian flag on top. Scott crawled in first. He found a name-plate with five names on it. He read them slowly. Something ground to a halt inside him. It wasn't so much that he knew the glory wouldn't be his. It was something rising in his throat; he saw the crowds in his mind's eye, but they weren't acclaiming him—and the newspaper headlines didn't carry his name. He struck his head against the tentpole. Worse than the fact that he had lost was the thought that he *could* have won. Was this an inherent failing in his character? He should have planned the journey in a way that would have *made* him first, shouldn't he? Was he morally in the wrong, as well as having failed the physical struggle? Five names. Read them slowly. There was a little bag at the foot of the tentpole, and he opened it. Two letters—one from Amundsen to Scott. When he read it, he had to clench his teeth. 'Would you be kind enough to take this letter to His Majesty, King Haakon of Norway?' Then Scott swore aloud. This was sheer mockery. He'd been appointed postman. They were at the Pole, weren't they? They realized that it would all be in the papers, that the loser had brought back a letter from the winner of the Pole, a letter to the King of Norway. A loyal officer couldn't avoid complying. He had to click his heels here in the cold and snow and declare to God and man that he would take the letter with him.

Amundsen had known this. He'd been shameless. Scott cursed, dismissing someone who was trying to crawl in. Even his close friend, Wilson, wasn't welcome here. He didn't want to leave, he didn't want to stay. He took the bag and scrambled out through the narrow opening, noticing the way the tent flap closed, annoyed that it was fixed in such a simple, easy way.

So they had reached the Pole. The leader forced himself to keep calm. The others sensibly stayed away from him. Everyone was sensible and steered clear of each other. They scattered. They did what they had to do—or they did nothing, just stared at the snowdrifts and swirling fog patches, held their gloved hands in front of their faces and thought about their families back home—would they ever get back? Were they at the Pole?

Oates was a millionaire, a hero from the Boer War. He had given money to the expedition, seeking adventure. He had defied the cold, completed his task, knowing he was at home here among these tough, almost indestructible men who had reached the Pole. But he would have liked to get there first. Wilson picked up a handful of snow and took it over to Scott. 'Look at this,' he said. 'I see the consistency of the snow is different here on the plateau from that down on the barrier.' A gentle reminder to the leader —*this* is why we are here. First or last, what does it matter? We came to observe and to examine. Our assignment is of a scientific nature. But the wise Wilson understood Scott. He also recognized his own underlying ambition, silent, discreet, barely noticeable. He analysed it here at the Pole and wondered whether the disappointment he felt would reduce his stamina on the return trip, which they had to embark upon right away. And what about the others?

What about Evans? Something had happened there, hadn't it? But what? Blisters had suddenly appeared on Evans's frostbitten hands and couldn't be explained away. He had difficulty holding his ski-sticks. His feet seemed to be getting worse. Most sinister of all was that the appearance of the blisters came at this particular moment—as if a mental force (or lack of it) had made the physical injuries manifest themselves just when they would do most damage. They put up their own flag at the Pole. Then they turned the sledge and left the spot—the least hospitable place on the map. To them, only five men had been there.

Now it was a matter of returning successfully. They had to reckon with over forty travelling days back to winter quarters. Scott gave orders for double rations that evening. The order was given when they started out in the morning as an incentive. Their creeping, nagging despondency was to be whipped under control with the help of a little frozen fat. He saw the problem clearly. The human animal would plod northwards in the hope of being able to put a lump of fat in his mouth at the end of the day. That said something: exhausted muscles, empty stomachs, open mouths, burned faces—which would flare up bright-eyed at the sight of a half-thawed piece of fat.

The wind was behind them. They hoisted a sail on the sledge and followed the slope. They made good progress. If only Evans had been capable of keeping up with them. But he slowed them down, sometimes deliberately it seemed—though the blisters on his hands had to take some of the blame. He had trouble holding on to his ski-poles and was limping a bit too. He'd also undergone a metamorphosis, spurning the others, bitterly turning his back on them.

They heard him mumble. A touch of unpleasantness entered the atmosphere, a hierarchical atmosphere, true, but that had always suited both parties best, a friendly, half-cheerful tone, an acknowledged inequality which had relaxed both sides. Now that was gone.

Evans is supposed to have said: 'Will I get my money?'

He probably meant to ask whether Scott would be in a position to pay what he owed them when they got back to London. *When* they got back, or *if* they got back? But the money wasn't what troubled Evans most. He had broken away and was no longer one of the party. He didn't do his assigned tasks. Scott spoke to him. As was his habit on board ship—it was the same here except that the sea was frozen—he took Evans aside and reprimanded him sharply, keeping the incident between the two of them. He let him know that this was the first warning, and that there might be more. There would inevitably be more. Evans simply wasn't pulling his weight. He lagged behind as they hastened northwards, their backs to the wind. They moved away from him, then had to wait while he caught up, and thus lost time.

In the tent that evening, Scott delivered a public reprimand, the others uncomfortably silent. Evans took it like a beaten dog, without replying, sitting there quite dejected. This would ruin the atmosphere for the rest of the trip. But the leader was the leader. The next day, Evans was still lagging behind. That evening he showed them his foot. It was horrible. Two toe nails were so loose they could be pulled out. An unpleasant thought struck Scott—we may have to leave him behind. But I couldn't do that, could I? Perhaps a tougher man would have been able to.

Evans said: 'You might have to leave me behind.'

He grimaced. The words had been spoken and violently opposed, but now the problem had been raised it oppressed them completely. If it became necessary ... or if they knew they ought to, but couldn't ... in either case, it was an added burden.

It was the end of the slope, the following wind and the

good speed to the north. Wilson fell and pulled a muscle. He limped and wasn't much use pulling a sledge. Then both Scott and Evans fell down a crevasse, not a deep one, but Scott struck his shoulder awkwardly and Evans hit his head. Both lay dazed for a moment, then Scott crawled up and put the sledge rope over his shoulder. 'We must go on,' he said. He grimaced; it hurt abominably. That evening his handwriting wasn't as clear as usual.

Evans should have been put in his sleeping-bag and allowed to rest, as he had hit his head quite hard, and was now vomiting. It could even be concussion. He mumbled about their having to leave him, so they hustled him on. He stumbled along, leaning on his ski-poles, the blisters on his hands torturing him. Scott fell once or twice. Wilson was limping after his fall the previous day. Bowers and Oates did most of the work alone.

'Double rations this evening,' said Scott.

But the food was scarce. Now they were among murderous crevasses. They trudged on, poking, scrambling across, losing the tracks from their trip south. Losing their heads, too. They didn't know if the depot should be here, or to the east or to the west. They found it the next day, by which time they had only enough rations left for one meal.

The moment they saw the cairn at the depot, they also caught a glimpse of the mountains in the north which had to be crossed again. It was a glimpse of hope. But at the depot, a day's ration of biscuits was missing. It was incomprehensible, and Bowers lost his head. The cool Wilson, always a careful observer, although so humane, told Scott quietly when they had crawled into their sleeping-bags and Bowers was asleep: 'You see, Scott, he seemed to crack up. I was standing beside him. He lost all control, drooling and raving—you should have heard his language! He stood stamping in the snow, swearing in a way I've never experienced before. It was as if his best friend had betrayed him and mockingly eaten the last biscuit knowing that we would—well, die of starvation.'

'Could that really happen to Bowers?'

'I suppose it could happen to anyone.'

'Who could have taken the biscuits?'

'No one. Faulty counting when we packed the supplies, probably. Or it could have been anyone. Who knows what men will do when they're starving?'

Outside, a blizzard was raging.

They were now on the bare mountain, where the snow hadn't managed to adhere to the precipitous screes. The mountain was devoid of any kind of smell. Everything was frozen, but they crawled on their hands and knees over the bare rock, pulling off their mittens and imagining that they felt warmth. As they relaxed and took half an hour off to chat, two of the men imagined they saw another stick his tongue out and lick the bare rock. They knew he couldn't have done that, as his tongue would have frozen fast, his skin loosened and the man would have been irrevocably linked to the frozen mountain, ten thousand feet above sea level. He would either have lost the tip of his tongue or met his death with his tongue out. But they each felt gripped by a kind of reckless courage, their last free evening before each one headed off on his last journey.

Here comes Wilson, still limping but his face alive with delighted, naked joy. He reckoned he'd found a fossil. He had raved about this before, impressions of plants and animals in the rock down here. It proved ... then he held forth in his gentle, measured voice in the tent one evening on their way south. They hadn't taken notice of what it proved. Now he thought he'd found the evidence. He didn't notice that his hands were bare, his leather jacket open, and that his cap was hanging over one ear, the wind blowing icily from the northwest. He thought he had the evidence. He was carrying it. Today the sun was out over

the Antarctic, wild peaks protruding, black precipices with
avalanches, glaciers glistening blue. Here was Heaven and
Hell—in colours, swirling wind, mortal danger, bare rock,
men in heavy boots, breathing deeply, sitting with their
backsides on snow-free ground and sighing. But it was a
long way from England.

Wilson had come up to the others, gasping with delight.
This was proof! They listened this time. He'd found evidence that plants had once grown here, and perhaps even
animals lived. 'And people?' Evans asked. It was the first
glint of humanity he'd shown for several days. Was he on
the way to recovery? Quick as a flash, Wilson realized that
he couldn't disappoint the man, so threw all scientific
criteria overboard for the moment. 'Yes,' he said with dignity to Evans. 'Human feet once trod here.'

'British feet?' asked Evans.

A quick smile, an apologetic shrug of the shoulders—
perhaps it was before Her Majesty Queen Elizabeth I ...
we don't know. Someone stifled a laugh. Was Evans stupid,
dangerous, or had he simply been transformed into a piti-
ful, half-dead creature before their very eyes? They didn't
know. His face was covered with swellings: one of them,
on his right cheek, was bright red. It looked as if it were
about to burst. Then blood might trickle out. The other
cheek was as white as wax. It looked hard, as if it wouldn't
puncture if they stuck the point of a knife into it. The
swellings half-covered his eyes, so Evans had to tilt his
head backwards to be able to see straight ahead.

Wilson walked round collecting various samples. He
couldn't get enough of them. Scott came. There was fog
again on the horizon and snow to the south. Soon they
would be caught between two extremes of weather—the
worst possible combination—mild from one quarter, cold
from another. In ten minutes, they might be pressed down
by a steadily increasing sheet of ice. They had to go on.
But Wilson wanted to take the stones with him. 'Fourteen

kilos,' said Scott. He remembered that according to a table
he and Wilson had drawn up in winter quarters, there
should be a calculated quantity of supplies at this place.
Weight of sledge, so much. Increased by stones, fourteen
kilos. They had no scales, and began to wrangle. Wilson
wanted to take his evidence. Both of them wanted to. But
how many kilos could they afford? 'You know it may be the
only thing we bring home, don't you?' said Wilson, un-
characteristically cruel to his friend. Harsh words—now
both were losers on their way home—death surrounding
them and the fog closing in from the north.

They loaded the stones on to the sledge.

No one complained about the increased weight. This
salvaged their pride. This was what they were here for.
They were to make the journey and die. One man still
had his strength: Bowers. He was a bit like a horse,
becoming stronger the heavier the load. He was as silent
as a horse. He had no skis. He had walked to the Pole and
now he was walking back.

They came to rough ice and crevasses. The transition
was too abrupt. Suddenly they were upon it and there was
no turning back. They had marked out a course but the
fog had overtaken them. It was as if God couldn't really
make up His mind—was it to be fog, which saturated
everything, or the blizzard, which could hurtle a fully-
loaded sledge with five men down into the abyss? It turned
out to be the latter. They couldn't get the tent up.
They had to go on, but there were crevasses everywhere.
They roped themselves together, and then to the sledge—
they couldn't let themselves be snowed in or they'd freeze
to death. They had to keep moving. But every moment
brought them dangerously close to the crevasses. One man
fell. They knew only that someone had fallen, they didn't
know who as they couldn't distinguish each other in the
swirling snow. They hauled in the rope. They shouted.
They could no longer control their words, and uttered cries

of the last judgment, curses, and brutal, earnest prayers to the Lord. One man let himself down. Two came back up. They were like faint shadows. One voice dominated the others, trying to count the blurred outlines: 'Keep together! Keep together!' They were already tied together. Scott felt something spring to life inside him—the cold economy of words which had always been a characteristic of his. No histrionics; that would weaken respect for the Empire's Navy. He cried to the men, 'Keep together!' They probably didn't know in which direction the others were going. They pulled on their ropes. Then someone laughed aloud, harshly and coarsely. Who was laughing—Death or Evans, a man on his knees in the snow, laughing loudly and stridently, gusts of wind hurtling down from the mountainsides? They were being forced into crevasses of unimaginable depths. Steer away from them. The tent on the sledge must have come loose at one end. If it were whipped away from them, death would be certain. Two men fell on to it, holding it down with their weight. Two others sat on the prostrate men, but then they heard a voice, a man calling for his mother. Was it Evans? Or was it someone else who had cracked for a second, and who later took comfort from everyone else's ignorance of who had cried out. They went on.

One of them went out of his mind. He clung to someone else's clothes and struck him on the back of the neck. He screamed: 'Stones! Stones!' A third man tried to separate them. They wrangled. No one knows who the two were. The blizzard had turned into a whirlwind—or that was how it seemed—and they were in the centre of it. If they could get the tent up, they'd be able to crawl inside, roll into their sleeping-bags, tie up the tops and let themselves be snowed under; die with the last delusion that they were somewhere else....

But they were here ... they struggled on. They could just hear terse cries behind them, stinging them like whip-

lashes. Someone was whipping them into line. He was at
the back urging them on. There must have been fewer
crevasses here, as no one had fallen for a while. The man
behind—whoever it was—shouted at them, cursed them,
cried out to the Almighty, praying that they would hold
out. Or could they hear something else? The Navy's brief,
curt words: 'Go on or be shot.' It took twelve hours before
the storm blew itself out. Scott said: 'We must reduce the
rations.' He should have been in a position to say: 'We'll
increase the rations.' That would have been good medicine
just then, but that would have necessitated their having
sufficient food for such a happy decision. They hadn't.
They had enough for one meal only. Reducing the rations
made it stretch to two.

And so, curtly, mercilessly, when they were already at
their lowest ebb—reduce rations; don't delude yourself.
No one gives up. Reduced rations until we find the depot.
It should be somewhere here, shouldn't it?

They had raised a red flag on a pole to mark the spot,
and now they stood scanning the horizon. False alarm.
'The depot!' False joy, ugly suspicions that the man who'd
cried out hadn't done so in good faith, but in order to
torment them with false hope. The rational part of them
knew it wasn't so, but they believed it all the same—when
you have no resistance, you let your deepest negative
instincts gain the upper hand.

Bowers and his sharp eyes: 'There it is!'

They were saved—for a while at least. They took three
hours to get to the depot and an hour to get the tent up.

They dug out supplies and oil. They lay in their sleeping-bags and struggled with their wet clothes, trying to dry
them with their meagre body-warmth, at the same time
hearing the storm blow up again. Then Scott said: 'Would
it be appropriate to hold a short service now?' But his
hands were too stiff to hold the Bible. He couldn't even
get them into position to pray. His fingers were out of

control. One little finger was sticking out at right-angles
and wouldn't get back into line with the others. He sat for
a while in the grey light and stared at his hands. They
were cut about by the storm and the snow, the wind and
the cold; covered in blisters, sores running with pus. He
hadn't noticed when he had been eating. He gave up the
idea.

Then Bowers shouted: 'There isn't enough oil!'

He had found the can, shaken it, but the cold had made
the oil viscous. He suspected something, but his thoughts
came too slowly. He shook the can again. He realized what
had happened—but nevertheless couldn't comprehend the
incomprehensible. So, miles and miles from civilization
—yes, they were to come past here on the way back, weren't
they—in a can laid down on the way south, the quantity
carefully measured, there was now too little oil. Bowers
knew it. He scrambled to his feet. He found the can and
shook it. Then he struck his head with his fist. Evans stared
at him with delirious eyes and laughed coarsely.

Scott, quickly and sharply: 'Keep calm!'

He examined the can, set it aside, turned to Wilson,
knowing that he had no answer either. Scott said: 'We've
established that the quantity is reduced. I'll note it in my
daily report. It means,' he went on calmly, 'that we must
reduce our rations. Perhaps from now on we should eat
pemmican without thawing it.'

That night Evans began to crawl round the tent. This
was difficult enough in such cramped quarters, but he
crawled over the others, lifted a knee, sat on someone's
stomach, laughing quietly and darkly. Scott and Wilson
had crawled from their bags. The weather outside sounded
better. They talked calmly to Evans to get him under control. Wilson offered to sing a bit of a song to him, and Evans
nodded. So the mineralogist from the Antarctic, now on his
way back, a man who'd never spoken a harsh word to anyone,
started humming. Once he had had a pleasant singing

voice. There wasn't much left of it now. He held the sick
man's hand and the others lay awake listening. It was only
a snatch of a song. He hummed it again and again.

'Will I get my money?' sobbed Evans.

'Yes, yes. I have His Majesty's word for it.'

'Did he tell you so himself?'

'Yes, yes.'

After a while, Evans fell asleep. But he woke again and
again, ready to leap up at the slightest sound. It was quite
light in the tent now, and they could see his eyes shining
with a deep, wild glow. He cried: 'We didn't make it, did
we? I won't get my money, will I?'

They went on northwards.

It was best when they hitched Evans to the sledge like
a horse and urged him on. But again and again he had
to rest. He fell and remained lying in the tracks. Once or
twice they tried to kick him up. It helped. Scott knew the
moment of decision had come. He knew what the others
were thinking. He was plagued by his conscience. You're
the one who has to decide. A tablet, put him in his sleeping-
bag, then he won't notice anything, and give the order:
we're going on; no one is to look back.

If you do that, you know you'll never be rid of him.
He'll always haunt you, whether you get home alive or
not. He'll be with you when you die. But it may well be
your duty to do it all the same. If you drag him on with
you—well, then you won't have to give orders to abandon
a man to his death, but on the other hand, that means you
condemn everyone to death.

It's your choice. You wanted to lead the expedition,
didn't you?

Evans was lying in the snow. But suddenly he scrambled
to his feet without assistance. He stared at them, smiling
foolishly. 'There's something wrong with my boot,' he said.
'You'll have to go on.'

They went on. He lagged behind. He'd done this kind of

thing every day lately. He let them get ahead. Perhaps in his sick mind he wanted to reduce their speed and make the day's marches even shorter. He knew he was going to die, and perhaps he reckoned that if he had to go, they all should. He realized they were trying to find a way of getting rid of him, but he realized too—his perceptions heightened by the imminence of disaster—that they daren't leave him, even though they wanted to.

They've got their doubts. Ha, ha! They daren't, but they want to. Abandon me . . . they're waiting for me. . . .

Perhaps that's how it was, or perhaps the others plodding on in the snow gave him that impression. They didn't meet each other's eyes. They didn't trust themselves. Wasn't he coming today? Was that him, that dark dot far behind?

Scott gave his weary order: 'We must go back and fetch him.'

They left the sledge there. It took an hour to walk back. He had loosened his trousers and was standing half-naked in the cold, stumbling round like a dog with one foot torn off. 'What's the matter with you?' asked Scott.

'Nothing.' He was grinning.

Now they had to take him with them. But the sledge wasn't there. Two men fetched it, one staying behind with Evans. At last they got the tent up—the whole operation had taken three hours.

The decision Scott hadn't the strength to make was taken out of his hands. Evans slowly faded away. He died in the early hours of the morning without regaining consciousness. They covered him with snow and Scott spoke a cursory Lord's Prayer. They went on.

'I should have given orders to leave him earlier,' he thought. 'But I am proud I did not do so.'

They moved slowly away from the scene of death.

They had a minor storm at their backs and could hoist a

sail again. It helped a bit, but they were filled with an emptiness which made every step a torment. And they suffered from a growing irritation with each other which they couldn't keep in check. Bowers's skis should have been somewhere in the vicinity. He'd left them behind on the trip south. One morning they began to bait him: 'Have we to waste time looking for your skis? Why did you leave them behind? You never think of us, only yourself. You left the skis behind. If we don't find them, I suppose you'll slow us down by walking all the way back?' One said: 'All the way back? Who knows if we'll get there?'

They found the skis. Bowers said nothing and fastened them on. Scott, unable to bite the words back, knowing he was being hurtful and unjust, but forced to get it off his chest, said: 'You can't ski, can you? What were you doing all last winter? You were supposed to train yourself to ski properly instead of wasting time.'

But they went on, fleeing from the place of death. There should have been a small depot somewhere here in the blizzard, at thirty degrees below zero, between ice hummocks and deep crevasses which made the route longer than it would otherwise have been. Later on in the day they found the depot. Here was the horsemeat from their trip south. There was food for several weeks, but here too was less paraffin than there should have been.

It was a mystery and an added mental burden. But Scott grew in stature as he shook the can and made the discovery. He wore the exhausted, almost weak expression on his face which had often fooled men into believing he was in despair, but then he seemed to brace himself somewhere deep inside, stretching out a frostbitten finger to silence the others: 'The shortage of oil is just something we'll have to face, and something we'll have to overcome. Wracking our brains to find out what's become of the missing quantity won't bring us any more oil. Secondly, we mustn't be too petty. That will quickly impair our ability to survive. There are several possible answers. Perhaps there was a leak in the can, which later sealed itself when the cold was severe enough and the oil thickened inside. For the time being we've no right to blame anyone for what's happened here. But we must reduce rations.'

Here they had quantities of horsemeat, but on the trip south they had neglected to cut the meat into small pieces while it was still fresh. Now it was as hard as stone. It was a considerable task to hack off small bits, and they hadn't enough oil to cook it properly. Nevertheless, they could eat their fill. They felt their strength and courage returning as they chewed worn-out old horse, as if there was still life in the horse. Again it became their best friend. They could have stayed here and eaten their fill, resting in the storm, if only they had had enough oil. But they had to go on the next day.

Then Scott was guilty of an incomprehensible mistake. He failed to give orders for the horsemeat **to** be taken with them. It might have been the forgetfulness of a lethargic brain, its efficiency reduced by exhaustion and cold. For when the worse came to the worst, they would have been able to chew frozen meat and extract some strength from it, if they hadn't left it behind. The nutritional value of the meat would have been a greater advantage than the disadvantage of the added weight. But they abandoned the meat.

It was the last time that Scott proved incapable of making a decision: he lacked the necessary mental energy. Should they press on northwards, taking every chance, neglecting to take the meat with them as they hadn't any oil anyway? Or should they take the meat with them, chewing their way forward, knowing that at least they wouldn't starve, as long as they had pieces of horsemeat on the sledge?

He didn't take a decision. They just left the food. Again, they were hidden by swirling snow and blizzards. When it cleared, the temperature dropped. As they moved farther away from the supply of horsemeat, they began to have fantasies about food. Time and time again they were tempted to lean on the sledge, their faces down in the leather brims of their hoods, whispering to each other about food. This worked like a small injection of strength, if an ear caught faint voices talking about food. When we get back ... just one good meal ... tea and hot food, eating slowly, gladly chewing everything thirty times ... knowing it has to last a long time ... I remember that dinner....

When I get back, I shall enjoy every mouthful of an ordinary meal, because it's just as valuable as a fancy one ... I can imagine myself chewing some cold pemmican ... I'd like some hot cocoa....

Four wills were fighting on. They forced each other up. They didn't goad each other on with sharp words, but appeared to support the weakest from behind when he began to lag, then a moment later it was his turn to help his helpers. It was a slow business, eight to ten kilometres a day the most they could manage, constantly staring at the compass needle, their eyes smarting, knowing that they might be off course, noticing that the others weren't in agreement in their estimates. One of them said they were too far west, another thought they were too far east, but they couldn't split up. Overcoming Scott's own doubts, they took a course he didn't trust. He tormented himself step by step, keeping quiet about his doubts, because doubts use up the last reserves of strength. ... He discovered with a little spurt of joy that it was the right way after all. Here was the track from their trip south. But in a short while it had disappeared again. They had now reached what they called the Middle Barrier depot. There was a shortage of oil there, too. As they were breaking camp to go on, Oates showed them his feet.

He had been silent for the last two days. They had

noticed that he was limping. They looked in horror at what had once been feet, and were now two stumps with no toe nails, swollen with fluid, essentially decaying, with no strength in them to carry a man onwards. It was a miracle they'd carried him so far. That morning it took Oates an hour and a half to get his boots on.

Scott bowed his head and said: 'God help us all. Amen.'

They went on northwards. Oates often had to lean on the sledge. The others waited, trying to get him on top of the load, but they hadn't the strength to do it. He rolled off voluntarily and stayed lying in the snow. They told him to get up. He got to his knees, hauled his body forward, grasped the sledge, with all of them helping, and the next moment he was standing swaying on his feet. Then they went slowly on.

When evening came and they had the tent up again—it took twice as long now to strike camp—Oates leaned over towards Wilson and asked: 'Have I got a chance?'

'I honestly don't know.'

It was a difficult night. When morning came, Oates asked them to let him stay in his sleeping-bag and leave him behind. Scott replied that they couldn't. He asked Oates to see if he could go on with them one more day. But before they broke camp he ordered Wilson, the man responsible for medical supplies, to hand out the tablets. They had morphine tablets with them, and it was now a matter for each man to decide individually whether he was going to use them or not. Wilson did as he was ordered.

They managed another short day's march, again struck camp and had a bad night. Early next morning, Oates said: 'I'm just going outside and may be some time. . . .' There was a blizzard outside. He crawled out of his sleeping-bag. Scott said to him: 'You can wait. . . .' Oates didn't answer. They knew what he was doing. He staggered out. He was some time.

From then on Scott betrayed no sign of weakness. He

wrote with a firm hand in his diary: 'Oates died like an English gentleman.'

What they didn't know, in that tent in the Antarctic, was that by then Amundsen had reached Hobart, Tasmania, on the *Fram*. From there, cables with the news of the conquest of the South Pole went out all over the world. They reached London. For a while there was confusion, people thinking that it was Scott who had reached the Pole. The papers brought out extra editions with incorrect headlines ... later they were corrected.

But the three men went on. They knew that at One Ton depot, which should now have been only twenty kilometres away or so, there was enough food and probably oil too. According to the plan, they would be met there by a dog-team from winter quarters. They thought they could hear dogs barking already. They knew it was an illusion, and they also knew what it cost them to flare up with hope and then collapse with disappointment. But it was impossible to stop. They leant on the sledge and rested. They re-assured each other: 'That's a dog barking. They're on their way ...'

But no one came.

So far, Scott had been the strongest physically. That evening he said: 'I'm the weakest of the three survivors.'

He studied his feet—the right one looked especially bad. He wrote with seeming calm in his diary that amputation was his only hope. They managed to do one more day's march. Then the blizzard returned. They crawled into the tent, with food for two days and oil for one.

They agreed that their only chance was for Wilson and Bowers to try to get to One Ton depot, and if they found it, to turn back for Scott. They tried the next day, but the blizzard was worse than ever. They had to give up and go back to the tent.

It was during these days—we don't know exactly how many—that all three of them showed their last calm nobility, all hostility evaporating in this situation. Bowers and Wilson tactfully retreated into sympathetic silence for a few hours to allow their great leader to stand alone on the stage in the glare of history. Scott wrote. He was sitting in his sleeping-bag, with two aching, suppurating feet, the last paraffin gone. It was thirty degrees below zero. He couldn't wear his mittens. He wrote in his elegant, handsome script, perfectly legible even now, with a calm choice of words, and undertone of desperation, but no hysteria; he revealed complete clarity of thought, making no excuses, the naked facts laid bare. Thus he put on paper his explanation to the British people. The leader of the expedition showed in his last hour that he was still born to leadership. Then he wrote his private letters, which were warmer in tone. Here, in the chill of death, his words contained a warmth seldom matched by the literature of the world. He wrote to Wilson's wife and thanked her for his friendship with her husband. He wrote to Bowers's mother and praised the son now dying beside him. He wrote to his own mother. Finally he wrote to his wife and asked her to take good care of their son.

Everyone received a few words from him—the suffering, who didn't yet know their suffering. But he knew they would suffer, and he knew his own suffering.

The blizzard raged on.

Bowers and Wilson had got down inside their sleeping-bags.

They were both quiet.

He dozed and woke; hours or days had gone by, he didn't know ... no one knows. For the last time he got out his diary and pencil.

'For God's sake, look after our people.'

Then he stretched out an arm and placed it over Wilson, who was now asleep.

It was good to sleep.

He smiled faintly.

EPILOGUE

The *Fram* reached the Great Ice Barrier on 8 January, 1912. On 30 January, the ship sailed north with Amundsen and his men on board.

After a good journey, the *Fram* reached Hobart in Tasmania. Amundsen told the world that he had conquered the South Pole in December 1911. He also sent a cable to the Geographical Society in Kristiania:

'Johansen mutinied. Therefore had to be excluded from the Pole party. His arrival home must take place quietly.'

Johansen took his own life the year after.

On 30 October, 1912, a rescue expedition left the British winter quarters in McMurdo Sound, the Norwegian, Tryggve Gran, with it. On 11 November, the expedition reached One Ton depot and went on southwards.

They found the tent.

Scott had thrust one arm out of his sleeping-bag and had laid it across his friend Wilson. In a finnesko, they found Amundsen's letter to King Haakon. On 18 January, 1913 the *Terra Nova* sailed into McMurdo Sound to fetch Scott's expedition. Until then, the tragedy had been unknown to all except those overwintering there.

The course was set northwards and on 12 February, cables went out all over the world. Mrs Scott was on her way to New Zealand to meet her husband there. The wireless cable didn't reach the ship. On 14 February, 1913, the ship had arrived at the coast of New Zealand. Mrs Scott was sitting in a folding chair on deck. A cable reached the ship. The captain went up to her.